HAUL THE WATER
HAUL THE WOOD

by Doris Stensland

Illustrated by Doris Stensland

Library of Congress No. 77-84862
Copyright © 1977 by
Doris Stensland

Sixth Printing 1986

Printed by

 North Plains Press
Aberdeen, S.D. 57401
Printed in U.S.A.

Order From
Doris Stensland
RR 1, Box 120
Canton, S.D. 57013

Preface

This fictional work is grounded in historical fact, and follows the general outline of the lives of Johanna and Ole Overseth, early pioneers in Lincoln County, South Dakota.

Several years ago I found my great-grandmother's old Norwegian hymnbook. Inside she had written, "Johanna Overseth, 1887, Philippians 3:20." On looking up this Bible reference I read, "For our citizenship is in heaven." I became curious to know more of her life and times. This research has held a special fascination, for her life is, in fact, a root to which I am attached.

I am grateful to many people for their assistance in this project. To my mother, who first had the idea of this book, and for all of her help in acquiring information for it.

A "thank you" to nonagenarian, Carl Carlson, a neighbor who supplied me with much useful information on the times of which I wrote, and to Rev. Neale Thompson for locating a copy of an old journal of the early pastor, Ellef Olsen. It offered much material on the community and the people I was concerned with, beginning with the year 1869, and thereafter.

My appreciation goes out to the Archives of Norway for the quick, willing replies to facts I needed; to the National Archives for all the material they sent; to the Canton Lutheran Church files, and the Canton Public Library for their help and for information gleaned from old Sioux Valley News and Dakota Farmer's Leader newspapers; to Gustavus Adolphus Archives and the museum at St. Peter, Minnesota, for their kind assistance, and to numerous other people who have offered bits of family history.

There are several people who gave me assistance as I attempted to put the information into a book; namely: Shelly Hartsook and Jane Hunt, for their advice and suggestions, and Paul Bjorneberg who edited the book for me. I am very grateful to each one.

Also, I wish to thank my friends and family, especially my daughter and two daughters-in-law who have at times had more confidence in this undertaking than I have had, and they have kept me going, and most of all, to my husband, Hans, for his concern with this project and the contribution he made to it.

TO

My mother, without whose help
and inspiration this book would
never have been written.

Aa kjøre vatten aa kjøre ve'.

Folkevise.

Allegretto.

Aa kjø - re vat - ten aa kjø - re ve', aa kjøre tømmer o - ver
A kjø - re aa dem kjø - re vil, je kjøre kjerringa mi

hei - a! aa kjø - re va dem kjø - re vi', je
ei - a! Hu er saa god, og hu er saa snill, de

kjø - rergjen - ta mi ei - a. De rø - de ro-ser aa de
kan visst al dri bli lei - a. De rø - de ro-ser aa de

ø - ne blaa, de vak - re gjenter haaller je ut - aa, helst
ø - ne blaa, mi ei - a kjerring holder je ut - aa, Naa

naar je faar den, je vi' ha, saa ær 'e mar-ro-somt aa le - va.
har je faatt den, je vil ha! Naa er det mor - o - samt aa le - va!

HAUL THE WATER
and
HAUL THE WOOD

a Norwegian folksong

1. Haul the water and haul the wood
    and haul the lumber over the hill!
Let everyone haul what they like to haul,
    I'll haul that girl of mine!

   Refrain: I love the pretty girls
      With the red rosy cheeks and blue eyes.
      Especially when I get the one I want,
      Then it is fun to live.

2. Let everyone haul whatever they want,
    For my part, I like to haul my own wife!
She is so good, and she is so kind,
    I can never get tired of her.

   Refrain: I love the pretty girls
      With the red rosy cheeks and blue eyes.
      Now I have gotten the one I want!
      Now it is fun to live!

(translated from "**Aa Kjøre Vatten**")

Most of the Norwegian words found in the text are indexed in the glossary in the back of the book. A map of Norway and of Norway Township, Dakota Territory, are included there also.

Part I

Johanna Narum, age 16.—circa 1865.

Chapter I

The rolling land of Vestre Toten was dressed in harvest garments. The wheat fields and barley tracts were turning a light gold, and the last cuttings of hay hung drying on racks. August was almost over.

Across the countryside on each little hillock a farmstead stood. Surrounding it were patches of green and gold, representing each different crop. Beyond, far away in the distance, stood the greater hills, looking as if they touched the sky. Norway was known for her fjords and **fjells,** but here lay her breadbasket, and here lived the people who produced most of her grain.

Situated on a knoll overlooking a valley was the **gaard** called Overseth. From this point the Narum farm buildings could be seen. Ole Overseth quickened his pace as he headed down the slope in that direction. He put his hand in his back trouser pocket and felt the letter that was there. The thought of its contents made him lengthen his stride.

Ole Overseth was a well-built young man, 20 years of age and standing close to six feet in height. His rolled up shirtsleeves gave a hint of the muscles in his arms. He ran his fingers through his thick auburn hair, pushing it back from a wide, prominent forehead. This evening his deep-set, penetrating eyes shone with excitement.

The fields he skirted were heavy with grain. In some areas portions had fallen under the weight of its product. He uttered an **"Uff da,"** under his breath, and shook his head. "Harvesting shall be difficult this year," he thought. "Just what Pa was afraid of."

He climbed over the fence and turned onto the road that would lead by the Narum home.

This section of Norway was still enjoying the long daylight hours of summer. The farmers had all finished their work for the day and bedded down their horses and other animals for the night, and the womenfolk had completed their chores.

As Ole passed the house of the Dystes', he saw the family sitting by the back door enjoying the end of a fine day. Soon it would be replaced by the raw weather of winter and its long nights. In fact, he could already feel the chill as evening fell, and he buttoned up his vest and rolled down his shirt sleeves.

Ole had soon covered the distance, and the two-story Narum house stood at his left. He always paused to admire the twin birches that grew by the entrance, their graceful branches arching out over the path that led up to the door. This house had been built on the highest elevation of its land, and gave a good view in all directions.

Behind the house stood the big barn, and to the north was the shed with the bell upon it. This place was almost as familiar to Ole as his own home. There were people living here that he had spent much time with down through the years.

"Ole," a childish voice called. Running down the path to greet him was little Hans, the youngest member of the Narum family. Ole responded with a big, friendly **"God dag,"** which was also directed at Hans' big brother, Christian, who followed right behind.

"And how is it with you tonight, Ole?" Christian asked in a very cordial manner. "You covered the ground in good time. We've been watching you ever since you passed the Dystes."

Christian was the same age as Ole, a young man of 20, and one of Ole's good friends and neighbors.

Ole quickly answered, "If a man is going visiting he cannot spend all the time on the road."

They laughed and walked over to where the Narum menfolk were relaxing. The father of the family, Paul Andreas Narum and his eldest son David were conversing about the farming operations. **Herr** Narum was a man of 51 years, with sideburns and a fringe of whiskers that edged his face and a full mustache.

Ole stopped a minute while they exchanged comments on the weather. The younger Narum sons, Peter Anthon and Martinus, rose to greet Ole. Little Hans, with a seven-year-old's speed, had run ahead to the house to announce his arrival.

Ole took this opportunity to break his news to Christian, as with a twinkle in his eye he remarked, "You'll never guess what I have in my pocket!"

"Well, I bet it isn't money," was Christian's quick reply.

"Ja, you can be sure of that!" Ole gave a slap to his back pocket as he announced, "I have a letter from America."

"Have you?" Christian exclaimed. "Will you let me read it?"

As he opened the door to the house, Christian invited, **"Velkommen.** Come on in." They went into the big kitchen with its painted carved furniture. Ole's eyes quickly settled on Christian's 18-year-old sister, Johanna, who was bending over the stove in the corner. She had seen him coming too, and had hurried to put a pot of coffee on the fire.

Ole called to her. "Mmmmm, Johanna! Something smells good in here."

As he spoke, she turned around. Ole took in her simple beauty. Johanna, her brown hair parted in the middle and drawn back into a soft roll on her neck, stood tall and slim, and the long, plain homespun dress she wore didn't detract from her pleasing figure. He had to admit that her serious big eyes always affected him. She greeted him with a smile.

Older sister, Helene Marie, was getting the dishes down from the shelf. **Tante** Berte sat in her rocker, knitting as usual, her cane hung on the armrest. Ole greeted her with, "You're looking well tonight, **Tante.**"

When little sister Helmine heard him come in, she pushed back the whisps of hair around her face and straightened her dress. It was so much fun when Ole was there.

"Hey, everybody, I got a letter from America!" Ole announced.

They all gathered around.

"Well, read it!"

"Who sent it?"

Far Narum and David were now in the kitchen too, and everyone found places to sit around the well-worn table.

America was the main topic of conversation nowadays. Already many people had left the community and more were making plans. This restlessness was like a disease, a fever that spread from one person to another. Curiosity about this far away country was in all their minds. The letters from those people who had already left were coming back to Norway and giving the others first-hand reports and information.

"It's from our former neighbor Sven," Ole said, and took the letter from his pocket, pulling it from the envelope and giving it to Christian.

Johanna moved over and stood where she could hear Christian read.

i Nordamerika
1 July, 1867

Kjaere Ole,

I am come to Amerika, and that was a big land!

I am at Decorah, in Winneshiek County, Iowah. There are many Norske folks here in this town. I am glad for that, for I have a terrible time when I must speak with those who only **snakke** englisk.

I have a job and work on a farm out on the land southeast from the town. Amerika is a fine land, but it is very warm here. The man I am working for came from Valdres about eight years ago. Now I am helping him build a barn for his six cows. I even have to help him milk them. Can you believe that the men have to do this kind of chores in Amerika? He also has four fine horses, and six big pigs with 20 small ones. He is doing well, don't you think?

I was in town two weeks ago and I talked with a man who shall go west to find land for himself. This land is called Dakota Territory and it is opened up for "homesteading" now. A citizen or a man who has applied for citizen papers can go to Dakota Territory and take a place for himself, 160 acres, and plow it and if he lives there for five years it shall be his land. Can you think that it can be so? You do not have to pay more than a few dollars for it. But you must be a man who can work hard, he says, for it isn't easy. Perhaps I shall go west also. I must think about it.

There are not many girls over here, but I have my eye on a sweet one who lives on the next farm, so don't worry about me. You know me when it comes to the girls.

There is lots of room over here, Ole. Maybe you should be thinking about packing your trunk and visiting me.

Your friend,
Sven.

Christian laughed. "That Sven hasn't changed a bit. He can take care of himself."

"Ja," chuckled David. "I'd like to see him milking those cows."

Everyone smiled in agreement.

"Are you going, Ole?" little Hans piped up.

Suddenly, all the eyes in the room were on Ole, and he knew this was the question he had in his own heart to which he would have to find an answer.

He tried to dodge it with, "Do you fc.ks want to get rid of me?"

Looking at all the faces around him, he said, "Even you, Johanna?"

Before giving her a chance to answer, he turned to Christian. "What do you think about it, Chris?"

Ole was speaking in loud excited tones now.

"One hundred and sixty acres of land almost for nothing. Can you believe it? Even when you inherit the home place here you have to pay out a lot of money to your brothers and sisters."

"Such talk," **Far** Narum said, as if trying to pour cold water on the whole thing. "You cannot get anything any place for nothing. You will see there is a catch to it."

"Ole go to America?" Johanna heard only the blur of their voices now as she quickly turned and busied herself pouring up the coffee.

"Ole go to America?"

She must get some lunch on the table, but she moved as if in a dream. She set a loaf of bread and a knife on the table before her father, put the wooden crock of butter beside it, and went to the cupboard and took down a large bowl of beautiful red jam. This week, she and her sisters had been busy picking berries and making preserves, and she was proud of this strawberry jam. Johanna knew it was Ole's favorite, and she had been looking forward to serving it to him.

She spooned some into a dish, stuck a silver spoon in it and placed it beside the butter. But now there wasn't any enjoyment in it. This America idea was threatening her future. The bottom was falling out of all her dreams and plans.

"If Ole goes to America . . . ." she thought.

But she didn't want to think about it.

Sleep wouldn't come to Johanna that night. The tears began to drizzle onto her pillow. Here in the dark she could let her feelings go. Here she didn't have to act mature.

In two months she would be 19 years old. It had been six years now that Johanna and her older sister, Helene Marie Narum, had been trying to be the homemakers in this house, with five brothers and younger sister, Helmine, to care for. At least they had helped Papa keep their family together, except for sister Klara who had gone to live with Uncle and **Tante** Kyset.

During these last few years, Johanna had been living with her eyes on the future, and she pictured Ole Overseth in that future. There was not a more handsome young man in all of Toten—nor a better one.

Most of all, she knew what her heart told her. She wished she didn't care, then she wouldn't be so upset tonight. Still, she had no claims on him, so she guessed he could go where he pleased. Ja, even to America.

This wasn't the way Johanna had planned it. She had thought that in a few years when little Hans and Martinus, the two youngest, were older, and David was married, she could be free to have a life of her own.

Now she'd probably end up like **Tante** Berte.

Johanna buried her head in the pillow and tried to hold back another batch of tears.

"Oh, Mama, if you were only here," she quietly sobbed.

Then she lay still, trying to think realistically. After all, Ole hadn't said for sure that he was going to America. Finally she quit her tossing, snuggled up under her feather quilt and after a while sleep came.

✳ ✳ ✳ ✳ ✳

When harvest was in full swing, it took priority over all other tasks. Late at night could be heard the grating sound of the grindstone as the scythe blades were being sharpened for the next day. With the morning light all available help marched to the fields, some with scythes and some with horse and cart.

The grain had to be cut down and loaded into the carts, then brought home for winnowing. Every family member had a job, and the days were too full for such a thing as visiting.

But Sundays brought a change. Not that there wasn't any activity in the Narum house on the Sabbath. No, it was rather that there was a change of attitude.

This Sunday morning found the whole family in good spirits, and from the time the first members were up, the sound of joking, singing and humming could be heard.

Sister Klara had come over from Kysets last night to spend Sunday with her family. The chores were quickly completed and one by one the members appeared in the kitchen where Johanna, Klara and Helene Marie were getting breakfast.

The girls had always followed their mother's custom and made Sunday a festive day. On week days they served gruel, but on Sunday mornings the table was spread with bread, jam and cheese, and soft boiled eggs were served in their wooden egg cups.

Far Narum, David and Christian were dressed in their suits and white shirts, narrow black ties hanging neatly in place. Peter Anthon and Martinus had not yet been confirmed, the time that boys usually get their first suits, but they looked fine in their homespun shirts and dark trousers.

Tante Berte had on her black taffeta with its little white lace collar and Helmine was wearing the long blue wool that **Tante** Berte had just finished sewing for her.

All awaited the **"Vaer saa god"** so they could sit down to eat.

"Johanna," little Hans called from upstairs. "I can't find my shoes."

Johanna sent Helmine up the steps with them. Last night after he was in bed, Johanna had kept them in the kitchen where she cleaned and oiled them.

"Isn't **Bestefar** coming?" Chris asked.

"No, just sit up to the table," Helene Marie answered. "Klara brought him his breakfast in his room. He says he doesn't feel too peppy today."

Sunday was the Lord's Day at the Narum home, and when all members were seated around the big table, Papa opened his Bible and read a Psalm. After his prayer they all bowed reverently and prayed the table blessing together.

Johanna looked at the faces around the table. Today she was proud of them as they sat in their best attire, heads bowed. Her eyes caught Helene Marie's and they both nodded with satisfaction. Johanna wished Mama could see them today, happily enjoying Sunday breakfast.

But the girls didn't have time to sit, for after they were through eating and Papa had given thanks, the family would be boarding the two wagons that were tied outside and head for Kolbu **Kirke** as was their custom on Sunday mornings.

The table was quickly cleared. Johanna inspected little Hans and wiped the egg from his chin. Martinus had to be checked, and then she ran up to her room and gave her hair a few brush strokes and threw off her apron. This morning she had put on her gray checked dress which **Tante** Berte had sewn for her confirmation two years ago.

Glancing out the window, Johanna saw the menfolk waiting in front. She grabbed her shawl, picked up her Bible and hymnbook and ran down and settled back in the wagon with Klara and Helmine.

Older sister Helene Marie sat beside Papa on the seat of his wagon, with little Hans between them.

Their two finest teams of horses were hitched to the wagons. The horses with coats gleaming from a thorough currying, had the short legs and plump bodies characteristic of mountain horses.

Brother David drove the other wagon, and sitting beside him was **Tante** Berte. Christian had helped her up on the seat and now he sat beside her. In the back were Martinus and Peter Anton.

On Sunday morning all carts and wagons were being driven to the church. The Dystes were just driving out of their lane, and along the way they passed some of the people who were walking to church.

As the family drew near, they could see teams and people approaching the corner where the three roads met; the point where the white Kolbu Church was situated.

Whenever the church came into view, it gave Johanna a feeling of joy. It wasn't a large church, but set upon a knoll, the sight of it gave a sense of peace to the countryside. Its structure of double peaks—first the low one above the entry, and then the larger one, out of which reached the round steeple—stretched up to the sky.

Again this Sunday Johanna had this feeling of anticipation. It was like a person with an appetite who is eager to sit down to a meal. She knew that here she would receive food for her soul. This white church was as much a part of her life as her home. Here she had been brought in baptism as a baby, and here she had spent almost every Sunday morning of her life seated in the sanctuary while the good news of God's grace had been proclaimed. Yes, here she had heard of the love of God as Pastor Magelsen had opened up the Word so she could understand it.

The teams pulled up to the hitching rail in front of the church. From here a long path led straight to the church door, and on either side of this path lay the cemetery. Flowers were still blooming on some of the well-cared-for graves.

Papa helped the girls and little Hans down from the wagon and they waited while the boys assisted **Tante** Berte. Together the womenfolk and little Hans walked up the path and into the church. They found their favorite pew on the women's side and sat down.

It felt good to sit and relax in this holy place. Johanna studied the familiar furnishings—the delicate carvings on the altar, the pulpit, and the colorful altar painting of Jesus and his disciples as they ate the last supper.

All her life Johanna had been awed by this picture. As a child she had sat here and in childish fancy envisioned herself seated with Jesus around the table. She remembered how puzzled she had been when it occurred to her there were no women in the picture. She had even asked her mother about it. With little girl curiosity she had inquired why Jesus didn't have women disciples. Or, she thought, surely women should have been waiting table as they ate. Her mother had taken her then upon her lap and explained so simply, "We are all his disciples, Johanna, and when we partake of communion we too sit at table with him. You will see when you are older. It is a precious thing, Johanna."

And after her confirmation in 1865, she had been able to participate and kneel at the altar and find her place as a disciple. Each time since it had been precious.

The church was filling fast. Soon she saw brothers David and Christian, Martinus and Peter Anton find their places on the right side of the church. She thought to herself—"Papa is taking the long way in today so he can go by Mama's grave."

The bell began pealing, and Papa quickly slipped in beside his sons.

The **klokker** rose and gave the opening prayer, and the congregation joined together in the first hymn. Then Pastor Magelsen, in his black gown with the white accordian pleated collar, climbed the steps into the high pulpit.

Johanna wondered what message from God he had for them today. He opened the big Bible that lay on the pulpit and began reading . . . "From the evangelist Matthew, chapter 28, verses 19, 20 . . . **"Lo, I am with you always, even to the end of the world!"**

The light shining through the windows illuminated Pastor Magelsen as he stood in the pulpit. His kindly face revealed the joy he found as he shared the gospel.

The rays of sunshine lit up all the carvings and painted scrolls on the pulpit and on the little roof that hung over it.

Pastor Magelsen began, "Today we shall see how Jesus said farewell." He paused a moment and then went on.

"Goodbyes are difficult, and goodbyes can be so painful. Some of you have had to say goodbye to loved ones who have gone to America and you know how hard it was to say **'Farvel.'**

Johanna could see Sven's mother, seated several pews ahead, raise her hand to her face as if wiping off a tear Others nodded their heads in agreement.

"Now I ask you, what did **you** say?"

"You gave them instructions, did you not?"

"Read your Bible everyday, son."

"Say your prayers."

"Remember what we have taught you . . . ."

"And don't forget to write so we can keep in touch."

The words "gone to America" brought Johanna's thoughts to Ole Overseth. Today he was most likely sitting with his parents and brothers in the neighboring church, Aas **Kirke.**

Again Pastor Magelsen's voice boomed out, "Listen, this is exactly what Jesus did when He had to leave his disciples bodily. He gave instructions and provided them a way to keep in touch."

His voice loudened, "These words are for us also. He gives us instructions also, even as He did the eleven. 'Go, proclaim, baptize, and remember all that I have taught you.' "

Pastor Magelsen's voice became touched with emotion as he continued. "Now we come to the beautiful part," and he slowly spoke the words that meant so much to him. **"Lo, I am with you always, even to the end of the world."**

"I ask you—do you believe it? You must believe it if you believe that this is God's Word."

"Yes, Jesus had a better way to keep in touch than by writing letters. He would keep in touch with us by walking by our sides—always. We cannot see Him, but that does not mean He isn't there."

Here Pastor Magelsen turned and pointed to the altar painting of Jesus and his disciples.

"Let us ask the disciples who lived with Him for three years what it means to have Jesus with us.

"Phillip would probably answer, 'it means Jesus will be with me when I am afraid, and He will command 'Peace be still'."

Again the pastor turned and pointed to the people in the painting.

"I can hear John answer, 'It is having Him always near me so I am in His loving fellowship—a friend better than any earthly friend. He is there when I sit at the table to eat and when I rest and when I am working. I can talk things over with Him'."

Now, looking back over his shoulder once again, he continued . . .

"Andrew perhaps would say, 'It is having the assurance that He will fulfill my needs—even provide loaves and fishes in the wilderness'."

"Peter would interrupt in his loud outspoken manner, 'It means He will never leave me, even when I sin. He is always there to forgive. I know, He did it for me'."

Pastor Magelsen looked out over his little congregation and finished his sermon.

"My friends, don't ever forget, He promises these things to you, too. Now you ask, 'What must I do'?"

"It is so simple."

"Just believe in Him and in His words to us, **'I am with you ALWAYS.'** Oh, do not be afraid."

"Praise His Holy Name!"

Chapter II

C urlicues of steam circled up from the coffee cups that set on the Narum table. The Sunday **middags** had been eaten and now in an attitude of contentment the menfolk and **Tante** Berte were enjoying their after-dinner coffee. The girls were clearing the table and washing the dishes.

Far Narum filled his saucer again from the supply in his big coffee cup and waited a moment for it to cool.

"Papa, can I dip a sugar lump in your coffee?" little Hans begged. "Please . . . .?"

Far Narum winked at him, dusted his beard, and answered in a gruff tone as he gestured with his index finger, "Only one!"

Little Hans, still in his dark wool Sunday britches and matching buttoned shirt, had stationed himself at his father's elbow. He picked up a piece of sugar from the wooden container and after a second look at his father to be sure it was all right, dipped it into the coffee cup. As soon as it absorbed the brown liquid, he quickly deposited the dripping lump into his mouth.

Everyone around the table smiled as they witnessed the moment of ecstasy for little Hans. He closed his eyes and uttered a big "MMMMM-mmmmm," then licked his lips to capture the very last drop.

David went on with the conversation they were having, which mostly concerned reports from visits they had had with neighbors at church that morning.

"Magnus Rue is making plans to go to America next spring. He told us about the explosion that took place when he informed his folks. His father declared he wouldn't give him one **ore** to use for a trip like that, and his mother burst out weeping."

Chris interrupted, "That's what they get for trying to push him into marrying that Maalstad **jente.** Her father may be the wealthiest farmer in Vestre Toten, but I wouldn't want to spend the rest of my life with her either!"

"Now, now, Christian," **Tante** Berte scolded. "Is that any way to talk about your second cousin? Guri is a nice young lady."

"Ja, if you like them plump!" he added.

"Well," David went on, "Magnus says he will go over to Hurdal when harvesting is finished and try to get himself a job cutting timber so he can earn some money for his ticket."

"Ja, more power to him!" Christian cheered.

David puckered his lips in a moment of concentration. "I wouldn't be too surprised if he changes his mind. Magnus has been fired up about things before and then weakens at the last minute. And that Maalstad **gaard** isn't anything to sneeze at. I would rather have a fish in the pan than ten swimming around in Lake Mjøsa. Besides, I think Magnus is kind of sweet on Guri. There may even be more there than he himself knows."

Far Narum sat back listening to the conversation. Every now and then he picked up his saucer with both hands and raised it to his lips, slowly sipping the coffee from it. Johanna, standing nearby, watched the pleased expression on Papa's face. He seemed to be in a world of his own as he savored each sip. "Yes, I think Papa will be happy as long as he has his cup and saucer and plenty of hot coffee to keep it filled," she thought.

Helene Marie came back into the kitchen after bringing the food supplies out to the **stabbur.** She whispered to Johanna, "I think Ole Overseth is coming up the road. Someone is singing **"a kjøre vatten og kjøre ved"**, and the closer he comes the more certain I am, for no one can sing that last line "so is it fun to live!" with such gusto as Ole!"

Johanna laughed, for she knew just what Helene meant. When Ole got going on that song, he always put his whole voice and self into it.

Suddenly her heart was pounding. It had been more than two weeks since Ole's last visit. She wanted a few minutes to regain her composure, and she should put on a clean blouse and brush her hair.

Johanna hurried up to her room. She slipped into a white blouse, looked into the mirror and placed a dainty pin at the neck. Then she heard the door open downstairs, followed by much laughing and loud talking.

Ja, that was Ole! You couldn't mistake his jovial manner.

Out of the myriad noises came the voice of her brother Chris. "Johanna," he called up the staircase. "Johanna, come on down!"

The moment she stepped into the kitchen, Chris explained, "Ole wants us to go over to the Dystes this afternoon."

Ole filled in the details. His younger brother Peter had gone with him and stopped to visit at the Dystes. "When I went in to say hello, they insisted that I come over and get you folks. They say they never get to visit with their cousins," he said.

Then he added, "I was informed that they have a big pail full of fresh red strawberries setting out in their **stabbur.**"

He smacked his lips at the thought.

Before he finished speaking, Klara and Helene Marie had picked up their shawls and were ready to go. Johanna looked at **Tante** Berte, who insisted, "Go ahead. Helmine and I will fix something for supper."

The afternoon sun was bright as the happy group headed down the road. Ole and Chris kept them entertained as they covered the half mile to the Dyste **gaard.** Johanna's heart was light and all threatening thoughts of **Nordamerika** were crowded out by the laughter and merriment around her.

The afternoon sped by quickly. They sat on the grass by the Dyste house. This had been Grandma Narum's home place. Johanna liked to think of Grandma as a little girl running and playing on this very spot. Johanna had never gotten to know this grandmother, for like her own mother, she had died when still a young woman in her forties. Now Grandma's nephew farmed the Dyste **gaard.** His eldest child, Peder, was born the same year as Johanna, and several years ago they had both been confirmed in the same class.

Her cousins brought out bowls, spoons and the big pail of strawberries and a bucket of cream. Their mother appeared with a platter of doughnuts.

"Vaer saa god! Vaer saa god! Have another! Have some more," she kept saying with true Norwegian homemaker hospitality.

Ole eyed the beautiful red fruit. He filled his bowl, held it high and announced, "The jewels of Norge—beats cloudberries* any day!" There was no one who would argue with him about that.

Soon the fellows were back at the pail for second helpings. It didn't take long for the berries to disappear.

Mor Dyste, a scarf tied around her hair and a big apron covering her long full skirt, came out of the house carrying a milk pail.

"It's milking time again," she remarked as she headed for the barn.

Johanna and Helene Marie looked at each other because they were reminded there were some cows waiting for them, too. Johanna spoke up. "Guess we'd better be starting home."

"Just sit, Johanna," Helene Marie said. "It's my turn to do the milking this week. Take your time. It's no use for all of us to hurry home."

David volunteered, "I'll go with you, Helene. I should check the horses before it gets dark."

Johanna, Klara, Chris and Ole finished their lunch and the time came for them to leave, too. Ole walked alongside Johanna, letting Klara and Chris go on ahead. Brother Peter Overseth would wait till Ole got back.

They walked along at a slow pace, enjoying each other's company.

The last hour before twilight was a special time of day. The birds were flying home to their nests amid much twitterings and you could hear the distant sound of "moos" as cows were settling down for the night. On both sides of the road the wheat had been harvested and now these acres were covered with golden stubble. The road was edged with native grasses, and tucked here and there were colorful wild flowers. Ole stooped to pick several stalks of fushia bells for Johanna.

"I've had a wonderful time today, Ole," Johanna said.

"Ja," he agreed. "I had a special reason for coming today."

*yellow berries popular in Norway and known as the national fruit

Johanna glanced at him. His smile was gone, and even the twinkle had disappeared from his deep-set eyes.

"Johanna, there is something I want to talk over with you."

"Why, sure, Ole. What is it?"

They had almost come to a standstill as Ole hunted for words to bring up the subject.

· "Ever since I got the letter from Sven, I have been struggling. Now I have just about made up my mind."

Johanna's heart began beating rapidly as she waited for what he was about to say.

"Try to understand, Johanna. I feel that this is my chance of a lifetime. With five boys in the Overseth family, I have to be practical and realize that we cannot all live at home. Now is the time for me to make plans. In several months I shall be 21, and I can't expect to stay at home any longer.

"This Amerika challenges me. At times I feel strongly that I must go and see if I can get a place of my own there, and plow it and care for it, and who knows, perhaps I can make a whole new world there—a new **Toten,** Johanna."

She caught the sound of excitement in his voice as he shared his plans. And as if to strengthen his argument he pointed out, "At church today the Pastor read about the Israelites who were shown a new land, but they missed it because they saw only the uncertainties and dangers, and as a result they were punished for their faint-heartedness and had to wander forty years in the wilderness. It is dangerous to turn your back on opportunities. There comes a time when you have to step out or you may lose the blessing."

He was quiet for a moment and then spoke very gently. "Johanna, I want to see if I can do it. I must make up my mind soon so I can earn the money for my ticket before next summer comes."

Johanna realized he had put much thought into this decision. Now she knew he waited for a response from her, but what could she say? If she had a choice, she would not tell him to go. Yet she would not try to change his mind. There would be no happiness for her if as a result he spent a lifetime here in **Toten** and each day regretted his decision. It was his life and his future.

Yes, she could even understand his dream. Underneath she was rather proud of his courage. And really all she wanted was the best for him.

Yes, even if she wasn't included in it!

Finally, she said simply, "Ole, do what your heart tells you. You have to decide."

After several moments she sadly added, "There will be many here who will miss you."

Ole answered defensively, "Don't you think that this has bothered me? **Mor** and **Far** Overseth aren't very happy about it. It will be hard to leave them."

He went on, "It is a big step, but still I feel Amerika is beckoning to me and calling, 'Come and see what I hold'."

He looked at her. "Johanna, I think I **must** go."

Johanna bit her lip and swallowed. The afternoon that had been so bright and sweet had suddenly become bitter and painful. As she walked slowly along, she forced herself to look straight ahead, for she didn't want Ole to see the tears collecting in her eyes.

Finally she said, "I'll miss you,Ole."

They had reached the twin birches setting by the walk that turned into the Narum house, and here they stopped. Ole faced her, put his hands on her shoulders and looked straight into her eyes.

"No, Johanna, you don't understand. I want you to come too."

He paused a moment and then went on to explain.

"Maybe not right away, but Johanna, I need you with me if I am going to build a new life."

She looked at him with a pleading, hopeless expression.

"Oh, Ole," she questioned, "how can I go?"

It was all happening so fast. Johanna's head was swimming. She felt like a child with candy dangling in front of his face, but just out of reach.

She shook her head helplessly. "There's no way until little Hans gets older or David marries. Helene Marie depends on me."

She tried to hold back a sob. "I can't let Papa and Helene down."

Then the wells in her heart began to overflow.

Ole drew her into his arms and stroked her hair.

"Don't cry, Johanna. Please don't cry. Something can be worked out."

But to Johanna there was not a speck of hope shining, and when she realized how much she wanted to stay here in his arms, the hurt was only sharper.

And then she heard his kindly voice whispering in her ear, "I love you, Johanna. I want you for my wife."

* * * * *

The Narum kitchen was a busy place every day, but appetites were even larger at this time of year. Johanna had been up early and already mixed up a batch of bread. Now she was kneading it. She had the sleeves of her dark dress rolled up. On her nose was a smattering of flour. Her apron was soiled where she had wiped her hands on it.

Johanna had a very determined expression as she worked, digging the heels of her palms into the elastic mass of bread dough. Over and over again she kneaded, her little body moving with the rhythm.

Tante Berte sat on a high stool at the other end of the workbench, skimming cream that would be made into butter. Yesterday's milk had set overnight in a large, open wooden pan which was used only for this purpose.

"Johanna, today you work with the bread as if you are angry with it," she remarked.

Johanna raised her head, was about to say something, but changed her mind and went back to kneading.

"Helene Marie said you young folks all had a good time at the Dystes yesterday."

Johanna mumbled an "uh-huh."

Tante Berte, unable to get satisfactory responses to her questions, finally came right out and stated, "Something is troubling you, is it not, Johanna?"

There was stillness again as she waited for a reply. Johanna kept busy with the bread dough. Finally she appeared satisfied with this step of her work and placed the dough into the wooden bowl. She broke the silence.

"**Tante,** Ole from Overseth is going to Amerika."

Now she had said it! She knew that keeping quiet would make it no less a fact.

"Oh, **nei-da!**" **Tante** Berte exclaimed, slowly shaking her head.

"It has come to that, has it? **Stakkars,** Johanna!"

After a long silence, Johanna added in a defeated tone, "He asked me to go with him" . . . . but the rest of the sentence trailed off weakly with, "but how can that ever be?"

Tante Berte's heart went out to her brother's daughter, and she tried to comfort her. "Now, now, Johanna. It is not so hopeless."

"Yes, it is, **Tante.** You know I cannot leave Helene Marie here with all the work. It is too big a job."

In a scolding voice, **Tante** Berte said, "Johanna, you are forgetting about your sister Helmine. Do you remember what age you were when your dear mama died? Barely twelve and a half years old, and remember how you helped. I think Helmine could do a lot to help if she had to. I can't get around very well, but I can do a little. **Nei,** do not tell me it is hopeless!"

Tante Berte poured the cream into the wooden churn, and then questioned, "Let me ask you, Johanna, do you care enough for Ole to want to go to Amerika with him?"

"All I know, **Tante**, is that all the joy has gone out of my world now that he is going away."

"Give it time, Johanna. I'm sure something can be worked out. You give up too soon."

Johanna took the large container of rounded bread dough, covered it with a large white cloth and set it aside. Now she must let the yeast have time to do its work.

As she turned from the bread dough, a little hope, like a speck of yeast, began working in her heart. Perhaps things would work out if she gave it time. Perhaps **Tante** Berte was right and she had given up too soon.

The door opened and little Hans came running into the kitchen. Behind him were Helmine and Helene Marie carrying a big wooden pail full of new potatoes between them. They had been out in the potato patch digging up the first tender specimens of this year's crop.

"I helped too, Johanna," Hans announced.

Johanna smiled and encouraged him with a pat on the head.

"You're getting to be a big boy, Hans."

"What we need now is some water," Helene said. "Some for your hands, little Hans, and some to scrub the potatoes. If we hurry, we can get the potatoes ready for **middags.**"

"Boiled new potatoes," Johanna said in a pleased voice.
"Won't Papa and the boys be happy!"

Chapter III

O le pushed down his hat brim and pulled up his coat collar. It had started to drizzle again. All during September the weather had been like this. But this could be expected for it was fall in Norge.

He felt sorry for the few neighbors that hadn't quite finished their harvest. The Overseths were fortunate. Ole was especially glad that they had gotten the flax taken care of before the moisture came. Nothing could be as tough as flax when it is damp, and his mother had to have flax straw for her weaving.

Ole was just returning from Gjøvik where he had put into action his plans for Amerika. Now it wasn't only talk and dreaming. Today he had signed up for passage to Amerika on a ship that left in May. Also, he had mailed a letter to the Hurdal lumber mill, inquiring about a job for winter so he could earn money for his passage.

Now, if he could only find a way to make Johanna feel free to make some plans, too. He had spent much time these last few weeks trying to think of a solution to this problem. No matter how often they talked about it, Johanna always ended with the determination she would not walk out on her family.

The only thing to do was to talk to Johanna's father. Ole would have to speak to him anyway about his marriage intentions. He had been putting off the confrontation because he knew Mr. Paul Andreas Davidson Narum could make or break his dreams for the future, as far as Johanna was concerned.

Perhaps he should stop now on the way home. Yes, he decided, he would waste no more time being faint-hearted! If he was going to be man enough to go to Amerika, he would have to get used to doing difficult things. He had to know Johanna's father's feelings, and he hoped to receive his blessing.

So much depended on this talk. Ole pulled the horses into the Narum lane and drew them to a stop. Now the rain was coming down quite heavily. With his hand he wiped the rivulets of water from his face and jumped down from the wagon. Ole tied the team to the hitching post and went to the house. After a quick knock he stepped inside and slipped off his dripping coat and hat. The warmth of the kitchen was welcome after the raw chilly weather outside.

A good fire was burning in the open fireplace and the fragrance of baking bread was coming from the oven.

Far Narum was sitting at the big table drinking his afternoon coffee and reading a newspaper. And there **she** was—his Johanna. She was holding a tray with two steaming cups of coffee on it and a plate with several slices of bread.

Mr. Narum saw him first.

"Well, if it isn't Ole from Overseth! Come in and dry yourself off."

"**Takk for sist,**" he courteously replied. Turning to Johanna he teased, "I smelled your bread way down the road and it just drew me right to the door."

"Oh, Ole," Johanna laughed, "I think you need lots of hot coffee and bread to fortify you on such a wet gray day. Sit down and help yourself. I'll take this coffee to **Bestefar** Narum and **Tante** Berte and I'll be right back."

She went down the hall to the west end of the house.

Ole turned to Mr. Narum and decided he had better get right at his errand. He sat down at the table opposite him.

"Help yourself!" Mr. Narum said, as he motioned to the plate of sandwiches. Thin slices of goat cheese covered each piece of bread. Ole decided this was too tempting to turn down and reached for one.

"**Herr** Narum," he began. "Today I came because I wanted to talk to you."

"Ja, vel?" Mr. Narum responded. "And what is on your mind?"

"**Herr** Narum, I have come to ask you for permission to have Johanna for my wife."

Mr. Narum smiled. "Ja, Ole, I have been waiting for someone to talk to me about that. Tante Berte has been telling me some things."

Ole went on. "I am making plans to go to Amerika. In fact, I am on my way home from Gjøvik where I booked passage for next May. I would like your permission to marry Johanna before I go."

After a few moments of thought, Mr. Narum slowly answered.

"Well, now, Ole. I have nothing against you and Johanna getting married, but this crazy Amerika talk doesn't set very well with me."

He shook his head and muttered, "Amerika. Amerika. That's all I've been hearing from Christian lately. I wish I'd never heard of such a place," he said in a very disgusting tone.

"I suppose one of these days he'll be sailing away. Why can't you and Johanna just get married and live here in Toten?"

Ole's heart sank. He realized it wasn't going to be as easy as he had hoped. This older generation just couldn't understand the Amerika idea.

"Now, Ole, the way I see it, with your older brother Hans married and working in Valdres, you will probably have first chance at the Overseth **gaard** some day. Why don't you wait? It is such a fine **gaard**; it should be enough to keep you here. You will not find anything like that in Amerika."

Ole didn't want to argue, but he had to let Mr. Narum know how he felt.

"When will that be?" he asked.

"Do you realize that it may be ten years before I can get to take over the farm?

Pa says he won't be ready to retire for a long time—until my younger brothers have grown up. I cannot wait around that long before getting married and being on my own. With five sons, Papa will have no problem finding someone to farm it."

"Ja, I suppose that is true. But must you go off to Amerika? It is so far away. How can you think of taking Johanna to some place that you have never seen?"

"**Herr** Narum, I came to see if you couldn't help us work things out. Please listen to my plans. We could get married in the spring before I go and when I have a home for Johanna I will send for her and she can join me in Amerika . . . in perhaps a year or so.

"But my problem is that Johanna is reluctant about leaving you and her work here at Narum. I will come right out and ask you, can you get along without her? Would you let her go?"

Paul Andreas Narum emptied his coffee cup. He appeared very thoughtful as he sipped the last of his coffee from the saucer.

"Ole, I don't know what I would have done without Johanna these years since her mother died. Both Helene Marie and Johanna have been such fine daughters. Of course I need her, but I do want her to be happy. I want her to someday have her own home."

He sat still and thought for a few moments, then went on.

"In answering your questions, I will say that I'm sure we can work it out. Helmine is growing up now and will be able to help. If worse come to worse, Klara can move home again.

"Let me say it again, Ole. It is not that I have anything against you and Johanna getting married. But as a good father I cannot just let her go off alone into God knows what kind of dangerous country. Haven't you heard about the Indian massacres?

"No, I want to know it is safe for her before I let her go."

"No more than I, **Herr** Narum," Ole agreed.

"Ja vel, why don't you wait with the marrying until you have a home and we know more definitely what lies ahead. I promise you, Ole, then I will not hold her back."

* * * * *

Soon winter settled on Toten. The snow lay in deep piles on roofs, and rows of fenceposts were topped with soft white peaks. The evergreen branches were laden. The Norwegian farmsteads had taken on a new look as drab buildings were decorated with dabs of sparkling white. Winter beauty was everywhere.

When it is snow weather in a land that has little wind, this winter covering lays right where it falls—like a fluffy thick frosting over the winter landscape.

The year of 1867, was in the third week of December and all thoughts were of **Jul.** Klara had already come to spend Christmas with her family. In the Narum kitchen Johanna, Klara and Helmine were preparing for the festivities. The **stabbur** was stacked with lefse and flatbrød. The head cheese and dried beef had been made, and a batch of sugar-topped **berliner krans** waited in a corner of the

stabbur for holiday eating.

The Narum girls were in the process of making **fattigmand.** Klara had mixed the dough and was rolling it out. Johanna stood over the kettle of hot fat and turned each thin diamond-shaped cooky. Helmine sprinkled the finished products with sugar and placed them in large wooden boxes.

Fattigmand was one recipe that wasn't hard on the butter and cream. But the inexpensiveness of the ingredients didn't detract from its popularity, for the Narum family never seemed to get enough. **Fattigmand** meant "poor man", but to the family it was a rich man's treat.

Helene Marie had gone to town with Papa and the boys to finish shopping. Johanna had been watching the hours of the day for she was expecting Ole and Christian. They had been working over at Hurdal at the lumber camp for more than two months now, and didn't get home except on weekends. Chris was going to America, too, and was earning money for his voyage.

It seemed like the afternoon had only begun, but already a hint of dusk was coming over the December day. The girls were just finishing the last few cakes when they heard the sleigh bells outside. Johanna went to the door to check. When she opened it, she heard Ole holler, "Look what we have for you!" as he lifted a Christmas tree from the sleigh.

"We chose two of the most perfect trees up on the timber—one for you folks and one for us at Overseth."

Johanna grabbed her long shawl, threw it over her head, quickly wrapping it criss-cross over her chest and twisting the ends around and tying them in front. Then she stepped outside to inspect the Christmas tree.

"Oh, Ole and Chris, it's beautiful! I can just see it in the parlor on Christmas Eve with candles burning on it, and our family holding hands around it and singing Christmas songs."

Ole set the tree down by the kitchen door. Johanna went on, "This will make Papa glad, for we aren't as fortunate as most Norwegians who have an abundance of trees in their backyard. This will save Papa a trip to the timber."

Ole and Chris came into the kitchen with her where they discovered the **fattigmand** and helped themselves to several.

"After eating that warmed-over porridge for a whole week, I need to have something sweet," Chris explained.

Johanna lit the lamp and the shadows that were gathering in the kitchen disappeared.

"I've been thinking of you fellows every day as we eat our hot noon meal," she said. "That frozen batch of porridge that you slice from each day must get tiresome."

"Oh, it isn't that bad," Ole replied. "You get a good appetite when you are out in the woods, sawing and chopping and hauling timber, so even a chunk of old porridge tastes good. We heat it up everyday, you know."

Christian added, "When we go back after **Jul,** you and Ole's mother had better fix a bigger kettle for each of us. It doesn't go very far for hard working men like us."

They all laughed.

Then Ole changed the subject. "Johanna, do you realize that Christmas is almost here? I don't suppose I'll be over again now until after Christmas Eve."

He took a small package from his pocket. "I found something for you the last time I was in Gjøvik. Here."

"I have a gift for you, too, Ole. Come on into the parlor and we can open them."

Ole watched Johanna as she lifted the cover from the little box he had given her, and saw her face light up as she discovered the gold pin. It was molded into flower shapes, and when the lamplight fell on it, it shone with a soft brilliance.

"Oh, thank you. It's beautiful! It shall look lovely on my dresses. Thank you. Thank you."

Now Ole carefully tore the paper from the little oblong package Johanna had given him. It was a small photo of Johanna in a silver frame. It had been taken several years before at the time of her confirmation.

"I don't want you to forget me when you go to Amerika," she said.

"Don't worry about that, Johanna! This is the best present you could have given me. Now I'll be able to see your face every day."

Also in the package was a pair of knit stockings. Johanna had made them from fine woolen yarn so Ole could use them for dress wear. She had been very careful in knitting for she knew Ole's mother would see them, and no one in the community could do such beautiful weaving and knitting as Marte Overseth.

He held them up.

"These mean much to me, Johanna, for you made them yourself." Then he grinned and teased, "Maybe because you kind of like me? Isn't that so?"

Johanna was a little bashful about answering, but finally she laughed and admitted, "You know I do, Mr. Ole Overseth, and I won't deny it."

"That's what I'm counting on, Johanna," Ole said as he took her hand, and this dreary December day became a time of joy and commitment for this young Norwegian and his sweetheart.

* * * * *

The lights of dawn were filtering into Johanna's room. She opened her eyes and the first thought she had was, "Today is May!"

She wished she could hold back time. She had been dreading this month, for in a few days Ole would be leaving. And Christian, too. Only a week until their ship sailed from Christiania.

Suddenly Johanna was wide awake. She sat straight up in bed. She remembered the ring that encircled the middle finger of her left hand.

She was engaged!

She lifted her hand in the semi-darkness and tried to examine the gold band. Yesterday Ole had come over and given it to her.

"I want Toten to know you are promised to me," he had said.

"Then I can leave confident that one day, not too far away, we can move this gold band to the third finger of your left hand and make you Mrs. Ole Overseth."

The feel of the ring on her finger, and its meaning, gave her a flood of joy. Yes, it was twice as precious because he had parted with some of the money he had earned for his Amerika trip to purchase it.

These past days Ole and Christian had been busy packing their trunks and getting everything in order. On April 28th, Ole had been to his church to sign up for emigrating, a process which members had to follow in order to receive a transfer from the membership of the Church of Norway where all their vital statistics were recorded.

Christian also had done that at the Kolbu **Kirke.** The day after tomorrow they would board the train at Gjøvik and head for Christiania.

Johanna jumped out of bed. There was much work to do today. Helene Marie and she would have to pack a basket of food for Christian to take on his voyage— bread, flatbrød, spekekjøt, cheeses and jam.

"We must be certain that he won't go hungry," Helene had said to Johanna.

Soon May 8th would be here, the day when Ole and Christian would sail away from the shores of Norge.

But Johanna was not sad, for now her life had a plan to it and the closer it came to Ole's departure, the more time Ole spent talking of their future. And she believed him, for if anyone would make good in Amerika, her betrothed, Ole Overseth, could.

And it was exciting to be a part of his plans for a "New Toten".

Chapter IV

The funeral was over and all the relatives and neighbors had gone home. Helene Marie and Johanna were busy getting the house back to normal again . . . but the rearranging and dusting did not accomplish it.

Things just weren't the same because **Tante** Berte's rocker was empty. As the sisters worked they caught themselves listening for the sound of **Tante's** voice, but it was not to be heard for now her kindly overseeing eyes had been closed in death.

How fast things can change, Johanna thought. In just two weeks. She felt badly because she had taken **Tante** Berte's first complaints so lightly. As long as Johanna could remember, **Tante** had had trouble getting around. Her swollen joints and aching feet had been nothing new. She hadn't been concerned even though **Tante** sat more than usual and often mentioned that her foot hurt. Finally **Tante** Berte had admitted to Helene and Johanna that she had been trimming a growth on her foot, and perhaps that was what was wrong.

When it had gotten worse, they called the doctor, but blood poisoning had set in and nothing could be done. It was hard to believe that such a small thing as a corn could be the cause of **Tante's** death.

Johanna picked up **Tante** Berte's cane and carried it into the storeroom.

"How we will miss her," she thought. "We girls depended on her so much for advice. No one can take her place.

"Who will do the sewing and the knitting? And who will pray each day for each of us? Yes, this home would be different with **Tante** gone."

Johanna laid the cane on the trunk in the corner. "Well, **Tante** won't be needing that any more," she thought. "No, and **Tante** won't have aching joints anymore either."

Johanna could envision **Tante** Berte released from her infirmity. There would be no more slow shuffling around. Perhaps now she was dancing for joy.

But on second thought, Johanna was sure **Tante** would express her joy in another way, for Tante had always frowned on such activity.

Johanna wished Ole was here so she could share her grief and thoughts with him. It had been over three months since he left and she hoped that soon she would get a letter from Amerika.

During these last few days as relatives and neighbors paid their calls, everyone had been asking about Christian and Ole. Someone had brought along a letter from a neighbor who had gone to Minnesota, to a place called the Saint Peter settlement. Johanna had read it. It sounded like a nice town with many Norwegian settlers. Many Swedes too, they said. Brother Peter Anton said this was where he intended to go.

But reading the letter from America had made her feel better, and calmed some of her fears about the wildness of that far away land.

How her life had changed these past few months. First, with Ole gone—and now **Tante** Berte. Johanna hoped she wouldn't have to wait much longer for a letter from Ole. She quietly said a prayer for his safety, for it was the only way she could show her love for him at this time.

For now, she had to be content with the knowledge that God knew where he was, how he was, and in due time she would hear.

* * * * *

It was a crowded, shoving mass of people that began the process of disembarkation. Yesterday, June 21st, the Nova Scotia had docked at Quebec and now everyone stood with their possessions, lined up for processing at the Canadian port.

Ole Overseth breathed a deep breath of good fresh air and tried to forget the smells of the ship's hold where all these emigrants had lived for more than six weeks.

The stench of vomit had become commonplace because the majority of passengers had experienced seasickness. For some, it had lasted the entire voyage.

There had also been the odor of people living close together without bathing facilities, and the mixture of food smells, strong cheeses and even mold as both food and clothing had to contend with the damp sea air.

Ole could hardly wait to get his feet on solid ground. He had decided after only a few days on board that the life of the sea wasn't for him. He had longed for the smell of fresh dirt, of earth unturned by the plow, the smell of hay. Why, the smells of animals would be like perfume compared to the vile odors of the last weeks onboard ship.

Ole and Christian stayed close to a group of Norwegians whose destination was Winneshiek County, Iowa. This group from Valdres had made arrangements to have someone meet them here in Quebec and take charge of getting them transported to Decorah.

Ole was glad to be a part of them for he had had enough experience with foreign languages during this trip to realize that he would feel strange in a land where Norwegian wasn't the mother tongue.

The voices around him sounded like ancient Babel. People from many countries had crossed the Atlantic with him. When the Nova Scotia left England it was jammed with Germans and Irish, besides the Norwegians and Swedes. He had had many opportunities during the past weeks to discover the helplessness, confusion and misunderstanding that came when persons cannot communicate.

But now he had more than the language to contend with. Last night when the guide met with the passengers headed for Winneshiek County, he had informed them of the amount of money needed for this portion of the journey. They would go by rail, stopping in Chicago, and then the train would take them to the town of Decorah.

But here came the catch . . . it would cost $14.

Last night Ole had taken his money out again and recounted it. As far as he could figure, when he got his **kroner** changed into dollars, it would take all of his money. He would only have the loose change in his pockets and would have to live on that until he could get to Decorah and find some work. Ole hoped he could buy several loaves of bread and a chunk of cheese for that.

Just sitting around for almost seven weeks hadn't been good for Ole. He felt listless. Really he felt like a caged animal as day after day for so many weeks he had lived in cramped quarters. He was becoming anxious to get out under the sun and work. His muscles needed some good hard exercise to get them back into shape. "Then," he thought to himself, "I will feel like myself again."

Well, it wouldn't be long now—perhaps a week or ten days and he would reach his destination.

Ole looked around at some of the women who had been on the crossing with him and most of them were very weary and pale. He thought about Johanna and wondered how she would stand a trip like this. He hated to think of her having to go through it, but it was a necessary step in their plans. He hoped it would take more than sea-sickness to stop her from joining him.

Now he was an ocean and forty-five days away from her and his native land, but he was looking to the future, and had finished the first step in their plans. Soon he would see this land of opportunity he had heard so much about. In his pocket he had a letter addressed to Johanna Amalie Narum, Vestre Toten, Norge, and he would get it posted the first chance he got.

* * * * *

Once again it was Christmas in Toten. The fluffy snow decorated the landscape, and the hearts of Totningers had experienced the excitement of another Christmas Eve.

Klara had been spending several days in her old home with **Far** Narum and her brothers and sisters, and the spirit of Christmas and family love had seemed especially strong this year. Perhaps it seemed this way to Johanna because she needed love more this year.

The closeness the three older Narum sisters had experienced these past few days was special. Together they had visited and laughed and shared and worked. They had decided the three of them should go to town and have a photograph taken together. It had been mentioned to Papa and he had agreed it would be a good idea.

"I'll take you myself," he said, and the day before Christmas they had dressed in their best and off they went to the photographer. Johanna had put on her finely woven gray wool with the double rows of narrow black braid trim around the neck, at the wrist and around the armholes, and a dozen little black buttons placed down the middle of the blouse.

Sisters Klara and Helene had on their long black skirts and each wore stylish striped blouses. Klara had her little gold cross hanging neatly at her waist while Helen's hung on a long chain around her neck.

The photographer had Johanna sit on the chair with one of her sisters standing on each side. She gracefully laid her hands in her lap with her left hand laying on top so the ring on her middle finger could be seen.

All three sisters posed in their most serious, grown-up manner. Mr. Narum watched while the photographer got behind his black cloth and took their picture. He was proud of his three oldest daughters. It made him happy to know that his girls felt this strong family bond. Paul Andreas Narum had always felt a little guilty because he let Klara live with her mother's brother's family—the Kysets. He had feared she would grow away from her brothers and sisters and from him. But having her with them on holidays and many weekends had kept her a part of his family.

"When do we eat?" the Narum boys were again asking.

On this second day of Christmas, Johanna decided her brothers regarded Christmas as mainly a time for food. It seemed the girls were always laying the table with the Christmas bakings—The **lefse,** and **flatbrød, krandser** and **fattigmand,** and the cheeses and sild. Now the family again bowed their heads as Papa asked the blessing on the food.

"Well, Johanna, how do you think Ole is spending his Christmas?" David asked.

"Oh, Ole is perhaps celebrating with some nice Norwegian family in America," she said.

Peter Anton teased, "Ja, maybe some pretty girl over there is helping him celebrate."

Peter Anton received a stern look from Helene Marie.

Johanna glanced down at the ring on her finger to get some reassurance. It had been seven months since Ole left and all she had now to show for this engaged relationship was this ring and three letters from America that ended with "All my love, Ole."

Klara, sitting next to her, patted her hand and with words directed to Peter, said, "Ole can't find any girl anywhere that could take Johanna's place, and you know it."

Peter went back to his eating, but the mischievous grin was still on his face.

When you were the in-between child in a large family, you had to find a way to get attention once in a while.

He heard Helene Marie's voice. "I'm sure Ole is lonesome this Christmas now that he is so far from Norge . . . and even though Christian may not admit it, I am sure he is lonely too."

"And so are their parents," Papa added.

"One of these years I intend to spend Christmas there," Martinus piped up, "and then you can sit and feel sorry for me."

Johanna was quiet for a moment and then said, "Who knows, maybe I'll be there next year."

Far Narum loudly cleared his throat, and with a tone of authority stated, "Let's talk about something else. America is far away and now it is Christmas here in Toten, so let's enjoy it together."

The jolly atmosphere changed to silence, and then little Hans spoke. "I'm enjoying it, Papa," he said as he reached for another **krandser** with one hand, and more **fattigmand** with the other.

After **middags** was finished and the table cleared and the dishes washed, Johanna went to her room. She couldn't help but think about Ole during these days of Christmas. She took the letters out of the little painted chest on her trunk and began rereading them one by one.

My dear Johanna,

I arrived in Quebec June 21st on the Nova Scotia. It took us six weeks plus three days to cross the Atlantic. I used my last $14.00 to pay for the train ride on the Grand Trunk line to Winneshiek County, Iowa, so I am a **fattig** man as I reach America. But Chris has a little money left so I'm sure we'll get along until we find jobs. We are both O.K. Will write when I reach Iowa.

All my love,
Ole

My dear Johanna,   15 July 1868

We reached Winneshiek County, Iowa, two weeks ago. We came to Decorah and I looked up Sven and he helped me find a job at a neighboring farm. Chris also has a job.

It feels good to get to work again. That six-week voyage made my muscles weak and now I am trying to get back into shape. It is harvest time here in America, and so there is much work to do.

I imagine you are wondering what Amerika is like. The country around here has many bluffs because it is close to the big river called the Mississippi. This river is so big that ships go on it. Several creeks run through this area, and it is beautiful country. I wish there was land here for homesteading because I know you would like it here. Now I must work a while and earn some money. Other Norwegians are so willing to help me and share but I like to feel I am man enough to be independent. I will never forget the kindnesses I have been shown as a newcomer in this new land.

Let me assure you that I have your picture beside my Bible and you are never far from my thoughts. So far, God has been good to me, as I have a nice Norwegian family to work for and I am learning many things about American farming. The weather here is different than Norge's—much hotter and drier—so I earn my wages by the "sweat of my brow" these days.

There is a little church here that I attended last Sunday with the family I work for and even though I was in a different land, when I sat there on Sunday and heard the same Word of God that I heard at home, and sang the same hymns, I did not feel like I was in a strange country.

I hope you are all well—and I hope you are missing me because I know I certainly have been missing you. Greet everyone, and I have learned a few new words—one is "Hallo", which means **"God dag"**.

Write as soon as you can.

> All my love,
> Ole Overseth
> from Amerika

Kjaere Johanna,   15 October 1868

Soon it will be your birthday and I want to send my best wishes. Are you really twenty-one years of age? You will be catching up to me soon.

Do you know how I spent my birthday last month? It was on a Sunday and there was no services in the church. You see, the **prest** here serves several congregations, so Mrs. Oleson got out the large sermon book and Thorvald read a sermon for us. Later I read all of your letters over again, so I had a good visit from you that day too.

After **middags** I walked over to where Christian is working and spent the afternoon with him. He had some news. He and some of his newcomer friends are leaving soon for Minnesota where they plan to work in a lumber camp this winter. They will headquarter in St. Peter as some of the fellows have relatives there. I'm sure he will send you his address so you can keep in touch with him. There is also alot of railroad building going on in that area so he hopes to get a job on that in the spring. He has given up the idea of homesteading. I guess if you do not have someone special to build a house for, it is of no interest.

Tell **Far** Narum that Decorah is a very progressive town for there is a university there called Luther College. Men are being trained there to be preachers.

The other evening I walked over to Nordness where there is a store and blacksmith shop, and where there are usually some men sitting around and visiting. I learned the latest community news. The settlers around there are from Toten, Valders, Sogn, Sigdal and Hadeland. We got to talking about Norge too. That is both good and bad, for I do get lonesome for home and especially you. They said two brothers who had a piece of land here had sold it and were going back to Norge again. Some people expect America to be heaven, which it is not, but it has so many possibilities that a person can put up with a few hard things now when the future holds so much.

I want to tell you a little about the family I am living and working for. Mr. Thorvald Oleson is a little man—but so much energy! I must go in high speed all day to keep up with him. Mrs. Oleson is very quiet and leaves all decisions up to him, but she, too, is a very hard worker, and keeps six children and us two men well fed and clean. She reminds me of you. Her love and concern for others are shown in many quiet ways. You would like her very much I know. That reminds me, before you come to Amerika you must try to buy a book of sermons, for when we get to our homestead I know we will not have a pastor to listen to every Sunday.

When I start to think of what we have ahead, the challenges, and adventure I become very excited. We have much to look forward to—especially being together, and building a home of our own. Can you believe it, Johanna? It **shall** be. Just be patient.

All my love,
Ole

Chapter V

The bright Iowa sun was shining once again after several days of spring showers. May 1869 was almost over. It had been a busy month with plowing and planting. At the breakfast table Thorvald Oleson announced, "Ole and I shall make a trip into Decorah today."

They hurried with the chores, hitched the team of horses to the lumber wagon and loaded up several bags of wheat. Then they headed northwest on their journey to town. Ole was glad for a change after putting in long days of spring work. He was aware of an inner excitement today, too, for this meant stopping at the post office.

Mr. Oleson held the reins and they followed the trail which had become muddy from yesterday's moisture. As they drove, and sometimes splashed along, Ole found himself humming an old familiar song. The happy melody of "Haul the Water and Haul the Wood" had been dancing around in his head ever since he arose that morning. When he came to the last line, "so is it fun to live," he really meant it, for this was how he felt today. The sun was shining on a fresh green world and he was sure he would have a treat in store at the post office.

As they reached the outskirts of Decorah, they heard hammering. Workers were busy building more houses. Mr. Oleson headed the horses toward the river and over to the mill where the wheat was to be ground. They were relieved to see there weren't many wagons waiting in line today.

After the wheat was ground, sacked and loaded in the wagon, Mr. Oleson pulled the team to a stop on Main Street. It was very wet and muddy. He gave Ole his instructions. "Go to the post office and pick up the mail while I go to the blacksmith and have some repairs made," he said.

"Enjoy yourself in the big town. Meet me at the hotel dining room about one o'clock and we'll have some coffee before we load the other provisions we need. We should still have plenty of time to get home so we can get the chores done before dark."

Ole jumped down from the wagon seat and stepped up onto the board sidewalk and headed in the direction of the post office. He walked in the door and looked around. The postman had his back to him, so Ole cleared his throat and ventured a jolly "Hallo."

The postman turned and answered, "Good morning," in crisp English. "What can I do for you today?"

Ole had decided he would try some American words, and he remembered that here in America "post" was called "mail," so he spoke up, "Have you any 'mail' for Ole Overseth?"

The postman turned back to his packets of letters and soon returned with several for Ole. "It looks like the people in Norway haven't forgotten you, and here's one from Minnesota, too."

Ole was a little puzzled as to the meaning of the English word "forgotten," but continued with his assignment.

"Have you any 'mail' for Thorvald Oleson?"

"We'll see," the postman said as he returned to his assortment. Again, letters were found. Ole accepted them with a "Many thanks," and went out onto the boardwalk with all the precious envelopes he had received.

It was still about an hour before he was to meet Mr. Oleson so he decided to walk down by the river behind Main Street and find a quiet spot where he could look over his mail.

The river was rushing along its way from the new rain that had filled its channel today. Ole found a spot of grass that looked dry and settled himself and began sorting through his mail.

Today he had a letter from Johanna and one from his mother, and what do you know, one from Christian.

Ole opened the one from his mother first and quickly glanced through it. It was dated February 1st. Everyone was well at Overseth. "We miss you and send our greetings and hope this letter reaches you. Your older brother Hans and his wife Marianne were home for Christmas and they have returned to Valdres again."

Ole was glad to know everything was all right at home.

Now what could Christian have on his mind? He wasn't a letter writer. He took a quick look at it.

St. Peter, Minn.

Kjaere Ole,

    I am working on the railroad now. There is a lot of work available here, and the pay is better than working hired man. Soon you'll be able to come to St. Peter by rail. It really would be good to see you. Keep me in touch with your plans.

Christian Narum

Now Ole held Johanna's letter. He had saved hers until last. He would always recognize her beautiful handwriting. When he opened it, a photograph tumbled out.

What a nice surprise! There she was, his Johanna, with her two sisters Klara and Helene Marie. He inspected the picture more closely and noticed his ring on Johanna's finger. That made him feel good. He unfolded the letter. He had to find out what she had to say.

Kjaere Ole,

Thank you for your letters. You don't know how I wait for them. And I am very happy when the envelope is very fat, for I am anxious to hear about you and your life in Amerika. And if each letter really costs over $.50 to mail, you should make it long and get your money's worth.

Helene Marie and I are very busy now as **Bestefar** has to be in bed all the time. It makes many, many trips down the hall to his room each day. We have to be both nurse and cook and housekeeper these days.

I got some goose down and i am making a feather quilt for our home in Amerika. It will go into my trunk with the other things I am gathering up. I will be waiting to hear when you get some land of your own, so I can finish packing my trunk and sail to you.

Last month we all attended Magnus and Guri's wedding at the Maalstad **gaard.** It was a big celebration that lasted a whole week. They have moved into one of the houses at Maalstad already.

The water lapping in the background made a melancholy sound. As he read the words she had written to him, he became more and more lonesome for her. Had it already been over a year since he had seen her?

Ole put the letter back into the envelope. He would read it more thoroughly when he got back to Oleson's. He looked at the photo again and studied her dear face. His eyes traced its structure—the well-placed cheekbones, and nicely shaped chin. Her lips were parted in a relaxed, thoughtful mood. "Was she thinking of me?" he wondered. She still wore her hair parted in the middle and drawn back, her ears bared and her eardrops hanging. How he wished he could look into those large, serious eyes again. She seemed so far away now. But Johanna had reminded him that she was waiting.

Things hadn't moved along as quickly as he had hoped. Money didn't come so easily in Amerika. This hired-man job earned him only $13 a month. That didn't add up very fast.

During the winter, hired men only received their board and room, so last winter he had found some extra jobs cutting timber. He was saving every cent so he would have enough money to make a claim down payment when the time came, and he also would be needing money for Johanna's voyage.

Well, maybe this was as it should be. He was sure Johanna wouldn't feel like leaving her sister alone with all the work now that **Bestefar** had to be cared for.

Ole put the mail in his back pocket and walked along the river to the mill. Then he turned over to Main Street. It was a little early for Mr. Oleson. A group of men were sitting outside and he stood near them for a while and listened to their conversation. Their dialect sounded like that from northern Norge—perhaps Trondheim. They were talking about a group of settlers that had passed through Decorah last week on their way west.

Mr. Oleson soon came, they had their coffee, loaded their supplies and headed for home. Ole gave Mr. Oleson his mail, and he looked forward to rereading his own that night. After supper he must begin another letter to his Johanna.

* * * * *

Ole's thoughts had been in Norway all day. It was Midsummer's Eve, 1870, and he was remembering the long hours of daylight and the bonfires of June 24th. He wondered if Johanna and the Narum family were having any special activities.

This had been a special day for him, because Vilhelm Hove, the neighbor, had stopped by with mail. There had been a letter from Johanna, and it had made him very excited. He had read it immediately, and now was going over it again by the light of this summer evening. Yes, there were longer evenings here in Amerika now, also.

It felt good to sit down. It had been such a busy day. Haying was in full swing and all day long Thorvald and he had been helping a neighbor with his work. As Ole looked west across Mr. Oleson's wheat field, he could see the tops of the haystacks they had been making.

What a hot, sultry day it had been, and such an itchy job! The hay chaff had stuck to his damp body as he perspired from this hard labor in the midsummer sun. It was never like this in Norge!

Now he had washed up and was content after a supper of **tykmelksuppe** and fresh strawberries for dessert.

He went back to Johanna's letter.

4 May 1870

Kjaere Ole,

I have so much news for you today. Can you believe that brother David has finally found himself a girl? Her name is Johanna Marie and he seems to be pretty serious about her. Maybe it won't be too long before there will be a new housewife here at Narum.

It looks like there may be many weddings coming up. Sister Klara and Ole Grevlos are engaged and Johannes Stikbakke has been coming to see Helene Marie.

About a month ago we got a letter from Christian in Minnesota and he mentioned that there is a big demand for hired girls in St. Peter. He thinks he can find me a job when I get ready to come to Amerika.

Neighbor Johan Narumshagen and his sister, Anne Mathea are planning to go to Amerika next year. It sounds like they will go to St. Peter for they have some relatives there.

You should see how little Hans has grown. He was 11 years now and you wouldn't believe how he has changed since you left. He is going to be a husky, big man. He follows Papa and tries to help with the outside work, so he doesn't spend much time in the house with us any more.

Write soon,
Love, Johanna

Ole sat with paper and pen in hand. The two years since he had come to Amerika had gone by so quickly. It was good that they had been able to keep in touch. He had to answer her letter right away.

Midsummer's eve 1870

My darling Johanna,

My, you certainly had alot of romantic news. I have some, too. Sven is getting married this fall. The neighbor girl that he has been going with is a fine young woman and very pretty, as you might guess. Her father was killed during spring work this year. His team was frightened and ran away, dragging him over the countryside. Her mother wants Sven to take over the farm and he is already helping there. So, guess he won't be going west with me either.

I was glad to hear that Johan Narumshagen and his sister were coming to Amerika. I think this is a wise move for Johan as he has no future staying on his home farm with only such a small acreage, where they only had four cows, one horse and seven sheep when I was home.

My plans aren't definite yet, but I will go west either this fall or in the early spring. I must find a group to travel with as I do not want to spend any money on train fare, although there is a train that goes to Sioux City now; this town is just south of Dakota Territory and many settlers are headed for that area.

I made my application for citizenship when I was in Decorah last month so I am now eligible for homestead land.

It is good that I have had this job with Mr. Oleson. I have learned so much about American farming. For instance, today we have been haying, but we do not hang the hay on the racks like farmers do back in Norway. Here it is cut and raked in piles and then put into big stacks.

I have had to get used to handling oxen, also. You know that at home we had only horses. Oxen are much cheaper than horses here in Amerika, and cheaper to feed, and they are very strong when it comes to breaking prairie. I am sure I will have to begin farming with them. Mr. Oleson has one team of horses and two teams of oxen which he uses for field work.

Also, I have had some experience with growing corn. Pigs do well on it, and it can also be a food for people. In August before the kernels get hard, it is boiled and served hot with butter on it. It tastes very good! I think it takes the hot weather of Amerika to make corn grow.

I will let you know as soon as I make a move so you can keep in touch with me. After I take a claim I will probably have to get a job on the railroad or lumbering for I will need many things to start farming, and everything takes money.

I am very lonesome for you tonight. I want you to know that I haven't forgotten about you, so you had better not get any romantic ideas about anyone else.

I love you, Johanna,

Ole

* * * * *

The harvest was finished, and now it was plowing time. Ole and Mr. Oleson were busy getting some of the fields ready for the following year. Walking behind the oxen all day, as they plodded at the same slow pace, around and around the field, was a tiresome job.

Ole had decided that he definitely would not be here to see this plowed field planted. As soon as he had helped Mr. Oleson get his corn picked, he was leaving. The September weather had been very warm and windy, and it was beginning to dry some of the stalks already.

One evening when he came in from walking behind the plow all day, Mrs. Oleson had a letter for him. It was from Johanna.

30 August 1870

Kjaere Ole,

Bestefar died the 22nd of August. The funeral was in Kolbu **Kirke** yesterday. Many relatives were here so Helene and I have been busy baking and cooking. Poor **Bestefar** was bedfast so long. He got to be an old man of 78. We will miss him.

The way things are working out now, I feel that I should be making plans for my trip to Amerika. We have been far apart for so long. I am no longer needed here at home so I would like to come next summer. What do you think about that?

I could come when Johan Narumshagen and Anne Mathea come so I would have some neighbors to travel with. If Christian can find me a job in St. Peter, I think it is all settled. I know you really would like to have me near to you. Let me know right away if this is all right.

Love,

Johanna

What great news! Ole could hardly believe it. Things were finally working out. It would be so good to see Johanna again. Ole had hoped he would have a nice little house on a piece of land all ready and waiting for her when she came.

Perhaps it still could be. In one year many things could be done. Well, anyway, he had money for her ticket, and he also had money for his claim. Now it was time for him to make his move, too.

30 September 1870

My darling, darling Johanna,

What great news your letter brought me. You couldn't have given me a better birthday present. All day tomorrow I will surely be singing with happiness.

Yes, I believe it would be best for you to come next summer when you have Johan and Anne Mathea to travel with, and being they are going to St. Peter it will work out fine for you to go there. By then I may be in that part of the country too, for I will probably be working on the railroad. There is alot of railroad building going on in that area. Ask Christian to find you a job with a Norwegian family, for it is rather hard to work with someone who doesn't speak your language.

I will right away send you money for your ticket so you can begin making definite plans. Now I have something wonderful to look forward to, and I know you must have some time to get ready for such a big move. Perhaps you will need more than one trunk.

All my love,
Ole

Chapter VI

It was early in the afternoon of May 24th, 1871, that Johanna went to her room to prepare for her visit to the Overseth **gaard**. Marte Overseth had invited her to spend the afternoon with her.

Johanna carefully combed her hair and dressed. She slipped her earrings into place and finally took out the gold pin Ole had given her and pinned it to the neck of her white blouse.

Johanna was excited today, and also a little tense. She had been to the Overseth home several times before, but that was with Ole. Well, Peter Anton Overseth would be here soon to get her so that would be a help. She heard the carriage wheels in the drive now. Peter, five years younger than his brother Ole, was sitting in the carriage waiting for her. He was getting to be a fine looking young man. They had always gotten along well together, so Johanna was soon at ease.

The drive to the Overseth **gaard** was very pleasant. As the horses trotted along, Johanna took in the scenery. May in Norge was a lovely time. The birches had leafed, and the grasses had turned their beautiful bright green again. All nature was young and happy.

Streams were flowing again, and Johanna knew that beyond, in the **fjell** country, waterfalls had begun their cascades down the mountains, as the winter snows began to melt. Up on the **seters** the sheep and lambs, the goats and their kids, together with the cows, were getting settled down to luxury living again after a winter of being penned up. Johanna felt a little stab in her heart as she thought of leaving all this.

She was brought back from her thoughts by Peter who asked, "Are you ready for your trip, Johanna?"

"Oh, I suppose I'll be packing and repacking until the day I leave," she answered. "It is so hard to know what I will be needing. Ole says it is hard to buy some things in Amerika. These new communities don't have many stores yet."

Peter interrupted her, "I've got it figured out, Johanna. I think I'll go to Amerika and be a businessman. It sounds like they can use some storekeepers in those new towns. Perhaps my brother Hans can find me a job in Valdres this fall. When I get some experience, I may follow you and Ole to Amerika."

Johanna looked surprised. "I didn't know that you were interested in going to Amerika."

"I have never really cared for farming, but working or running a store sounds exciting to me. I'll be twenty-one next year, and then it will be time for me to shift for myself. I must get something figured out."

Soon they turned into the lane of the Overseth **gaards.** Two farms set side-by-side and two different Overseth families lived in them. The cherry trees and apple trees behind the house were in blossom, and Marte already had flowers blooming by the door. This attractive middle-aged woman stood in the doorway waiting for them.

"Velkommen, Johanna," she greeted, and in her gracious way led her daughter-in-law-to-be into the house. Here in the parlor she had laid out the little table with a lovely cloth and some fine cups and plates. It was set for two people.

"Sit yourself down," she said and then quickly moved into the kitchen.

Marte Overseth came back with hot coffee and a wooden tray covered with a cloth. She set it down. "You must have some coffee, Johanna, and then we can sit and talk."

A napkin lay beside each plate. Johanna slowly took hers and laid it on her lap. Marte uncovered the tray, and Johanna saw the dainty waffles on it. Marte passed a bowl of sugar and a beautiful ladle-like silver spoon, with a design cut through it.

"Sift some sugar on your waffles with this," she said. "Or perhaps you would rather have some lingonberries on them."

Johanna sugared her waffles and began eating. This world of Marte Overseth was like a fairyland to her. Everything was lovely and Marte was such a refined woman. Her talents were displayed all around. On the wall was a woven wall hanging that Johanna was sure Marte had made, and colorful woven pillows were on the bench. This, she thought, was the world that Ole had grown up in.

"What have you heard from Ole lately?" Marte questioned.

"He was still in Winneshiek County when he last wrote, but he was getting ready to go west. Several families from around Decorah were going to look for land to settle out in Dakota Territory. He is probably on the prairie now. He will meet me in St. Peter, Minnesota, later this year. I can hardly believe that we will finally be together again."

When they had finished lunch, Marte got up and soon came back with her arms full. She laid the things on the bench. "I want you and Ole to have these for your home in Amerika."

Johanna arose from her chair to inspect them.

There were two tablecloths. One was white linen with six napkins, and there were two colored woven woolen runners and some woven linen towels and pillowcases.

"I've made these things for you," Marte said. "I want you to take them with you to Amerika."

Johanna choked up when she saw all these lovely things, and she felt the love Marte Overseth was trying to express to her through them, and also the concern Marte had for the home Ole and she would be making.

"How can I thank you?" Johanna asked.

"Just use them, and think of me, and of our love for you both. You know, we do hate to see you go so far away, but both Ole's father and I wish you and Ole the best."

If this woman had been her own mother, Johanna would have embraced her to show her appreciation, but she couldn't do that to the woman who would be her mother-in-law, so Johanna put out her hand and said, "Many thousand thanks. You are so kind to me."

"It was fun for me to do it. You know I have no daughters of my own to fuss over."

She put her arm around Johanna. "God be with you, dear Johanna. I am happy that Ole chose you to be his wife, and not someone who is a stranger to us. Now we will be able to picture the two of you together making your home—even if it is in far away Amerika. **Farvel.**"

Johanna saw a tear trickle down Marte Overseth's cheek.

"Give Ole the dearest greetings from his Mother and Father in Norway. We do miss him."

* * * * *

Johanna checked off another day on the calendar. May 31, 1871, had come, and there would be only a few days left before she would leave for Christiania and her voyage to Amerika. It was becoming real now, this trip that she had been planning for three years.

Today Johanna would take a tour to Kolbu **Kirke** where she had to register for emigration. Little sister Helmine wanted to go along, so brother Martinus harnessed the horse to the cart and the two sisters loaded the three plants that Johanna had been tending so carefully in the Narum kitchen all winter. They climbed up on the seat of the little cart and the pony trotted off down the familiar road to the church.

Johanna stopped first at the parsonage across the road from the church, and signed the register. She took the pen, dipped it in the ink, and carefully wrote the date—"31-May-1871"—followed by her full name, "Johanna Amalie Paulsdatter Fogd Narum."

"Now it was done." She was no more a member of this little church. She shook hands and said farewell to her beloved pastor, **Prest** Magelsen, who finished the entry in the church records with "gone to **Nordamerika**". He gave her his final words, "Remember all that I have taught you, Johanna, and don't ever forget that Jesus will always go with you and be your friend through both good and bad days. God bless you, Johanna."

Johanna had to force herself to hold back the tears. It was almost as hard for her to say goodby to her church and her pastor as it would be to say farewell to her father and her home at Narum. Everything was so final now—she had signed the register.

Outside, Johanna looked across the road to the peaceful scene of the white church and the quiet cemetery. Many graves already had flowers blooming on them. Helmine helped Johanna carry the plants she had brought along. They were bright red flowering begonias.

First they went to **Bestefar's** grave. A new marker had been erected there. "David Paulson Narum-born 1792, died 22-8-1870."

The girls set one plant there.

Next to his grave was **Tante** Berte's. Johanna stood there for a while as her thoughts went back to that day when **Tante** Berte had told her not to give up. Now Johanna's dream was coming true, but **Tante** Berte was not there to share in it.

Johanna would never forget **Tante's** advice. She could still hear her voice, "You give up too soon, Johanna. It is not so hopeless. Give it time." It had been almost four years since **Tante** Berte said that, and soon Johanna would be married to her dear Ole.

"Goodbye, **Tante** Berte. **Takk for sist.**"

Now Helmine held the last plant. Together she and Johanna walked to Mother's resting place. There on the stone was etched the name "Helene Marie Hansdatter Kyset, wife of Paul Andreas Narum, born Nov. 3, 1820; died May 5, 1861." At the bottom were the words **"Vi skal møte i himmelen"** that Papa had chosen.

Johanna dug a hole for the flower and planted it. She gave Helmine her little spade and told her to take it back to the cart. Johanna wanted to spend a little time here by herself. This was a farewell she had to make alone.

Johanna packed dirt around the roots of the plant. "This is perhaps the last thing I can do for you, Mama," she said. "I have missed having you to talk to and to advise me through these past ten years. You gave your young life for one of your babies, but you gave all of us so much."

Johanna looked again at the words on the stone—"We shall meet in heaven". "I guess it doesn't really matter whether I am in Norge or in Amerika, we shall meet again in our home in heaven," she thought.

Johanna knelt there for a long time, loving thoughts and painful thoughts intertwining together with her prayers. Then she got to her feet and took one last look at this spot.

"Thank you, Mama. **Farvel** for now."

Johanna turned and headed towards the cart. There were so many hard goodbyes to be said. The more one had loved, the harder farewells were to say. Helmine was already on the seat of the cart. Johanna took the reins and directed the pony away from Kolbu **Kirke** and from the cemetery. Inside her heart was assured. "We shall meet again."

That evening after supper Johanna went to her room. Her departure was getting so close now, and tonight she was riddled by fears of the future. There were so many unknowns in the days ahead of her. She wished Ole wasn't so far away. The world was so big and the ocean so wide. She needed some words of comfort. She opened her Bible to the book of John. She would reread the 14th chapter and see what Jesus said before his departure from his disciples.

She read, "Let not your hearts be troubled."

Yes, this was what she needed tonight. Johanna had heard about the hardships of ocean voyages, the epidemics, the Indians and all the things that could go wrong. She looked at the verse once more.

"Let not your hearts be troubled. Believe in God, believe also in me."

Johanna read on about the home Jesus was preparing for her and she smiled. "That is just what Ole is doing for me, too—preparing a home for me. The two who love me most are both preparing places for me. I will have a home no matter what."

She went on down the chapter to the 23rd verse where Jesus said, "If a man loves me, he will keep my word, and my Father will love him, and we will come to him and make our home with him."

She closed the Bible and bowed her head.

"Kjaere Gud,
Dearest Jesus,
   Please come with me on this voyage, and make your home with Ole and me in Dakota Territory."

* * * * *

Christiania was an exciting city. In its big harbor ships from many lands were moored. On one side were fishing boats where fishermen were busy unloading their daily catch of shrimp and mackerel.

Far Narum, Johanna, Johan Narumshagen and Anna Mathea stood looking at the nautical scene. Their eyes tried to take it all in. Beyond the other ships was the one they had a special interest in. It was the ship Johanna, Johan and Anna Mathea would sail on the day after tomorrow. This world of boats, ships, fish and fishermen symbolized Norway to most people, but to these inland folks it was a sight to which they were not accustomed.

These four Totningers had spent several days in the capital city and now felt somewhat acquainted with its cobbled streets and rows of shops. On June 8th, they had left Gjøvik on the railroad. **Far** Narum had insisted on going along. "I'll feel better if I know that you get off all right," he said. "Christiania is a big city, Johanna."

They had spent the afternoon shopping. Johanna and Anna Mathea had browsed in a bookstore, and Johanna found what she wanted. Ole had asked her to bring a book of sermons along to Amerika. She had chosen one written by a Swedish pastor, Linderots.

Before the bookstore, they had gone to the photographer's. Papa insisted on having Johanna's photo taken in the fashionable white dress, trimmed in black braid which he had purchased for her yesterday.

"When you are in Amerika I must have a picture so I can see your face once in a while."

Johanna had begged for a photo of him, also. He had finally agreed to a little daguerretype. But Papa would not take off his knit cap. Dear Papa, after his hair had thinned on top he always tried to keep his head covered. Well, at least, she would have a picture to take along.

Papa had brought Johanna into a Goldsmith Shop where he had her help him choose six silver spoons.

"Do you like these?" he questioned. Then he had the goldsmith engrave her initials—JPN—on the back of each of these lightweight silver coffee spoons, and had him wrap and pack them into a little box.

After their afternoon of shopping, they walked back to their rooms. The narrow streets held much activity. All sorts of people, in all sorts of carriages and carts, drawn by all sorts of horses and ponies were each on different errands. Finally they climbed the steps to their rooms.

Far Narum took Johan into a corner and began giving him advice again. Paul Andreas Narum would be placing his daughter Johanna in Johan's care when the ship sailed day-after-tomorrow and he had many things to counsel him about.

Johanna got out the book she had purchased and carefully wrote on the flyleaf, "Johanna Amalie Paulsdatter Fogd Narum. Purchased this 10th day of June, 1871, in Christiania." She rearranged her trunk until she found a corner where she could pack it. The leather-covered book took up a large amount of space.

When Papa noticed she had her trunk open, he came with his box of spoons. He cleared his throat and said, "This is for your home in Amerika, Johanna. I want you to take it along when you go."

Johanna could hear the emotion in his voice and it made her want to cry. Dear Papa. He had never been a man who displayed his feelings, but she had always known how deep his love was for his children, and for her. Then as she knelt over the trunk, he tenderly patted her on the head.

"Thanks so much!" she said, and placed the box of silver spoons in an empty spot in her trunk.

Far Narum quickly reverted to his stern business manner.

"Ja vel, tomorrow the trunks must be delivered to the ship," he reminded them. "We shall hire a cart and load all of them on it. Have you everything packed now?"

He thought a few moments, and then went on, "Tomorrow we must fill up your food baskets. Ja, tomorrow will be a busy day."

* * * * *

It was early dawn when **Far** Narum, Johanna, Johan and Anna Mathea got to the harbor at Christiania. It was sailing day. The gulls were busily flying in confusion over the water. Their cries gave atmosphere to the harbor. Many people were on the dock this morning because the ship to England was loading and in an hour would be pulling anchor and moving south with many emigrants bound for Amerika on board.

Everyone was tense. Papa had wakened at four o'clock and kept prodding them all to hurry! hurry! Here on the dock he had a few minutes alone with Johanna and he placed a note for 50 **kroner** in her hand.

"I don't want you ever to go hungry," he said, and added,

"If things don't work out in Amerika, don't be too proud to come back. Remember, I'll always send you money to get home again. Please write us often. You know I'll be worrying if I don't hear."

"Yes, Papa. Yes, Papa," was all that Johanna could say.

The cries of the gulls rang in her ears and the pain of separation tore at her heart. The shadowy activity of sailors and passengers in the foggy, early morning light made her wonder if it was just a bad dream. But then she heard the call.

"Everyone aboard," and she knew the time had come. She threw her arms around Papa and said, "I love you, Papa. Thank you for everything."

He only answered, "My Johanna. My Johanna," and tenderly patted her shoulder.

Johanna picked up her food basket and her long bag filled with all the things she would need on the voyage-blanket, pillow, clothes, her Bible and other personal things. Then Johanna, Johan and Anna Mathea stood on the deck and waved to Papa. As the ship moved away, Papa appeared smaller and smaller, and finally the people on the dock disappeared in the fog.

"Will I ever see Papa again?" Johanna wondered.

She looked out to sea and remembered that at the other end of her voyage was someone she loved, too, and this love was greater. It was just like the Bible said. "You shall leave Father and Mother . . . . ."

"Yes, that love was greater.

Part II

Mr. and Mrs. Ole Overseth, wedding date, Dec. 8, 1872.

Chapter VII

Johanna, Anna Mathea and Johan stood in the railway station at St. Peter, Minnesota. They had finally reached the end of the journey that had begun nine weeks earlier in Christiania.

Johanna was hot and dirty. Never before in her life had she been so miserable because of the heat, and never before had she felt so filthy. One thing she knew— she must get some cooler clothes if she was to live in this climate. Her wool dress was sweltering. She longed to find a place where she could let down her hair and wash it, and scrub herself with soap and water. Never in Norway had summer been nearly this uncomfortable.

Johan found a man who spoke Norwegian and obtained some information.

"He said we must go across the swinging bridge to get into the town," Johan told the girls. "I asked about Christian's room and this man said the house is right behind the Main Street. It is better we get going."

They took their bags of soiled clothes and empty food baskets and headed west over the Minnesota River bridge. The August afternoon sun beat down on them.

"So this was the hot weather that Ole had been writing about," thought Johanna. Well, Amerika was certainly giving them a warm welcome. She wondered how far away Ole was. At least there was no longer an ocean between them.

Johanna looked at Anna Mathea whose face was rosy and flushed. Yes, this weather was really hot. She could feel the penetrating rays. Even Johan's face was red. Well, they wouldn't have to walk much farther, for the buildings of Main Street lay just ahead.

They found the rooming house, and the landlady took Johanna and Anna Mathea to Christian's room. When she opened the door, they were met by more hot, stuffy air.

"It is frightfully warm," Anna said.

"What have we come to?" thought Johanna. "It seems to get worse and worse."

The landlady pulled up the window and a little fresh air came in. She had another vacant room that Johan could use until the Narumshagens could get in touch with their cousins who lived **"ut paa landet."**

Johanna was thankful the lady spoke Norwegian and she shyly asked if they could clean up.

"You poor people," Mrs. Anderson said. "I know just how you feel. You are not the first emigrants I have had at my house. There is plenty of water in the pump by the back door and there are basins in your rooms. Find something cooler to put on. The sun will soon be going down and then it will be better."

Johanna sat on Christian's bed. She was tired from the hot walk into town. Anna Mathea tried to fan herself with a paper that lay on the chest. She kept mumbling, "It is like an oven. It is like an oven."

"Nei, this will never do," Johanna thought. "We cannot just sit here and suffer from the heat."

She turned to Anna. "Come, let's get busy. Things won't get better this way. You find yourself something cooler to put on and I'll go down and get the water."

Anna Mathea only kept blowing **with her** lower lip as if hoping it would cool her, and again she muttered, "It is like an oven."

Mrs. Anderson was out by the pump. Johanna hung her pail on the spout, and then worked the handle. Soon the cool water spurted into the pail. Johanna put her hand in it and splashed some on her face. What a relief! She already felt better.

Mrs. Anderson watched her and laughed. "You'll get used to it. When winter comes you'll wish you had some of this warm weather. You mark my words." Then she became more serious as she questioned, "Christian told me that when you came, you would be looking for work, is that right?"

Johanna nodded.

Mrs. Anderson placed both of her hands on her hips as she assumed a position of advisor and informed Johanna, "Only yesterday I heard about a family that is looking for a girl."

"I want a Norwegian family," Johanna said.

Mrs. Anderson continued while nodding her head. "Yes, this will be just the place."

She went on to explain. "Nils Gaarden who works at Evenson's Hardware Store is looking for help for his wife. **Stakkars** Kari! She has three small ones and already she is with child again."

Mrs. Anderson paused and pursed her lips as she thought the matter over. "It will be barely a year between them. She will not be able to manage by herself. She has never been very strong. The Gaardens may not be able to pay very much, but you'll get board and room and a little spending money—and a good home."

She wiped the sweat off her brow, and then continued. "I have a feeling that Christian will be coming one of the first days. Every other week he comes to pick up supplies. Those men working on the railroad have to eat, too, you know. And they must get their mail. Ja, when Christian comes, he can help you look into it."

Mrs. Anderson finished her conversation very emphatically, "But if it's money you want, you must work for an English-speaking family."

Johanna picked up her pail. As she walked through the kitchen door, Mrs. Anderson called after her, "When you get cleaned up, come down and eat with us.

After supper we'll sit outside. There we can get all the breezes."

* * * * *

Christian had come and gone. The second day after Johanna's arrival in St. Peter, he checked into his room. She didn't realize how much she missed her family until she saw him again. Now everything was much better because she knew her brother wasn't far away.

Christian was working on a railroad-building job northwest of St. Peter. He told her that Ole had been up there in early June looking for a job. He couldn't get on his crew, so he had gone to Heron Lake where more construction was in progress. Christian hadn't seen anything more of him since then, but a letter had come for Johanna in Christian's mail, and this letter put Johanna much more at ease.

She caught herself several times considering what she would do if she couldn't make contact with Ole. In this big country, how could she look for him, especially if he was in some wild, unsettled area? She thanked God that now she knew approximately where he was.

The weekend Christian spent in St. Peter, he was busy getting the newcomers settled. He had their trunks picked up from the railroad station. He helped the Narumshagens make contact with their cousins in the country. Then he had gone down to Evansons' Store and talked with Nils Gaarden about hiring Johanna.

It was all settled. Tomorrow Mr. Gaarden would come to pick her up and she would begin her first job in Amerika. She had been apprehensive, but Christian was very encouraging.

"I know both of them and you'll like it there, Johanna. And as far as housework is concerned, that is nothing new for you."

Tonight Johanna sat in the twilight and reread the letter from Ole that Christian had brought her. She had to admit, getting that letter had made everything look rosier.

30 June 1871

My dearest Johanna,

Velkommen to Amerika! I know that when you receive this letter you will be here in your new country. I wish I could have been there to greet you personally, but I know you didn't really expect to see me. We will have our reunion later this fall.

Everything has been gradually working out. I came west in March with others from Decorah. We went to Sioux City. There I met a land man who told me about some homestead acres about sixty miles north of Sioux City. I got a ride up there with some others who were also interested in this area.

You should see what I found, Johanna! It is a nice-lying 160 acres with a creek running through it. Right now it is prairie grass—all but five acres that I got plowed. I hired a neighbor's team of oxen and plow. I had to plow some so people would know I had staked this claim.

Several of the neighbors—two batchelor brothers, August and John

Johnson who are Swedes, live on two neighboring claims. They were very willing to help me and are keeping their eyes on my claim this summer while I work on the railroad. I could not get on any crew in Minnesota, where I tried first so I would be nearer you when you came, but I was very fortunate to get on the Sioux City-St. Paul line that is building north from LeMars. LeMars is a town east across the river and a little south of our homestead. It is in Iowa. This summer they plan to lay the roadbed from LeMars to Sheldon, Iowa. Four of us took a sub-contract and organized our own crew. I am getting much better pay this way, but it is our responsibility to keep things rolling.

When October comes I think we will have reached our destination and then I will go back to our homestead and build a shanty. August and John Johnson said they would help me. I helped them a little with some of their work when I was on the claim this spring. They are going to pick up lumber when they make a trip to Sioux City. After I have our first home built (I warn you it will be small) then I will come up to St. Peter to find you.

I have discovered that it takes much money for everything. The lumber for the house will take quite a bit, so I think it would be best if I go with Christian this winter to the lumber camp in Minnesota. That is a good paying job, and this is an occupation that I have had experience in. I hope you have found a job—one that isn't too hard for you, and one with pleasant people.

Johanna, I want to remind you that I look forward every day to seeing you again. Step by step our plans are working out. Won't it be wonderful when we are in our own little home by the little creek in Dakota Territory? Be patient. It shall be. There are still things to be done before this comes true.

Think of me out under the Amerikan sun, directing a crew of men and teams as day by day we plow and dig and level the roadbed. I am really helping to build this country, for some day trains will pass on this roadbed on their way between St. Paul and Sioux City. We have a tent we set up for sleeping so we do have a little protection from rain and other bad weather.

I will be seeing you around the first of November. It sounds like a long time, but if we both keep busy, the time will go by before we know it. You had better be thinking of all the things you will be needing to start up housekeeping in our little shanty. Oh, Johanna, then you can believe "It shall be fun to live!"

May our Heavenly Father keep and protect both of us while we are absent one from the other.

All my love,
Ole.

Chapter VIII

Johanna turned the pork chops in the hot frying pan. They sizzled and their aroma filled the house. She was finally becoming accustomed to Kari Gaarden's kitchen. Johanna reached for the wooden spoon and stirred the red fruit pudding, and finally poured it up. One thing she had learned—Nils had to have his dessert.

Sometimes Johanna thought Kari spoiled him. No wonder she had too much to do. Even with Johanna's help, the two women didn't have a spare minute. Ja, between the three little girls and Nils, Kari had her hands full. And with one more on the way, it wasn't going to be better very soon.

Johanna heard the door open and knew Nils was home from work. She was glad she had supper ready, for Nils liked his meals on time. Kari and the two older daughters were at the door to welcome him. It was fun to see the way the girls worshipped their daddy.

Nils laid down the newspaper and took off his coat. Then he went to baby Mari's cradle and picked her up. He sat down at the table with her in his lap.

"It smells like something good for supper," he remarked.

Johanna had begun dishing up the potatoes and creamed cabbage, while the family got to their places.

"Well, how did everything go today?" he questioned.

"We had a great day today," Kari said. "Mari took her first steps. I wish you could have seen her."

"Yes, so do I." He gave Mari a piece of bread to chew on, then went on, "You should see the headlines in the paper today. There was a big fire in Chicago Sunday night. That's all people have been talking about in the store today. You'll never guess how it started!"

He took a swallow of coffee while Kari and Johanna sat intently listening and waiting for him to give them the information.

"A cow kicked over a lamp in a stable," he explained.

Then turning to Johanna, he said, "You must be careful when you are milking, Johanna. We don't want anything like that in St. Peter."

He went on to give the details. "The wind was blowing so the fire spread quickly and by Monday night the entire business portion of the city was wiped out. Just think! October 8th and 9th, 1871, will be remembered by Chicagoans for a long time. Why, all the hotels, printing offices, depots and stores within miles are gone."

Again he turned to Johanna. "You were in the depot there in August when you came, weren't you?"

"Yes," she answered. "It was a very busy place. So many people. You have to go through Chicago if you are going west." Then she asked, "What will they do now?"

"Oh, they'll have to rebuild. No question about that."

He took a few bites of his food and then added, "I have a lot of respect for fire. It can be a friend or it can be an evil thing. They said over three thousand people died and over one hundred thousand people are left homeless. Just think of that! And with winter coming on, too."

"How terrible!" Kari sympathized.

"Cut my meat," little four-year-old Betsy Marie demanded. Johanna was right there to help her, and she also mashed the potatoes for her.

Johanna was tired. It had been a long day. She had been up early to carry water for the clothes washing and then scrubbed them all by hand. Some of the children's clothes took a lot of rubbing today. When she finished that, she had to use the good lye water to scrub the floors.

Besides all of this, she had to milk the Gaarden's cow, and today was the day to churn butter. She wasn't even hungry tonight. All she wanted to do was to get the kitchen cleaned up and then climb the steps to her little room. She hoped the children would be in bed by then. Tonight she yearned for a little time to read her Bible before she went to sleep.

Tomorrow was bread baking day again. Also, they should try to get at the barrel of apples. Kari had been talking about that for several days now.

* * * * *

It was the first of December before Ole got to St. Peter. Johanna had been looking for him every day for almost a month and had begun to fear that something had happened to him. It had taken him so long because he had gone the whole distance from his homestead to St. Peter by foot. Now, two weeks later, their meeting was still very vivid in her mind. That day she had opened the door and he was standing there, and she was in his arms immediately.

How good it was to see him again. The excitement was still there. This love hadn't died over the months and years. Three and a half years it had been since they had seen each other. And it was still the same. Enfolded in his arms was still where she always wanted to be.

But the reunion was only a brief one. He had spent several days in St. Peter and they had a chance to catch up on each other's activities and plans, and then he had gone with Christian and Johan Narumshagen up north to work in a lumber camp. Now Johanna waited for Christmas when the men planned to take a week off and come back.

Ole seemed almost driven by his ambitions. He had put his heart, soul and muscles into his dream. She would have to be patient. The day would come when they would have time for each other.

December 21st, 1871, was a happy day in the Gaarden home. Nils had been parading around and beaming all day. He was the father of a son.

Last night he had to go after Dr. Daniels. He had awakened Johanna and she was soon busy helping the doctor. Nils had stayed home from work today and Johanna was glad for that, for today there were four little ones to care for.

And after being up most of the night, she was tired.

Yes, everyone was tired, but happy today.

All had gone well with Kari, and the boy was a sweet little fellow. Johanna had never taken care of such a new arrival before. She couldn't help but admire God's handiwork when she looked at the perfect little body and delicate little hands.

"What are you going to call the boy?" Johanna asked Nils.

"Kari and I have been talking about it and I think we have finally decided to call him John—not Johannes, mind you! He was born in America and we will give him an American name—John.

"That's a fine name," Johanna agreed.

"Yes, he was a great Christmas present. Kari couldn't have given me anything better."

"I hope Kari will be strong enough to be up by Christmas Eve. It is good she had all her Christmas sewing done, and we finished our Christmas baking only yesterday."

"By the way, Kari said to tell you to invite your Ole and your brother Chris to spend Christmas Eve with us. We want you to."

"Thank you. Kari is very thoughtful."

"Yes, that's my Kari!" Johanna could detect the pride and delight in his voice as he added, "She's quite a woman!"

* * * * *

St. Peter
Dear Papa,   Friday, 21 June '72

I think it is about time that I wrote you another letter. I was glad to hear that all of you at Toten are well. It is a year now since I left Norway. God has been with me, Papa, and I have a nice home to work in. Kari and Nils make me feel like one of the family. I am glad for that because this summer Christian is working so far away I don't see him. He is on the same crew as

Ole. They are laying tracks from New Ulm, Minnesota to the Iowa state line. Johan Narumshagen is working with them too.

I think I wrote you at Christmas about our homestead and the little house Ole built on it. In March Ole went down to check on it and he tried to do a little more plowing. He went by foot from Mountain Lake by way of Sheldon to Dakota Territory. He had a dangerous experience on the way when he tried to cross the Sioux River. It was full from spring thaws and he was soon waist deep in water. Someone came along and offered to give him a ride across in their wagon. In the middle of the stream the harness of the horses broke and the wagon and its occupants went sailing downstream. The current carried them past a mill where they were rescued by some men working there. Oh, Papa, everyday I pray for Ole's safety as this country has many dangers.

While Ole was in Dakota he went to a town called Vermillion and made application for homestead. That was on April 18th. He made his down payment of $14.00 for 160 acres of land. Now it is definite that we have a home. One hundred sixty acres sounds like a big farm, doesn't it, Papa? Ole returned by foot to the construction crew at New Ulm, and he had to walk many miles without a taste of water.

Ole must keep on working because he needs to buy many things to begin farming. A team of oxen in this country costs about $150. One horse costs about $150. The money doesn't go very far with those kind of expenses. I suppose it is hard for you to imagine farming with oxen, but many things have to be done differently here in Amerika.

Tonight I went with Kari and Nils and the children to a strawberry-ice cream festival. I wish Ole could have been here. He loves strawberries. I suppose your strawberries at Narum aren't ready yet. It will perhaps be another month or so. The ladies at the Episcopal Church here in St. Peter had this event to raise money. They made $100. In Amerika the members of the churches have to earn money to run the churches themselves. It isn't like Norway with the government paying all church expenses.

Have Klara and Ole Grevlos gotten married yet? I haven't heard from Klara since Christmas.

It has been very warm today, but I think we may have some rain tonight as it has been clouding up and I can already hear some thunder in the distance. I hope it doesn't storm like it did Wednesday.

I don't think I'll see Ole and Christian again until fall. I hope Ole will have raised enough money then so we can be married and move into our little house in the spring. In the meantime you can think of me helping to care for four small children. I do enjoy it even though I have much work to do. There is something sweet about rocking a little child to sleep.

Well, I had better get to bed. I will probably dream about strawberries. This morning we made strawberry preserves and then this evening we filled

ourselves with strawberries and ice cream as did other St. Peter citizens.
Good night, dear Papa.

Love,
Johanna Amalia Paulsdatter

Johanna looked out of her bedroom window. She could see lightning flashing in the south and the thunder was getting louder. She hoped they wouldn't have bad weather like they experienced Wednesday. That was terrible. It had become dark in the afternoon. The wind came up, the thunder rolled and the lightning cracked, and there were even some pieces of ice that came pounding down. Johanna didn't think she would be able to go to sleep tonight until this weather settled down. When it rained back in Norway, it just rained, but here in Amerika all of these fearful elements accompanied it.

Johanna got herself ready for bed. Then she spent a few minutes in her Bible and read about Jesus stilling the storm. She got down on her knees by her bed,

"Kjaere Gud,
Dearest Jesus,
My heart fears for the weather, but I know you still are in control. Quiet my heart.

Amen."

Johanna got up and blew out her lamp. She stood at the window and studied the sky for some time.

Yes, the lightning was further away now. "Thank God, tonight it will miss us," she said, and then she laid down and went to sleep.

* * * * *

July 4th was a holiday in Amerika. The town of St. Peter was going to celebrate it too. Early in the morning there was a booming salute of 37 guns, for the 37 states of the United States.

Wagons had been going by all forenoon. People from the country began showing up in town before 8 a.m.

About 10 o'clock, Nils, Kari, the children and Johanna walked over to Minnesota Avenue to take in the parade. The music of the band could be heard several blocks away. The St. Peter band led the procession. They approached in their uniforms, all marching in step.

Nils waved to several of the men. "Just listen to them!" he said. "They have the reputation of being the finest band in the state of Minnesota."

Next followed the wagons. In each wagon rode a girl representing a different state. Johanna didn't realize there were so many states in Amerika. There was New York, Virginia, Georgia, Florida, Illinois, Wisconsin and many many more.

People had surely gone to a lot of work for this parade, she thought. Finally, when a wagon carrying Gov. Austin passed by, people began to clap.

"He is going to speak this afternoon," Nils explained.

As the procession moved down the street and turned onto Mulberry Street, Kari and Johanna and the children headed for home. Suddenly raindrops began falling. Johanna put her scarf over Mari's head and Kari covered the baby with his blanket, but soon they all were soaked. It was good they didn't have far to go.

The parade was just the beginning of the celebration. Many people were going to cross the bridge in their wagons and picnic in Spring Lake Grove. Nils was going along. He wanted to hear Gov. Austin and listen to the band again, but Kari and Johanna decided that it was no place for four little children who needed their naps.

This was the first July 4th that Johanna had spent in Amerika. Nils had told her that it was a birthday party for this land, and was a time for every citizen to be excited about his country.

* * * * *

Johanna scratched a little spot through the frost on her bedroom window and looked out.

"Oh, **kjaere meg!** It is snowing again today."

All night she had heard creaking noises in the house as the temperature lowered and pulled everything into its icy grip. Her first thought this chilly morning was of Ole and Christian. What was happening to these men now that such wintery weather had come upon them? Why, it was only the middle of November and already it had been snowing off and on for a week. The ground of St. Peter had a deep covering, and the temperature had fallen to way below normal the last three days.

"Surely the railroad workers couldn't survive in a tent in this weather. They surely couldn't build railroads when the ground had such a deep snow covering," Johanna thought.

"Oh," Johanna sighed, "I hope those men have sense enough to keep from freezing to death."

"Why, even toes and ears can be frozen if they aren't careful." She had seen raw patches on many faces that hadn't been protected.

"Maybe today I will hear something from them."

She went down into the Gaarden kitchen and began preparing the oatmeal gruel for breakfast. She was glad Nils had offered to milk the cow now that the weather was so bad. Johanna shivered as she put more wood into the stove. She had to get it warm around the house before the little ones were up.

While the coffee and oatmeal were cooking, she reached into her apron pocket for the letter she had received from Ole last week, and read it again.

My dear Johanna,   30 Oct. 1872

Well, I am back again on the railroad crew after taking a little tour over to our homestead. I left the first of October and went by foot as usual, but it wasn't as far this time because we are working only a few miles from the Iowa border and not far from Sheldon.

Everything was all right there. I visited with the Johnson brothers and used John's oxen to do a little more plowing. I put together several benches and a table from left-over lumber that I had. We must have some furniture when we move in, don't you agree? I also dug down some poles and made a frame over them which I covered with prairie hay. This will be a shed for the livestock.

I stayed ten days and then started back again. I am getting so familiar with that trail that my feet know the way by themselves. Dakota Territory isn't so far away anymore.

We are getting close to the end of our work here. It is good to have a tent to sleep in for there have been some chilly nights already. When the work is terminated for the season, Christian, Johan and I will come to St. Peter. I plan to see you in a month or so.

All my love,
Ole

Johanna spent three more days of deep concern for Ole, Christian and Johan before the men finally showed up in St. Peter. On November 20th, when Johanna was right in the middle of preparing a batch of lefse, there was a knock at the door. Kari opened it, and Johanna heard a jolly voice say, **"God Morn!** Have you a girl here that is named Johanna?"

It was Ole! Johanna dropped her rolling pin and hurried to greet him.

"Oh, Ole, you are all right!" she exclaimed. She stood there wiping the flour and dough from her hands unto her apron. He laughed at her.

"Oh, ja," he teased, "you mean you were worrying about me?"

Her heart warmed as she listened to his familiar voice again, while he filled her in on all the details.

Johanna learned her fears hadn't been without foundation, because the men had indeed experienced many hardships because of the cold and snow.

Why, the snow, Ole said, lay three feet deep on the sleeping tent and wagons when they finally had given up and left for St. Peter.

Then Ole grinned at her. He had a twinkle in his eye as he enthusiastically proclaimed, "I have good news. The whole crew has been hired to do snow-shovelling at St. Peter. The snow is already so deep in some gorges along the railroad lines that are in operation that it threatens to block train travel. The railroad company is hiring us to do shoveling this winter. I have rented a room at Mrs. Anderson's house where Christian has been staying, and I plan to find out when Pastor Johnson will have services in the church in town because I think it is time that you become Mrs. Overseth. Will that be all right with you?"

She threw her floury arms around him, and all she could say was, "Of that you can be sure!"

Johanna realized they had an audience when she felt a little one tugging at her skirt. Ole gave her a good squeeze, and matter-of-factly said, "You get back to your lefse and I'll drop in later today and let you know what I find out."

Johanna went back to the kitchen table and to the lefse dough. She had not felt such happiness since she came to Amerika. She could hardly believe it! Soon she was going to be his wife! Yes, soon she was going to be his wife!

Chapter IX

Johanna's head was in a whirl. The past two weeks had flown by. Tomorrow, December 8th would be her wedding day. She had her trunks all packed and tomorrow Ole was hiring a team and sleigh to take her to church and then he would bring her trunks to Mrs. Anderson's rooming house, for it was here that they would make their home this winter. It was hard to believe it was finally going to happen.

Her new dress lay on her bed. Johanna fingered it gently. The soft black silk had been pleated into neat folds around the waistline. Anna Mathea had sewed it for her.

When Anna heard of their wedding plans, she had insisted. "Just tell me how you want it," she had said. So Johanna purchased the material and Johan brought Anna into town for a few days while she did the sewing.

Anna was a wonderful seamstress. That was mainly what she had been doing since she came to Amerika. As different families needed sewing, she would move into their homes until she got it done. Now she had gone to another job so she would have to miss the wedding. Johanna was so thankful for Anna because she had to admit that fine dressmaking was not one of her own talents.

Johanna inspected the pleated ruffles at the bottom of the sleeves. Down the front of the bodice was a row of tiny covered buttons. Anna had done such a fine job. She had made white cuffs, and around the neck she had fashioned a white collar. It was tied in a bow in front and she had daintily fringed the ends of the ties. Now the dress waited in Johanna's bedroom all ready to slip into tomorrow.

Ole had been getting ready too. He had bought himself a new suit.

"Johanna, you should see how fine I shall look on our wedding day!" he had teased as Anna was busy with Johanna's dress.

"There are two times in a man's life when he must have a new suit. One when he is confirmed, and one when he marries."

Dear Ole! He was just as excited about their wedding plans as she was. He had made arrangements for a wedding dinner at the hotel. She could still hear him inform her of it.

"This is a big day in our lives, Johanna, and we must make it festive."

The first of the week they had gotten their license. Now everything was ready.

This afternoon Kari had gone downtown to do some shopping and the children were all sleeping. The house was quiet. On this day before her wedding Johanna had been doing a lot of thinking, and she was so full of joy and expectation that she just had to share it with the one she loved the very best. She knelt by her bed.

Kjaere Gud,

Tomorrow is my wedding day. I want to thank and praise you for bringing me this far. When I look back to see how you brought Ole and me half way around the world, and kept us safe and kept us well, and helped us find each other again—it is a miracle, Lord! For this I praise you!

And you have preserved in us our love for each other through many years already. For this I praise you and thank you.

Dearest Jesus—Be at our wedding tomorrow as you were at Cana, and we will be happy indeed.

Amen.

Sunday, December 8th, was a crisp, bright day. The sun shining on the white snow made Johanna squint. The world was beautiful today—but a little nippy. She pulled her shawl around her face to protect it from the wind. The horses plodded through the snow as Ole, on the seat beside her, held the reins. Christian and Johan Narumshagen sat behind them on the other seat.

Ole drove up to the little brick **kirke** in the northwest part of St. Peter. This church had been built just five years ago when Norwegian Lutherans living in St. Peter decided it was too far to journey out in the country to Norseland **Kirke** for services. Now Pastor Thomas Johnson was serving both churches, besides several others. Today he would have his regular services and afterwards he would conduct their wedding ceremony.

The little church was almost full. Johanna watched Ole as he took off his overcoat. He was so handsome in his new suit. It had gray striped trousers and a gray striped vest, with a dark suit coat, and he wore the smartest looking necktie with a bold wide diagonal stripe.

Johanna took off her shawl, but decided to leave on her wrap. She noticed a seat on the women's side next to Kari, who had left the children at the neighbor's today. Ole, Christian and Johan found places on the men's side.

Johanna didn't know how to describe her feelings. There was happiness, to be sure, and joy, but she wondered about the future and the primitive life on the homestead, and also she caught herself wishing for Papa, Klara and Helene Marie today. And wouldn't it be great if little Hans and Helmine could be here for her wedding too?

Kari reached over and patted Johanna's hand. Johanna reprimanded herself for thinking thoughts that could only make her sad. She smiled at Kari, who had been so kind to her this past year. She had been a real friend to her. Johanna would still be helping in their home this winter, even though she wouldn't be staying there.

The **klokker** began the first hymn **"Velt Alle Dine Veie"**. Johanna sang along with the congregation, and it was like God himself had read the fears in her heart and was speaking to her. "Leave all your ways with Him—with Him!"

It was a little drafty in church this morning. It seemed like the raw northwest wind had found some openings around the windows and doors. Johanna was glad she sat with her wraps on.

Today Pastor Johnson read and preached on the men of faith in Hebrews 11.

"There was Abraham," he said, "who dared to go to a new land because he had trusted his way to God. And his eyes didn't see only this world of tents and sod-houses and shanties, for he was looking for a house without foundations which had been prepared for him—his heavenly home."

Pastor Johnson closed his sermon with, "Leave all your ways with Him—even as these men and women of faith did. May this be true of us all."

At the close of the service Pastor Johnson announced that the marriage of Ole Overseth and Johanna Narum would be held following the service.

Kari and Nils stayed, together with others. They all went to the front of the church. Brother Christian and Johan Narumshagen were to be their witnesses.

Johanna took off her wrap and stood in her wedding dress beside Ole at the altar rail. Pastor Johnson faced them, and for his wedding message to them he read Psalm 128.

"Here you will see that the family that fears the Lord is blessed and happy. Today as you two become a new family, why don't you step out on these promises from God's Word and see if God doesn't keep His promises? Each year on your anniversary reread this short chapter and I am sure each year you will agree that the family that fears the Lord is blessed."

Pastor Johnson turned to Ole, "Now I ask you, Ole Overseth, before God and this Christian gathering, will you have Johanna Amalia Narum, who stands beside you as your wedded wife?"

Ole spoke loudly, "Yes."

"Will you live with her according to God's Holy Word, love and honor her and in good and bad days remain true to her until death do you part?"

Again he answered, "Yes."

Likewise, Pastor Johnson turned to Johanna, and asked her the same questions. She gave her affirmative answers also, and then Pastor Johnson instructed, "So give each other your hand as a witness thereto. As you have consented to live together in holy wedlock and openly declared the same before God and this Christian gathering, I proclaim you man and wife before both God and man, in the name of Father, Son and Holy Ghost. Amen."

"For the closing hymn," Pastor Johnson announced, "we will sing 'So Take My Hand, Dear Father'."

"My dear friends, as you have given each other your hands as a witness to your commitment to each other, even so, may you together put both of your hands into God's hand. May this be the prayer of all of our hearts as we sing this hymn.''

After the hymn was finished, the people gathered around, congratulating them. Pastor had them sign the wedding certificate and the new Mr. and Mrs. Ole Overseth, Christian, Johan, Nils and Kari headed off to the Nicollet Hotel for the wedding dinner.

Johanna felt like the whole world was rejoicing with them, and Ole could not keep his happiness to himself for as he drove the horses down town, he began singing his favorite song, "Haul the Water, Haul the Wood".

The last verse went . . .

> "Let everyone haul whatever they want,
> for my part, I like to haul my own wife!
> She is so good, and she is so kind,
> I can never get tired of her."
>
> The song got louder and louder as he came to the last lines . . .
> "Now do I have just the one I want
> Yes, now is it fun to live!
> Yes, now is it fun to live!"

Chapter X

The shops of St. Peter were displaying their finest wares because Christmas 1872, was only two weeks away. Johanna could sense the holiday excitement as Ole and she walked along the boardwalk and stopped in some of the stores.

The snow lay in huge piles here and there where it had been shoveled from the fronts of the stores and from the street in the downtown district.

Johanna and Ole had on their wedding garments for they had just come from Jacoby's Photo Gallery where they had posed for their wedding pictures.

They turned into S. O. Strand's Dry Goods, Millinery and Notions. Here Johanna purchased some yarn so she could keep her fingers busy in the evenings, for now as Ole's wife she would have to keep him supplied with mittens and stockings. She also bought some gray twill and dark flannel because she must get everyday clothes sewed for herself before they left for the homestead.

It was easy for her to do her shopping in Strands for Strand himself was from Norway and she could use her Norwegian in conversing. Johanna had been proud of Ole in the photo gallery. He was getting very good at speaking English, and she depended on him to translate for her.

Johanna stuck her purchases in her bag and headed for the door where Ole was visiting with some men who were also waiting for their wives.

Ole and Johanna walked past Casper Baberick's Merchandise Store and when they came to Ludcke and Rhodes, Ole stopped. "Johanna, let's go in and look around. We have plenty of time."

They opened the door and entered the music store. There was a piano and an organ on display and musical instruments and stacks of music.

Johanna watched Ole as he wandered from one thing to another. The salesman followed him, explaining and answering his questions. Finally they stopped at the organ.

"Sit down and see for yourself how easy it is to play," the salesman invited.

Ole sat on the bench and pumped the pedals with his feet. He touched several keys and the music swelled forth.

The salesman sat down and began to play. He looked at Johanna and remarked, "Here is something I think your wife will like," and he played a hymn for them.

Ole and Johanna stood and listened to the majestic sound. Ole was enthralled, and kept repeating, "Now isn't that fine? Isn't that fine?"

When the music stopped, Ole took out his pocket watch, studied it a moment, and said, **"Nei,** we must be getting on our way."

"Remember," the salesman called after them, "if it's anything you want in the line of music, we have it."

Ole and Johanna crossed the street to Evanson's Hardware. Ole was going to pick up a few tools that he would be needing, and they had to say hello to Nils now that they were downtown. Johanna had been wondering how Kari was getting along. Tomorrow Ole would be back at work and she would be helping Kari again.

The winter of 1872-73 had begun early and snow had followed snow. The first week in January 1873, a fierce blizzard descended on central Minnesota and added more snow.

The day it began had seemed to be a normal winter day, but along about four o'clock in the afternoon it darkened and the wind came up with a roar and the snowstorm was upon them. Johanna hurried home from the Gaardens and she was glad to see Ole there, just inside Mrs. Anderson's back door, shaking the snow off his coat.

The strong wind and snow did not let up for three days. Then the call went out for the railroad snow-shovelers. All the trains were blocked. The Sioux City-St. Paul train was snowed in below Ottawa and seventy-five men were sent up to shovel a cut about 700 feet long. The snow was about three feet deep and was no longer soft and fluffy, for the wind had packed it so solidly that it almost had to be chiseled out piece by piece.

Another crew of men that had been gathered from St. Peter, along with some from Mankato, set to work on a drift about a mile long between Mankato and St. Peter.

Two gangs of men had been sent to work on the Winona-St. Peter road. A deep snow lay in a cut six to eight miles west between New Ulm and St. Peter. The whole community was shoveling out and trying to get back to normal living again.

Every evening Ole came back from riding the snow shoveler train and told of more tragic results of the storm. Many people who had tried to travel had lost their lives. The community was glad to find that Dr. Asa Wilder Daniels had been found safe.

"You know," Ole related to Johanna, "God was looking after Mrs. Loomis and her children, too."

He went on to explain. "Dr. Daniels had been out to Norseland on a sick call when the storm came up. With the wind at his back he thought he could reach home, but it was worse than he thought. He reached the woods north of the Loomis farm, and here he left his cutter. He loosened his team to shift for themselves, and found his way to the Loomis home.

"Poor Mrs. Loomis was home alone with the children for her husband had gone into St. Peter and she was extremely worried about him. She took Dr. Daniels in and gave him food and shelter.

"The storm kept on day after day and Dr. Daniels had to saw and split wood to keep them from freezing to death. At night he slept up in the loft under the roof where the snow came in and piled on his bed."

Finally Ole came to the end of the account, "The third day the storm let up and a search party found him and brought him back, together with his faithful team that hadn't left the cutter. Mr. Loomis also was able to get back to his family again."

"Yes," said Johanna, "I wonder what would have happened to them if Dr. Daniels hadn't come along to help."

One night Ole came home with two letters. The mail had finally come through, after a whole week without service from St. Paul. Ole handed them to Johanna and he immediately sat down and pulled off his boots.

"My feet are like ice. It has been frightfully cold today."

He began rubbing them to get the circulation back into them again. Johanna went downstairs and got some tepid water. She poured it in the washbasin and had him sit with his feet soaking in it.

"Now I am finally beginning to have feeling in them again," he said. "Maybe when I get the chilblains feelings I will wish they were numb again."

"No, Ole," Johanna replied, "you mustn't say that. You must take care of yourself. You'll be needing your feet, of that I am sure."

She picked up the two letters. Johanna could hardly wait to see what they had to say. She gave Ole the one from his mother and she opened the one from Narum. Sister Helene Marie had written it.

20 Nov. 1872

Kjaere Johanna,

I hope this reaches you for Christmas as we all send you **Jul** greetings.

We are busy here getting ready for Klara's wedding. It will be December 13th and we have already started Christmas baking. This will be the first wedding here at Narum in over thirty years and Papa wants all the relatives and friends to be here. How we wish you could be with us. I suppose when you get this letter Klara will already be Mrs. Ole Grevlos.

I hope my wedding will be the next one. I am betrothed to Johannes Stikbakke now but we haven't set any definite date for marriage.

David and Johanna Marie are still seeing each other. I really believe that it will end in marriage some day.

There is lots to do as usual. However, Peder Anthon is making plans to go to Amerika and Martinus wants to go with him. Soon there won't be many of our family left here. I don't know how their plans will come out.

Papa is fine. Every time he goes to town he says, "Perhaps I shall get a letter from Johanna today." Hans is getting bigger every day, and he and Helmine are still going to school.

We wait to hear news from you and from Christian in Amerika.
Merry Christmas!

from
Sister Helene Marie

"Johanna!" Ole excitedly interrupted her reading.

She looked up from her letter and she had to smile. There Ole sat with his feet in the washbasin, his pants legs rolled up to his knees and so excited that he could hardly remain on his chair.

"Johanna, my brother Peter is in Amerika!"

Johanna gave her attention to his news as he continued.

"He and Peder Anton Dyste were going to leave Norway the first of November. They were going to Winneshiek County. I'll have to get Mother to send me his address when he gets settled.

"Can you believe it, Johanna? Pete is in Amerika!"

Ole laid aside his letter and said happily, "That was good news from home."

Johanna agreed.

Part III

Ole Overseth family.—circa 1884

Ole holding Martin, Johanna with Anna on her lap, daughter Helmina seated between them, and Johnny standing in rear.

Chapter XI

It was the first of March that Ole left for Dakota Territory in the year of 1873. He could wait no longer. He was anxious to get things on his claim lined up and ready for his bride.

He was very fortunate when he arrived in Dakota because a homesteader in a neighboring community had a pair of oxen and a wagon for sale. After inspecting them, he decided they would be worth the $120.00 price. The great gentle beasts were very tame. With all the sod he had left to break, he decided a span of powerful oxen would be the best buy at this time. The covered wagon was in very good condition, and well worth the $80.00 asked.

During the week he spent on his claim he took the wagon and oxteam over east to the Sioux River and picked up a load of wood and brush for firewood. He constructed a bed frame and laced it back and forth with a network of rope to hold the mattress that Johanna was making. This mattress of striped ticking would be filled with hay or straw when they moved in.

Now they were all set. A table and two benches were made last year. Ole knew Johanna would have liked a cupboard, but he had no more lumber on hand.

Ole had no time to waste. When he had finished these tasks he started back for St. Peter. His heart was light as he left the homestead to bring his bride home. However, travel turned out to be a struggle for it took him three days just to travel the forty miles to Sheldon. The frost had come out of the ground after he arrived in Dakota and with the melting snows in the lowlands there were places where it seemed as if there was no bottom for the wagon wheels and oxen to stand upon. At times they sank into lakes of mud. Ole spent a lot of time those first three days pushing the wagon out of the mire. There was one good thing—at least the wagon was empty on this trip.

Ole finally reached the St. Peter settlement where Johanna was waiting, and they packed the wagon with trunks, and the necessities and staples she had been collecting to set up housekeeping on the prairie.

They purchased a cast iron stove, and a good supply of candles and a buffalo robe. There was a special on coffee at Babericks—four pounds of Best Rio coffee for $1.00. Ole bought $3.00 worth.

"We'd better get in a good supply," Ole said. "I can do without many things, but I like to have my coffee. Just think how cozy the smell of freshly brewed coffee will make our little shanty."

Johanna had already acquired a coffee grinder.

They laid in a supply of sugar and molasses, flour, salt, rice and salt pork. Now all these provisions were packed in their wagon and the oxen were headed in the direction of their homestead.

The first week out of St. Peter was a hard one because of the trail's condition. Ole had traveled over this path several weeks earlier and the mud caused by the melting of the winter snows was no surprise to him.

It was now the 10th day of April and it had been another long hard day. The ride had been especially rough because the trail was full of hard deep ruts, and the wagon ride had been shaking Johanna all afternoon.

They had finally reached solid ground after plowing through the spring mud for several days. At least this dry ground made it easier for Ole as he walked alongside the team of oxen.

The sun was getting low in the west. For the past hour Ole had been searching the southern horizon for signs of the Sheldon, Iowa, settlement. It should be appearing soon.

Ole could tell the oxen were getting anxious to stop for the night because their pace had slowed considerably and his calls needed the touch of the whip to get much action.

Ole could see that Johanna, sitting on the wagon seat, was tired too. Her clothes were spattered with mud from travel on the trail. They had been sleeping in the covered wagon at night. At the end of each day, Ole would look for a high dry spot where they could camp, and here he would loosen his oxen.

Spending the night in the open was nothing new for Ole, but Johanna was apprehensive and had seemed quiet and tense the whole trip. Ole could tell she hadn't been resting well.

Finally Ole called out, "Look, Johanna, there it is."

His shouting gave the oxen a sudden spurt of movement.

"It isn't far now until we get to the Vangsnesses," he assured her.

Ole tried to prepare Johanna for these people who were strangers to her but not to Ole.

"You'll like Knud. He has a heart of gold, and he's a hard worker. Why, he was one of the best men we had when we laid the roadbed from LeMars to Sheldon in '71."

"Are you sure they won't mind us coming?" Johanna questioned.

"Of that I am sure," Ole answered.

"Only two weeks ago when I came through here I talked with Knud and he made me promise we'd stop with them when we came through. Ja, I'm sure you won't be sleeping out in the open tonight."

After a pause, he added, "It will be jolly talking over old times when we worked together on the railroad, and I hope he can help me find a good milk cow to buy tomorrow."

Johanna looked forward to the end of today's ride. She hoped Knud's wife and she would have a nice visit too.

Johanna hadn't talked to anyone but Ole since she left St. Peter a week ago. This prairie had an abundance of grass but very few people.

* * * * *

On April 12, 1873, the little Overseth caravan left Sheldon, Iowa, proceeding westward. A milk cow was tied behind the wagon, and a crate with six hens and one rooster was tied on the back. In the early afternoon of the second day they forded the Big Sioux River and Johanna got her first sight of Dakota Territory.

"It won't be long now, Johanna," Ole announced. Johanna was tense with anticipation. She was afraid to expect too much, and yet she had high hopes for this place that would be her home.

After leaving the banks of the river where bare willows, cottonwoods and other brush stood, the scenery returned to drab tall prairie grass. The green of spring hadn't yet descended upon the countryside, and beyond the river not a tree or building intercepted the horizon.

"Doesn't anyone live around here?" Johanna asked. She scanned the landscape for a sign of a house or a human being.

"They are there," Ole assured her. "Many of them live in dugouts or sod houses that blend into the scenery. There are many nice people living around here. You'll see."

The oxen plodded along. The milk cow was getting tired of the long walk and pulled at the rope and often emitted a "moo" to express her feelings. One of the hens cackled and Johanna wondered if perhaps she had laid an egg.

"I'm glad we have had such fine spring weather for traveling," Ole commented. The sun was shining on the tall grass as it gently moved with the mild April breeze.

This was a quiet world. Once in a while a prairie chicken or rabbit would rush out of the tall cover ahead of them. Here and there they passed a small spot that had been plowed.

The last few miles of their journey were the most exciting to Johanna because for months she had tried to imagine what this land she was moving to would be like. She tried to take it all in. She wanted to get acquainted with this new world that would be their home.

Ole began pointing out areas where people lived. Soon he told her to look to the northwest.

"When we get over the next little knoll we shall see our land."

The oxen pulled the wagon up the slope and Ole stopped them at the top. Stretched out before them was a broad expanse of gently rolling land, with a stream meandering through it. Back up above the creek stood a little building with a door and window in it, and a shed covered with prairie hay. A small plot of ground had been plowed, but otherwise the area was covered with tall dry grass.

Ole hollered at the oxen. He was getting anxious, and lightly touched them with his whip as he tried to hurry them along.

He glanced at Johanna, his deep-set eyes shining with excitement.

"We're finally coming home, Johanna!"

The oxen pulled up to the shanty and Ole helped Johanna down from the wagon. As he lowered her to the ground, he shouted, "Stand on it, Johanna! Stand on it! This is our soil—our land."

Then Ole grabbed her up and swung her around as he excitedly repeated, "Johanna, we're home. We're home!"

* * * * *

Ole and Johanna woke the next morning to find a gray and gloomy day. Johanna was glad Ole had set up the stove the night before. Their little shanty was warm and cozy as she went about unpacking and getting her little house organized.

Ole came in with another load of wood and piled it in the corner.

"It's good we got here yesterday. It's starting to rain outside. It's a cold nasty rain. I think our nice spring weather has disappeared. The livestock will need that shelter I made now."

Soon the rain turned to sleet and then fine snow, which was driven by strong winds. A late spring blizzard had hit, and it lasted into the second day. The temperature fell to low degrees and the snow piled into drifts.

The next two days Johanna and Ole spent a lot of time around their little stove, sometimes poking at the burning sticks to make them burn better, and this phrase was repeated over and over—"How thankful we are that we arrived in Dakota the day that we did."

And it was true, for traveling in weather like that could have meant tragedy.

But spring snows quickly disappear and in a few days it had turned to slush. The moisture soaked into the plowed field. Some ran down the little creek, and soon the sun was shining again on the Dakota prairie.

Chapter XII

Johanna stood in the doorway of the Overseth one-room shanty and viewed her little Dakota world. It was the first day of May. They had now had two weeks in which to get settled.

Along the east side of the house a stack of wood was piled. Here the chopping block also stood with an ax inserted in it. Ole spent his spare moments splitting firewood.

To Johanna this woodpile looked beautiful. Why, wood was more precious than money in this treeless land. Without it, their new stove was of no value, and no cooking or baking could be done either.

Johanna watched the chickens as they scratched in the plowed furrows that Ole had made around the house for a firebreak. They seemed contented.

"How cozy we are," she thought, "and how happy in our new home. It is wonderful to wake up every morning and realize that we are really here. God be praised that we are so well settled."

She looked at the room she called home. Built into the northwest corner was the bed, plumped high with the feather quilt on it. In the northeast corner was her new stove, still hot from the bread baking. The table had been placed in front of the west window, and on each side of it was one of the benches that Ole had made.

It had been fun to see how far a little could go and make do when need be. Her two trunks had been pushed against the walls. Johanna had put a small cloth over one of them and on this her Bible and devotional book lay. The other was stacked with her cooking equipment and plates and cups and silverware. She had to agree they could not have been happier with their home, had it been arranged and furnished with the greatest elegance, than they were now in all of its simplicity.

On the table were four loaves of bread that she had just taken from the oven. They were toasty brown and their aroma filled the whole room.

"We have food, a place to sleep and we are together and in good health. May we truly be thankful."

Johanna turned to look outside. She watched Ole as he went with his scythe, cutting down the tall prairie grass in the area he was going to break up with his plow. The grass would make good hay for his oxen. Last week Ole had finally gotten the wheat planted in the 15 acres that he had already plowed.

Johanna's gaze turned toward the creek where their golden-red milk cow stood drinking of the clear water. Guldenrosen had all she wanted. She spent the days feeding on tufts of old prairie hay. They had indeed been fortunate in getting such a fine cow.

It was Johanna's task to milk morning and evening. Today she had churned a batch of butter from Guldenrosen's cream. Yes indeed, they had much to be thankful for. There was bread and butter and plenty of milk—and an egg once in a while. Yes, and 160 acres of property that had the possibilities of a Toten-land.

Johanna was suddenly startled from her musings. She thought she heard a child's voice. In this quiet prairie where only the mooing of a cow, the shouts of the homesteaders driving their oxen, or the occasional crowing of a rooster breaks the silence, it was a strange sound.

Again she heard it. Johanna couldn't mistake the happy ring of a child's laughter. She walked around the side of the house to investigate. Northeast, toward the Larsen homestead, she spied a little girl crossing the creek in a spot where it was very narrow. Right behind her was a woman carrying a child, and they were coming her way. Johanna hurried down to meet them.

"Velkommen," Johanna called to them. "You must be Nils Larsen's wife."

This tall woman with the kind friendly eyes, answered, "Yes, I'm your neighbor, Lisabeth Larsen. Just call me Lisa. **Velkommen** to you! Welcome to our community."

"This is my Anna," she explained, pointing to the little girl who was running ahead of them. "She will be three years old next month."

"And this little wiggler in my arms is Lina. She had her first birthday only last month."

Now it was Johanna's turn. "My name is Johanna. I am so glad you have come to visit me."

They went into the Overseth's little shanty and Johanna graciously invited her neighbor to "Sit yourself down!" while she went over to her stove and pushed several more sticks into it and put the coffee pot on. Then she sat down beside Lisa on the bench. Johanna held Anna on her lap while they talked. The child's long, blonde hair hung over her little shoulders and her wide eyes examined Johanna and her home.

"You're the first woman company I have had," Johanna said. "The Johnson brothers were over several days ago. Neither one of them is married. August told Ole he would like to send a ticket to Sweden for a distant cousin of his to come over, but he hadn't made up his mind yet."

"Yes, it takes women to make these shanties into homes," Lisa agreed.

"Really, it's pretty hard for homesteaders to manage without them. For instance, take our neighbor Paul Gubberud. His work clothes were getting all worn out and he wasn't going to be able to make a trip to LeMars or Sioux City for a while. He was telling us about it. I had this big piece of heavy denim, so I told him I'd make work **bukse** for him. I sewed it all by hand.

"But you know, you can't get ahead of that Paul. He was so happy to get it, he brought me a nice little pig. Now we'll have something to butcher this fall.

"No, I think they will all agree that a woman comes in pretty handy now and then."

Little Anna had become restless and slid down to the floor where she was playing peek-a-boo under the table. Lisa went on, "I was so glad when I heard that your husband was finally bringing his bride. I have been so anxious to meet you."

"How long have you folks been here?" Johanna asked.

"We came in 1870, from McGregor, Iowa, where we were married in 1868. Nils did blacksmithing there after he arrived from Norway in 1866."

"We were married in St. Peter, Minnesota, last winter," Johanna said.

"Yes, we have heard all about that."

Johanna looked puzzled until Lisa smiled and explained, "Ole has visited with us every trip he has made to his claim, and he always talked about you."

"We both came from Toten, Norway," Johanna said. "We knew each other there."

Lisa laughed.

"Toten, Bergen, Opdal, Valders, Romsdalen. This settlement is getting to be a regular **lapskaus** of Norwegians and Swedes.

"Nils is from southern Norway. Right east of us is Paul Gubberud who is from Gran, Hadeland. August and John Johnson come from Sweden. Out west are the Romsdal people.

"The Ansten Odegaards, who live right north of you, are from Hedemarken. Ansten and Eli and several older children settled here in 1869. Their daughter Elisa is ten and some of the older boys were born in Norway too. Ansten was a tailor in Norway, and when he has time, he still sews clothes for himself. You'll like Ansten's wife, Eli. She's a busy mother with many little ones."

After a pause, Lisa went on, "You'll soon be acquainted with the people around here." The little child on her lap had gone to sleep as she gently bounced her on her knees.

"Yes, I'm especially anxious to meet some of the other women."

Johanna changed the subject.

"Ansten Odegaard stopped in last week and he told us about Pastor Ellef Olsen's services."

Lisa explained, "Many of the families around here have joined this group. So far we have no church, but we have baptism and communion in the homes, and Pastor Olsen gives us God's Word."

"When Ansten was here, Ole volunteered to have services in our home on the 11th," Johanna informed her. "Ole says that's a good way to start our life in this community."

"Last month we met at Stener and Thora Paulson's. They live several English miles northwest of here. They also settled here in 1870, coming from the

Gudbrandsdal valley of Norway. Yes, on May 11th, you will meet many of the people in the neighborhood."

Lisa went on, "This is mostly a settlement of young families. Many new babies have been born. Paul Hanson Graestadsmoe's wife, Ingeborg, is a mid-wife, and she has been kept busy.

"Over west a short way is the Thomas Twedt log house. They just had a baby boy last month—Ole Thomas. It is interesting how things have worked out for them. Both Thomas and Anna were married to others when they immigrated. They all came over on the same boat, but after arriving, Anna's husband died of pneumonia and Thomas' wife died of asthma in Iowa. So last year they married each other."

Johanna sat intent as she learned of the people in her Dakota neighborhood.

"It won't be long until you become acquainted, Johanna. You will discover that there is a bond between us all. We need each other and we are all in this adventure together," Lisa said. "Don't ever forget, if you need me, just holler!"

And Johanna knew she really meant it.

The fragrance of coffee was filling the room now. Johanna got up and began to prepare lunch for her new neighbor. Little Anna tagged along with her. Johanna took out her silver coffee spoons and she opened a jar of strawberry jam that Kari had sent along from St. Peter. She cut off several slices from her fresh bread, smeared them with Guldenrosen's butter and Kari's jam. Then Johanna, Lisa and Anna sat around the table and drank coffee and visited while little Lina slept.

Johanna was happy. She had found a friend in Dakota Territory.

* * * * *

The next month on the Overseth homestead was very busy. Johanna helped Ole plant a long row of potatoes and they dug down some corn in the sod. Potatoes would keep way into the winter if they got a good crop, and corn could be ground and made into meal.

The field he had planted in wheat was getting green now. This would be their food for next year. These 15 acres should make many sacks of flour. Yes, it looked like they would not be hungry next winter.

The voice of Ole shouting at the oxen directed Johanna's attention outside, where southwest of the house he was breaking sod. She watched as he struggled to keep the plow in the ground, bearing down with all his might on the handles while the oxen pulled.

A strip of prairie grass was slowly being uprooted, widening the portion of plowed ground on their property. At times when the plow share hit a snag of root networks or a stone, it would jerk the plow and pull at Ole's arms as he tried to keep it under conttrol.

Last night Ole's shoulders ached and Johanna had tried to rub them and relax the muscles in his arms. But he was back at it again today. Breaking of the sod was part of the cost of this land, and Ole had visions of all of it some day plowed and planted in wheat and corn. Johanna wondered how many years it would take. It went so slowly. He could only complete about one and a half to two acres a day. But little by little it would come.

* * * * *

It was a Sabbath morning and Johanna and Ole had been up early. Their breakfast was over and their chores taken care of. Now they proceeded to get their shanty ready for services which were to be held in their home again today.

Ole pulled the table over to the east wall. Here Pastor Olsen could place his Bible and address them. Johanna spread the white linen cloth that her mother-in-law had given her over the table. They lined up the benches in two rows on the west wall.

"Some of the folks can sit on the bed, too," Ole said.

Ole and Johanna were getting used to this arrangement. This was the third time the Overseths had had services in their home since they came in April. The first was on May 11th, then June 1st, and now September 21st.

Many of the settlers had sod houses and dugouts, which were very small. But mostly, the Overseths had services in their home so often because Ole was so quick to volunteer.

Johanna set a bowl of wild flowers on the table. Ole had brought these in from the pasture last night. Johanna got out a wooden bowl and placed it on the table, also, because there would be a baptism today. Katharina, the little daughter of Stener and Thora Paulson who was born August 16th, would be christened.

Johanna had to get everything organized before the people came so that she too could sit down and hear the message God had for them today.

Pastor Olsen was such a fine pastor. Johanna was glad they had someone who fed them God's Word. He reminded her of Pastor Magelsen back home in Nor-·way—only Olsen was a much younger man.

Johanna was getting acquainted with many of the people in the community. There were three new brides who had joined the fellowship during the summer. Marit Helgeson Rogness, Ragnild Tvedt and Oline Gubberud. The two couples—Halvor Helgeson Rognesses and Ole Tvedts had had a double wedding at Pastor Olsen's home and Peder T. Gubberud, their neighbor Paul's brother, had married Oline Lybeck. All of these families lived south and west of the Overseths.

This was getting to be a community of new brides and new babies. Almost every time they had services there were one or more babies to be baptized. The settler's homes were small, but they always seemed to find room for one more little one.

Johanna heard Ole's jovial voice outside the door, **"Velkommen, Pastor Olsen."**

Johanna's thoughts drifted back to Norway and to Kolbu **Kirke,** and to the bells that rang across the countryside, calling the people to worship on Sunday morning, and this all seemed so different. But then she remembered, "Where two or three are gathered in **My** name, there am **I** in the midst of them," and she went to the door of her little shanty and invited her neighbors and friends to join in the fellowship.

It was such a nice autumn day that after the services many of the people stayed around and visited before they went home. The men stood outside and talked and Johanna sat down with some of the women.

It was good to see Helene Marie Hegness again. Helene and Johannes Hegness had come to services today. They were from Vestre Toten, Norway, too, and knew some of the same people and places that Johanna and Ole were acquainted with. The Hegnesses had joined the Bethlehem fellowship and came to Pastor Olsen's services only occasionally.

Anne Raasum was telling the ladies that her husband was getting ready to make a trip to LeMars, and she dreaded staying alone with her little baby.

"No, don't you do it!" Helene Hegness spoke up.

"You go and stay with someone. I am still frightened when I remember what happened to me last spring. My Johannes left for Sioux City and I was home alone with the two little ones in our sodhouse." She stopped a moment and slowly shook her head.

"I am still frightened when I think about it. There was a rap at the window and when I looked up there stood an Indian peeking in. I didn't know what to do."

She looked at the other women sitting around her, and asked, "What would you have done?", and then continued with her account.

"What could I do? I grabbed the children and stood in the corner. He kept rapping and I knew he could see me so I thought maybe he wants some food. I didn't have any meat, but I had a loaf of bread. I set the children down on the bed and took the bread and went to the door. I could only speak Norwegian and I suppose he was speaking an Indian language because I couldn't understand him."

Again she looked at the ladies around her and asked, "How could we understand each other—one an Indian and one a Norwegian?" She slowly shook her head again.

"I held out the loaf of bread to him, but he quickly raised his right hand as if he wanted to push it away. He wouldn't take it. Then I was really afraid. I couldn't figure out what he was saying. Maybe he wanted our cow. I tried so hard to figure it out.

"The Indian began gesturing with his hands. He rubbed them back and forth, while he kept repeating the same word. Finally I thought it sounded something like the Norwegian word for grind or sharpen, so I went over in the corner and got Johannes' stone and gave it to him. The Indian took it and quickly went on his way.

"I still can't figure out if that was what he wanted, but anyway he left without any harm to us. But Johannes really misses his stone.

"I still wonder—how could an Indian know the Norwegian word for it—unless maybe some other settler had called it that.

"Oh, I tell you I was afraid. But he seemed to be peaceful enough." She stopped for a pause and then she said, "No, Anne, you go and stay with someone when Ole goes to LeMars."

Anne spoke up, "Well, I am afraid enough already. You know we live along the trail that the Indians take when they go to the hills six or seven English miles north of us. There have been several times they have stopped at our dugout. Ole always gives them some tobacco and they give us some "jerky" dried meat. We haven't dared to eat it because we don't want to take any chances on getting sick.

"Many, many, nights we have seen their campfires on the hill right southwest of us. Sometimes we can see them dancing and hear them whooping and hollering. I never sleep much those nights. Ole tells me not to be so afraid. The Indians have been friendly to us he says, and if we treat them nicely, he doesn't think we have a thing to worry about."

Now Johanna interrupted, "No, Anne, it's all settled. You and the baby come and stay here. My Ole won't be going to LeMars until later on, so you come and stay with us. I insist. You plan on that now."

"Thank you, Johanna. I'll talk it over with my Ole, but don't be surprised if I take you up on the invitation."

Chapter XIII

The December wind was howling around the corners of Ole and Johanna's shanty home. Winter was on its way. There was already a light layer of snow on the ground.

The Overseths sat at their table eating their evening meal. Johanna had made buttermilk mush tonight. This was a good, hot, nourishing dish for a chilly evening. She had tried all kinds of dishes that used milk—sweet milk, sour milk, buttermilk. This was the only food she had in plentiful supply. Guldenrosen had just had a calf several weeks ago and now the pail overflowed morning and evening with creamy, rich milk.

Johanna had made a batch of butter today and so had fresh buttermilk on hand. Nothing edible was thrown out when living on the prairie. Johanna prepared the mush by bringing the buttermilk to a boil and adding flour for thickening and salt to taste. Then some of Guldenrosen's creamy milk was poured over it and a dab of butter placed on top. Ole and Johanna ate this with their fresh bread, and it was very satisfying.

The little stove made the one-room home warm and cozy. A new piece of furniture had been added to their room—a wooden rocking chair. Ole, together with several of his neighbors, had made a trip to LeMars in October with some of his 1873 crop of wheat. Part of it was ground into flour and part of it sold so they could have money to buy other necessities. Johanna and the cow had stayed with Larsens while he was gone. It took the men over a week. The trip with oxen was two days each way, and they had spent a lot of time waiting their turn in line at the grist mill. Ole had brought the rocking chair along home for Johanna.

He had purchased some lumber, too, and in the corner of their shanty were pieces of a cradle that he was making. In the evenings he would sit and whittle on the runners.

Ole put the last bit of mush into his mouth, patted his stomach and remarked, "That tasted good!"

"Hauling and chopping wood always did give you a good appetite," Johanna said. "Remember all the porridge you would eat when you worked at Hurdal?"

Ole smiled and nodded.

Johanna went on. "I guess you should be hungry after all the exercise you've had today. The pile of firewood on the east side of the house is getting higher and wider every day."

"We will need all of it, and more, before winter is over," Ole answered, "if I am going to keep my little family warm."

Johanna picked up the Bible which was laying on the table and questioned, "Remember a year ago today?"

"December 8th will always be a red-letter day," Ole responded. "You have been Mrs. Overseth for one whole year now."

Johanna went on, "It seems like it all happened so long ago. Like it was in a different world."

"Yes. That it was. But the time has gone quickly. Usually I have felt that I didn't have time enough for all the things I have to do."

Johanna interrupted, "You have accomplished much."

"I am glad I got the well dug, and I'm glad I got a place fenced and fixed up for the livestock. They will be needing the extra protection from now on. Especially Guldenrosen's little calf. It's kind of cozy in there now. They have straw over their heads, straw to lie on and straw to eat."

He sat pondering a while, then said, "Yes, it has been a good year."

Johanna handed him the Bible as she reminded him, "At our wedding Pastor Johnson told us to read Psalm 128 on our anniversaries, remember? Why don't you have that for our devotions tonight?"

Ole turned the pages until he found the portion. Then he began . . . ."In Jesus' name," and announced, "first verse—**Blessed and happy is everyone who fears the Lord, who walks in His ways.**"

Ole paused while he studied it, then he nodded his head in agreement. "Yes, that is true."

Johanna interrupted, "Remember the hymn they sang the day of our wedding? **Velt alle dine veie paa ham.** The one who stills the storm, he shall find the way for us. How true it has been!"

Ole turned his attention back to the Bible, "Second verse—**You shall eat the fruit of the labor of your hands.**"

In an excited tone he exclaimed, "Ja, just see upon the table how true that is! The bread was from the wheat I planted, and it was made with the labor of your hands. The butter and the mush came from the cow you have been caring for."

He thought a few moments, then added, "Johanna, I think now I shall take care of the cow and do the milking. It is getting too cold for you to go out."

He went back to reading, "**You shall be happy, and it shall be well with you.**"

"Ja, so it is. So it is."

"Third verse—**"Your wife will be like a fruitful vine within your house."**

"Ja," he laughed, as he lovingly looked at Johanna and reached for her hand. "That can you see!"

"Your children will be like olive shoots around your table." Here Ole commented, "It won't be long now. Several more months and then this will also be true for us, God willing."

"That reminds me, Johanna. The school board will be meeting here tomorrow afternoon. Perhaps you can cook coffee for them. Maybe you can make sandwiches also. That would taste good. It will be Stener Paulson who is director, and Paul Gubberud, who is treasurer. As the clerk, I suppose I will have to take notes on the meeting. We must get something worked out for school for the children around here."

Getting back to his reading, Ole went on, "Fourth verse—'**Lo, thus shall the man be blessed who fears the Lord.**' "

Ole stopped here and with his big hand laying over Johanna's, he bowed his head and gratefully spoke,

"Kjaere Gud,

Mange tusen takk.

The wife you gave me has given me so much happiness.

Thank you for being with us and keeping us safe and well.

Be with Johanna when her time comes and give us a healthy child, if it be your will.

We leave our future ways with you. Guide us through the next year and its challenges and make us equal to them.

In Jesus' name, Amen."

* * * * *

Johanna and Ole Overseth started the year of 1874 with much enthusiasm. The future looked good. They already felt at home in this new community.

On January 2nd, their neighbors Lisa and Nils Larsen had their first son. He came to join their two little daughters, and was christened Adolph on February 7th, with Ole and Johanna serving as sponsors.

February 19th was a big day in the Overseth home for their first child was born. Ole had gone over to get Ingeborg Hanson Graestadsmoe who helped with the birth of their son.

Now it was Sunday, March 1st, and Ole bent over the cradle that set in the middle of the room. Johanna stirred in the pot on the stove as she went about preparing supper. The room was warm and comfortable.

"Johanna," Ole called to her, "come over here and see your son. He is a sweet little fellow when he is awakening. See how he yawns and stretches. Come here. He makes the most comical faces you can imagine."

Johanna laughed. "You'll find out how sweet he is when he doesn't get his food the minute he wants it!"

She pushed the pot to the back of the stove and joined Ole as they watched their new baby. Soon the child gave several little snorts, then a short little cry and finally he was fully awake.

When the little boy opened his eyes, Ole began to talk to him.

"Well, baby Johannes, you have been with us for ten days already. How do you like it here by now?"

Ole slipped one of his fingers inside the baby's little hand so that the baby gripped it, then Ole beamed.

"Now, my son, let me tell you about next Sunday. That will be your big day!"

Johanna smiled as Ole had this serious conversation with their baby, who lay there with his eyes wide open.

Ole went on, "Yes, next Sunday you shall be baptized. Your papa got it all lined up with Pastor Olsen yesterday. Yes, next Sunday you shall be named for your paternal grandfather Johannes Overseth."

". . . as is the custom in Norway," Johanna added.

"But," Ole went on, "I am going to call you Johnny."

"It is good I am not having the services here," Johanna said. "I don't know how Lisa did it—having church services at her own home when Adolph was baptized. She just seems able to cope with anything."

Johanna started to get up and Ole took her hand and gave her a pull.

"I have found out that babies are a tremendous lot of work." Then she smiled at Ole and added, "But they are a tremendous lot of fun, too. I get as much delight in watching him as you do, but I suppose that now he would like some dry clothes."

The baby began to cry and Johanna picked up little John and changed his clothes. Then she sat down in her rocking chair and began to feed him.

"I hope the weather will be nice next Sunday," she commented. "Not cold and windy—nor snowing or raining."

"We can always bundle the baby up in a few of the shawls you have been knitting," Ole teased.

"I've been wondering, who shall we have for sponsors?" Johanna asked.

"Well," answered Ole, "the meeting will be at Hans Dompedahl's house. Perhaps we can have him for one.

Johanna spoke up, "And we must have Lisa and Nils for sure!"

"Pastor Olsen said there would be two other baptisms at the service Sunday— Ole Tvedts' little son Iver, and Lars and Mari Sogn's little girl Louise."

After a few moments, Ole questioned, "Johanna, do you think when you make butter this week, that maybe we could take a few pounds along and give Pastor Olsen on Sunday? We haven't given him any honors since we came."

"That sounds like a good idea," Johanna agreed.

When Johanna finished feeding the baby, Ole offered, "Why don't you let me hold the baby? I can rock him while you finish the supper."

Johanna went about setting the table and Ole sang and rocked baby John. Suddenly he spoke up, "Johanna, I was just thinking. Paul Gubberud has been such a fine neighbor and he has been so concerned about this baby's arrival, I think we should ask him to be a sponsor, too."

Johanna added, "And Anne Raasum was so kind to come and bring me chicken broth after he was born. She killed one of her hens to make it. Next to Lisa, I think she is the woman out here that is closest to me. Couldn't we have her, too?"

Ole nodded. "If you want to, of course we can. The more sponsors we have, the more people we will have remembering our little Johnny in their prayers."

Johanna looked down in love at her husband and little son, "Oh, Ole isn't he wonderful? God surely has been good to us. And everything went so well with his birth, too. It's kind of funny, Ole, but as I look back, I think I was being prepared for this when I stayed with Kari and she had her little John. That experience helped me a lot."

Ole considered what she had said, and then he reminded her, "**Velt alle dine veien paa Ham.** He has purpose in the ways he guides us."

Ole rocked some more, and the baby closed his eyes. Ole laid him in his cradle and stood awhile just watching him.

"I am grateful to both God and you, Johanna, for our first-born. I am very proud of him."

* * * * *

Summer came and Johanna spent some time outside each day so that baby John could get sunshine. Often she would walk over to see Lisa. Several times she had walked across the field to visit Paul Gubberud's bride, Agnete. Paul and Agnete were married in March by Pastor Olsen.

The neighbors around the Overseths lived in many different kinds of houses. Paul and Agnete Gubberud lived in a log house with a dirt floor and no loft. The Gunder Tvedts and Thomas Tvedts each lived in log houses, too. August Johnson had a sodhouse; Ole Raasums lived in a dugout, and the Nils Larsens and Ansten Odegards had small frame houses, and Stener Paulson's house was the largest. When services were held with communion, it was often at Paulson's so there would be room for everyone.

Over west lived a settler named Solomon Mortenson and for a long time he had lived in a hole he dug in the ground. When the weather was bad he covered the hole with a blanket and kept his animals in there with him.

No matter what kind of construction the houses were, to each family it was home.

Ole had bought two little pigs from Paul Gubberud in the spring. He kept them in a pen by the straw shed, and the extra milk went to the pigs and they were fat and frisky. They liked to burrow their way out of their pen and often they were up by the door of the house. They would come right in if the door was left open. One day Guldenrosen had come up to the house, too. She licked on the windowpanes, and Johanna had been very upset. She ran outside and hollered, "Go! Go away!" But Guldenrosen nonchalantly turned and looked at her. Johanna became indignant and scolded, "We love you, and you are a very fine cow, Guldenrosen, but I will not have my doorstep for a barnyard."

Ole was just returning from the field when he saw all the commotion. Now Johanna had grabbed the bottom ends of her large apron and was wildly waving it at the cow. Finally Guldenrosen caught on, kicked up her heels and ran in the direction of the stable. Ole helped Johanna get her back in the pasture, and he laughed about the whole episode, as he told her, "I don't believe the animals want you to be lonesome."

Ole planned to butcher one of the pigs in November, and the other one he planned to keep for a sow.

Ole had planted ten acres of sod corn because it was good food for pigs. He had planted his wheat early and now it was getting ripe. It was much better planted on second-year plowing than on newly broken sod. He also had planted some oats, for if he got a good crop he hoped to get horses in the fall, and that would be good feed for them.

Having a little one in their home made each day an adventure. Now baby John was doing something new all the time. He had made their home even happier than before. The baby kept Johanna company. Ole was so very busy all the time. Always he was working on two or three jobs at once, and always there were two or three things waiting for him to get done. He had now broken up 45 acres on his homestead.

Johanna tried to take care of the garden and milk the cow. This year they had planted potatoes and carrots and beets. Ole had gotten some seeds in LeMars in the spring. The garden looked good, even if it had been hot and dry for the past few weeks.

On Sunday, July 19th, 1874, there were no services because Pastor Olsen was at Aal congregation, near Inwood, Iowa. He usually only held one service a month in each community that he pastored.

Sunday was always a welcome day to Johanna. It was a day of rest which Ole badly needed. She had taken out their Norwegian book of sermons and read a sermon from that.

Now while baby was napping, Johanna headed down to the well to get some cold milk and butter for dinner. Ole had built a box which she could hang down in the well, and keep the things she wanted cool. Cold milk and cool buttermilk were delicious on a hot day.

Yesterday John Johnson had been helping Ole put up the prairie hay he had cut. It was piled into a big stack. Next week they planned to get at the wheat.

Later than afternoon when the sun was in the west, and it wasn't so hot, Ole, carrying baby John, walked around with Johanna as they checked on their garden and crops.

Both the wheat and oats stood tall and the grain kernels were nice and heavy.

"Ja, it does look good, doesn't it, Johanna?" Ole asked.

She had to agree.

Ole and Johanna went to bed that night content that their days of labor had been worthwhile and they were ready for another busy new week.

Chapter XIV

onday, July 20th, 1874, was washday for Johanna. She had to keep a supply of clean, dry clothes for her baby, and she had been up early because she wanted to be through before the heat of noonday.

Their little shanty was still hot from the fire she had made in the stove to heat the washwater. Now she stood outside, bending over her tub and washboard in the shade on the west side of the house. Nearby on the ground her little John slept on a sheet she had spread out for him. It was too warm inside. She had the windows and door open, but she didn't know how much good that would do because it was a very hot sun that had risen in the sky.

From where Johanna worked, she could see Ole and John Johnson as they cut down the wheat. John went ahead with the scythe and Ole followed right behind, tying the grain into bundles.

Johanna used her wet hand to push back the strands of hair that had fallen over her face and wiped off the rivulets of sweat running down her cheek.

This was getting to be such a hot day that Johanna could see the blurry heat waves rising from the earth. It gave her a dizzy sensation.

She stood up, straightened herself and stretched her shoulders back. The bent position over the washtub had made them tired and heavy. She turned her head to check on the rest of the world after being buried in her soapsudsy washwater environment.

Johanna could hear the clucking of her hens, as north of the house they tried to guide their broods of little chickens on a hunt for food.

It was so hot. The shade was disappearing as the sun rose higher in the sky. If only there was a nice tree beneath which she could lay her baby. Oh, if only for one day she could enjoy the summer weather of Norway again. There the heat never got too uncomfortable and the evenings were cool and good for sleeping. Last night their little house hadn't cooled off one bit, and little John had been restless and hadn't slept well.

"No, Johanna!" she told herself, "don't think about it! It only makes you more uncomfortable. Thinking of Norway can do you no good. It will only make you unhappy." If it would only rain, then things would be better. She looked at the sky for a hint of some clouds. To the northwest she noticed a strange looking cloud. She watched it for a time. As the cloud neared, the air seemed to tremble and vibrate.

No, I musn't let this heat get the best of me, she told herself, and bent down to finish the last of her clotheswash. She scrubbed away but now the sky was darkening. She hurried to hang up the last of Ole's dark work clothes on the rope he had put up for her between the house and the cattle shed. She hoped her clothes would get rinsed again by a good rain. She wouldn't complain about that. It was what was needed after this hot, dry spell.

Now it seemed as if a cloud was covering the sun. Johanna looked up and something glittering fell. Several shiny grasshoppers dropped to the ground around her. Then they were falling just like raindrops. In a few minutes there was nothing but crawling, shiny, green bodies with long legs covering every growing thing.

Johanna picked up baby John, shook the grasshoppers from the sheet he was laying on, and hurried inside. Some of the insects had already come in through the open door and windows. She got her broom and swept them out, then closed both door and windows.

She looked at the clothes hanging on the line and they were covered with grasshoppers, too. She took them down, shook them, and carried them inside. Insects were already floating around in her washwater. That was a good place for them. She wished they would all drown.

Ole came running up to the house and John Johnson hurried to his own homestead.

"I've heard about these grasshoppers," Ole said. "They will eat everything. The settlers had them back in the 60's. We have to try to do something to salvage our crops."

Johanna remembered her garden. She grabbed the sheet and ran out and covered up as much of it as she could.

Ole went to his wheat field and began carrying back the bundles of wheat they had just cut down. Johanna helped him get it out of the field. They piled the bundles in the corner of the livestock shed.

The grasshoppers were getting thick outside. The ground was becoming a moving, shiny mass. Every step squished them. Now the chickens were busy. They didn't need to hunt for something to eat, for it was there in abundance.

Ole and Johanna soon had the small amount of wheat that had been cut down safely in the livestock shed. But there were grasshoppers in there, too!

At chore time Johanna went out to milk the cow and the grasshoppers even jumped into the milkpail. She got a clean cloth and covered the pail. She wasn't going to have grasshoppers in her milk!

The grasshoppers clung to Johanna's petticoat and dress. She had to keep brushing them off her arms and shoulders. "This is just like a nightmare," she said. "I can't believe what I am seeing."

But it wasn't simply a nightmare because by the next day the damage was beginning to become apparent. There was no way to stop them. After several days the green grass and corn and wheatfields were mostly black bare ground. They even chewed holes in the sheet Johanna had spread over to protect her garden, and they helped themselves to the green leaves of the potatoes, beets and carrots.

Ole had to remove his clothes and shake them before he came in the house. Sometimes Johanna would find one or two grasshoppers that had sneaked in, and she made a quick finish of them.

At night she thought she could feel their claws on her. Johanna and baby stayed inside most of the time. With windows and door closed, it was very hot and stuffy. But it was better than having those insects crawling on her and jumping at her in their irratic fashion.

The twinkle had gone out of Ole's eyes and he grew tired from fighting the losing battle with the grasshoppers.

"You know," Ole told Johanna, "I have never felt sorry for the Egyptians before. I have heard the story of Moses and Pharoah and the locust plague many, many times. But it has just been words before. Now I understand how awful it was."

On the fourth day the grasshoppers flew away, but they left behind black ground where several days earlier there had stood golden grain and fields of green corn, and gardens. They also left behind eggs which they laid in the black earth. But mostly, they left behind bewildered and distraught pioneer men and women who wondered what the future would be now that these hungry hopping red-legged Rocky Mountain locusts had robbed them of their 1874 crops.

These insects had done more than that. They not only stole the food the homesteaders had been growing from right under their noses, they also had stolen their enthusiasm and some of their dreams.

Conditions of life during the 1870's were harsh and rigorous. Most of the homesteaders had moved into the untamed prairie with usually just enough to enable them to take a claim and plant a few acres. Often they had to seek other employment to tide the family over until the first crop was harvested. Short crops spelled discouragement and failure for them, and at times even left them destitute.

When the grasshopper raid struck, it left the settlers with extremely limited resources. The grasshoppers had destroyed a large portion of the crops. Now credit was even harder to obtain, and interest rates were very high—often up to 18 and 24 percent.

"Hva skal vi gjøre?" was the question on everyone's lips. Each settler sat down with his wife and took inventory. They had to figure out how to pick up the pieces and go on. They had planned on this crop to feed their family . . . and their cows, and pigs and oxen.

Winter was coming and the cupboards were almost bare. Some settlers had been buying their plow, oxen and cow on installment and when they couldn't make payments they often lost them. Many of them talked of selling out and going back to civilization—or better yet—back to Norge!

"Oh, no!" Ole told Johanna. "We mustn't give up. We have put part of ourselves into this land—our sweat and muscle and time and energy. This is nothing that should be decided in a hurry."

One man sold his homestead for a wagon to take him and his family back east.

The settlers used what they had. And life went on. And babies were born. On September 20th, services were again held in the Nils Larsen home with five babies baptized—Ansten Odegaard's new daughter Tine, Halvor Helgerson Rogness' son Helge, two Asper daughters and Julia Blilie.

The settlers directed the question, "What shall we do?" to each other, and they also directed it to God.

With no threshing or corn to harvest, the homesteaders had time to meet with Pastor Olsen during the week. On Wednesday, October 14th, they gathered at the Stener and Thora Paulson home. As they sat around the room all eyes were upon God's servant as he opened God's Word.

Pastor Olsen adjusted his little wire-rimmed glasses, cleared his throat, then began reading from Matthew 18:23-27. "The Kingdom of Heaven can be compared to a king who decided to bring his accounts up to date. In the process, one of his debtors was brought in who owed him $10,000. He couldn't pay, so the king ordered him sold for the debt, also his wife and children and everything he had."

How well the little congregation related to this parable now. They knew what it was to be destitute, to owe money, and to worry about what would happen to their wives and children.

Pastor Olsen read on, "But this man fell on his face before the King and pleaded, 'Oh, sir, be patient with me and I will pay it all.' The king was filled with pity and released him and forgave him his enormous debt."

Then the pastor looked up, and with one hand smoothed back his hair. Pastor Ellef Olsen was without the customary full beard and sideburns that most of the settlers wore, but he had a trim mustache and a small beard that ended in a neat point beneath his chin. Now he fingered his beard for a few moments and then spoke to his little congregation. "You may owe money, you may be in hard financial straits, but today you can rejoice because your largest debt has been forgiven—the debt you have to God has been all taken care of by His son and has been marked 'Paid in full'."

"Now what does God ask of you? He says 'Have mercy on others, just as I had mercy on you.' "

And so the fellowship of the settlers that remained became stronger. The congregational records that fall showed that there was now a membership of 210 souls. Their homes were no longer big enough for services, but they assured one another, "Someday, when things are better, we will build a church."

But for now, their dream of building a church had to be given up.

Along the wagon crossing of the Sioux River, about eight miles southeast of the Overseth homestead, several buildings were coming up—a schoolhouse, a store, a hotel, and several dwellings. A post office had been established there, and it was called Eden.

One day when Ole stopped there for his mail, he found a letter from Johanna's father, Paul Andreas Narum, in Norway.

15 Sept. 1874

Kjaere Johanna,
Your brother David wants to take over the Narum **gaard.** He is married now you know. We have agreed on a price and this is being divided up

between all of my children.

Enclosed is your portion of the inheritance. Perhaps you can buy a team of horses or build a bigger house. I'm sure you will find use for it.

I now have the room that Bestefar had at the other end of the house and will be cared for as long as I live.

Johanna and Ole hugged each other and cried for joy. Then they got to their knees and thanked God for hearing their cry and for looking after them in their time of need.

That fall most of the homesteaders didn't make their trip to LeMars with their wheat because they had none to sell or grind. But Ole went and he took along the money they got from Norway. He bought the supplies they needed and hauled home three sacks of ground wheat.

In November they butchered the pig they had been feeding, and packed down the meat in salt brine.

That fall, the settlers went down to the river and helped each other lay in a good supply of wood for fuel. The shortage of prairie hay was felt in many ways—not only as feed for livestock but also as fuel. Because of the scarcity of fuel on the prairie many settlers had previously used prairie hay to heat their homes by twisting the long stems into tight bunches which burned quite well.

On November 26th, a **Takkedag** service was held in the Nils Larsen home. In spite of it being a clear, cold November day, many settlers turned out.

The pioneers were destitute of money and food, but they still had health, children, wife, home and friends to be thankful for.

They sat on benches and some had taken their wagon seats along in to sit on. The women had their babies on their laps. Many men remained standing. Some held toddlers in their arms. They all joined together in the ardent singing of several Norwegian hymns. That Thanksgiving Day, Pastor Ellef Olsen ministered to them from Mathew 16:7-10. He cleared his voice and glanced around the crowded room. then he began, "In Jesus' name":

"O men of little faith! Why are you so worried about having no food? Won't you ever understand? Don't you remember at all the 5,000 I fed with five loaves, and the basketfuls left over? Don't you remember the 4,000 I fed, and all that was left?"

The tears began to flow from men and women alike. This was just the Word from God they needed.

Yes, Pastor Olsen knew the question that was in their hearts as winter came upon them—"What shall we do?" and he turned their eyes to the supplier of all needs.

"Yes," Pastor Olsen assured them, "He is still able to provide bread. You can be thankful this day because you have such a great God that loves you."

When Ole and Johanna got home that day, they talked about the sermon.

"You know, Johanna," Ole said, "I'm sure trusting in the Lord and his Word doesn't come easy when you have a half-dozen children to feed and the flour sack is empty."

"Yes," she replied. "It well may be that believing what Pastor read today was hard for many." Then she paused. "But maybe when there is nowhere else to turn you have to put your faith in Him."

"Ja, Johanna, we know that God can perform miracles and we know He takes care of His children. But it seems to me it is much easier to believe that when there is some food in the cupboard."

Johanna had something she wanted to share, "You know, Ole, today I felt guilty when I saw the drawn, tense expressions on so many faces and I knew that we had three sacks of flour while many of the others were scraping the last few spoonfuls."

"Yes, Johanna, I guess I felt that way, too. I was especially sorry for those new families who just moved here this year and have nothing to go on."

Ole thought about it for awhile and then he said, "Johanna, I think sometimes God wants us to answer someone else's prayers. It is selfish for us not to have compassion. We could scrimp a little and share. We have sufficient ground wheat and a barrel of salt pork. We could share it now and put some of our neighbor's minds at ease. It isn't easy to worry about your children going hungry . . . and with winter coming on, too."

"Yes," Johanna agreed. "I think that is what we should do."

That afternoon Ole loaded one of the sacks of ground wheat and some salt pork in his wagon and stopped at the homes that he knew had the greatest need. And the Overseths weren't the only settlers that shared. Those that had, divided with those who had not. They were in this thing together.

The grasshopper plague had covered the whole Upper Midwest and in the East people heard of the plight of these settlers and a Territorial Relief Committee collected more than $4,000 for food, clothing and seed wheat.

During March and April 1875, the War Department distributed 75,000 lbs. of flour, and 25,000 lbs. of bacon to 4,000 persons in Dakota Territory, which was a twenty-five day's supply.

Congress passed a law in December 1874, permitting settlers in grasshopper-stricken regions to be absent from their homestead or pre-emption claims until the following July so they could find employment elsewhere. They also extended the time for making proof of their homestead claim from five to seven years.

But this wasn't the end of their troubles, for the winter of 1874-75 was unusually severe and prolonged, with an abundance of snow and stormy weather.

The only thing that .carried the homesteaders through was the thought of springtime.

"When spring comes," they said, "then we will begin over again."

But now when they made their plans they always added—"providing the grasshoppers don't come again!"

Chapter XV

Johanna sat at her table, a bottle of ink and a sheet of paper lay before her, and a pen was in her hand. She was alone in the house. Outside she could hear Ole hollering at the oxen as he plowed his wheat stubble. Often she heard the voices of baby John and the hired girl who was watching over him as he played outside.

Their little shanty seemed smaller than ever, for now in the southeast corner Ole had built another bed. A curtain was hanging on one end and could be pulled closed for privacy for Ragna, their hired girl.

Johanna dipped the pen in the ink. She intended to get a letter written to her father this afternoon. One of these first days Ole was planning to make a trip to Canton where he could mail it for her.

15 Aug. 1875

My dear Papa,

I have been thinking about you all day. This morning as baby Johannes was playing on the floor, I thought "how Papa would enjoy him now!" He is a fine little boy, Papa, and already a year and a half. I could see you bouncing him on your knee like you used to with little Hans.

I hope everything is fine at Narum. Have David and Johanna Marie had their baby yet? Ja, soon you will have a little grandchild there to hold in your lap.

Here in Dakota we are well and happy. And busy. The days seem to fly by, and we are especially happy because we didn't have to go through another grasshopper plague like last year. Only a few grasshoppers showed up in July. The crops look very good this year. We have high hopes for a fine return for our work.

The wheat has already been harvested, and they say that some Lincoln County, Dakota Territory farmers produced wheat that yielded 35 bu. to an acre, and we hear that some had oats at 109 1/2 bushels to an acre which we can hardly believe. What do you think about that? Crops like Toten, eh, Papa?

Everyone needed this to make up for the loss last year. With these good crops I wouldn't be surprised if Ole will soon be driving a team of horses. It has been hard on his patience to work with oxen. They plod along at one speed. They are so slow, Papa. And Ole always has so much to do. He has plowed up about 60 acres of native sod now and doesn't really need oxen any more for that. With horses he will get the planting and plowing done much faster. Not very many in the community have horses yet, but if they get some money I am sure many of them will try to buy some.

Did I write about our hired girl in my last letter? Ragna has been so much help to me. In April when we had church services in our home, some of the men were mentioning several families that were looking for homes for their oldest daughters. After last year's crop loss, they were short on food and money for shoes and clothes, and every person less to feed and clothe gave them some relief. We decided we could use some help with baby, and thanks to you, we had some extra money for food and clothes. Ragna is just 16 years old, and very sweet. She always tries to please, and she isn't afraid to work. This summer, baby Johannes is just big enough to get into everything—and not big enough to understand many things. When she watches baby, I am free to get the other work done—sewing, and taking care of the garden, and my cow and chickens.

The last of June we made a trip to LeMars. This was the first time I had been to a town in over two years and there were many things that I had to get. Ole is a pretty good shopper, but there are some things I can best pick out. We all needed shoes—Ragna, our hired girl, and Ole and I. And now that baby Johannes is walking he needed shoes, too. Just think, his first little shoes, Papa!

Ole thought we could all make the trip, although, of course, it did take a week. The June weather was fine and Ragna was very excited at getting the chance to go along. I packed a few loaves of bread and some lunch to eat on the way. We stayed in taverns the two nights on the way down, and also on the way home. The day we were pulling into LeMars it started to rain, and we were glad to get sleeping quarters at the Depot Hotel. It rained hard all afternoon and all through the night, but by the next day it was just sprinkling now and then. We had a fine time looking around in the shops, and being back in civilization.

The railroad arrived in LeMars way back in 1870, so they have had access to supplies from Chicago and New York, and have almost everything you could want in their shops. They also have a mill for grinding wheat into flour—the Gehlen mill. Ole says they have a fine hardware store and lumber yard, too.

We got all of our shopping done in one day and started back. The trail was a little muddy to start with, but the warm sunshine soon dried it up. The trip home will never be forgotten for when we got to the river crossing at Eden . . .

Here Johanna stopped writing. She put her elbow on the table and let her forehead rest in her hand, her eyes closed in a position of deep thought as she relived the events of that afternoon. The experience was still fresh and she became almost sick every time she remembered what almost happened.

The rains had raised the level of the river and given its current more force as the waters from upstream hurried south. Most of the water from the showers three days earlier had already had time to travel on, and the river didn't appear to be at a dangerous level. It usually was between three or four feet deep at that crossing.

As they approached the crossing they could hear the "gees" and "haws" of a man who was driving his oxen on the other side of the river. Ole started across leading his team, and at one point the water went up under his armpits, but he soon was in much shallower water. With the long rope he began tugging at the oxen and they started slowly into the river. The wagon box that Johanna, Ragna and baby John were riding in was set on a low running gear. The water coming downstream splashed at the north side of the wagon box. The team and wagon moved into the middle of the stream, and then, all of a sudden, the water lifted the box off the wheels and began moving it downstream, together with its contents. It hit something and tipped, dumping the three of them into the swirling waters. At first Ragna screamed, but with the water splashing all around her face, she decided it was best to keep her mouth closed.

Johanna had no idea how deep the river was there, but she quickly was carried within reach of some trees that were growing in the water and she grabbed hold. She held baby John in one arm, his arms clasped around her neck. She held on tightly to the tree with her other hand.

Not far away she saw Ragna had caught hold of a branch, too. Then she could hear Ole calling. Johanna tried to shout back, and after what seemed an eternity he came running to the edge of the bank and another man was with him.

"Hold on, Johanna! Hold on, Ragna!" he kept shouting. He was soon wading into the water toward Johanna.

Ragna was closest to the shore so the man helped her unto dry land first, and then he went to help Ole and took baby John while Ole assisted Johanna.

When they all were back on the bank of the river, Johanna threw herself into Ole's arms and they clung tightly to each other, little John squeezed in between them. Johanna began sobbing. Then she kissed her son and repeated, "Baby Johannes, oh, baby Johannes. Thank God you are all right."

Ole squeezed her again as he said, "Thank God you are all right, Johanna!"

Johanna's eyes caught sight of Ragna standing there, dripping wet, her clothes clinging to her body and her long hair hanging in stringy bunches, the water still trickling down her face. Johanna ran to her and hugged her. "Are you all right, Ragna?" she questioned. "Are you all right?"

They were a sorry sight, these people who were smiling through their wet clothes while the onlooker, who lived nearby, watched the glad reunion of a family that had felt the breath of death and escaped.

This man, who lived along the river crossing, went to help Ole rescue his wagonbox, and Ole couldn't stop telling of his relief that all were fine.

"You don't know how awful it was," Ole told him. "For a few minutes I was afraid I had lost my whole family. Thank you for helping me rescue them."

Now Johanna picked up her pen again and went back to her letter. Perhaps Papa will worry about us if I tell him all about our experience at the crossing. She dipped her pen into the ink and only wrote . . . .

"We were dumped into the water and our new shoes got wet.

Write again soon. May God keep you in good health, Papa.

Much love,
Johanna."

* * * * *

It was a bright May day. The sun shone through the south window on Ragna's bed where little Johnny lay taking his nap. He was now two years and three months, and a chubby little fellow with thick, dark, brown hair.

Ragna sat in the middle of the room beside a big sack of wool. Ole had gotten it from August Johnson when he helped him shear his sheep in April. Johanna had washed it and now Ragna was carding it, patiently working the wool with the two implements that disentangled and arranged the wool fibers ready for spinning.

Johanna sat in her rocking chair knitting. She hummed softly as she worked. She was making a little baby sweater. The reason for her project was apparent.

She spoke to Ragna, "That is a slow job, isn't it?"

Ragna replied, "Oh, I'm used to it. My mother has had me carding wool ever since I was old enough to sit on a chair."

"Are you sure your mother will have time to spin it into yarn for me?"

"Yes, she is planning on it. This weekend when I was home I told her about the wool, and she enjoys spinning. Really she does. My sisters are good to help her with the other work, so it won't be any bother. In fact, she would feel bad if you didn't let her. After sending that hen home with me last weekend, I know she would like to do something in return."

"I will certainly appreciate it. There are quite a few of us now to keep in stockings and mittens. Ja, and before long there will be one more."

Johanna finished her sentence with, "No, and you can't knit without yarn!"

Johanna rested a few minutes and then remarked, "I think we'll use the other sack of wool to fill a quilt. We'll be needing it when winter comes."

She began knitting again, and added, "But the wool will have to be carded just the same."

They both looked up as Ole opened the door.

"Is coffee ready?" he called. Johanna put her finger over his lips as a suggestion for him to speak more softly and not awaken Johnny.

"How is the corn planting going?" Johanna asked in a quiet tone.

Ole began to smile. "Did you see me go out in the field?"

Again he smiled to himself and then chuckled. "As I led the team out in the field, I said to myself, 'Are you crazy, Ole? Driving a sleigh on a beautiful May Day?'

"But, I do believe it is a good idea, and I'm glad I tried it. Neighbor Thomas Twedt knew what he was doing! The runners make such straight rows, always the same distance apart. I make several trips across the field and then I take my sack of corn kernels and plant corn in the runner tracks."

"Well," Johanna pointed out, "when the corn comes up we will all see how good an idea it was."

Ragna left her carding and poured up coffee and served Johanna and Ole a slice of bread with it.

It didn't take long to discover that corn planting was not the only thing that was on Ole's mind. He took his first sip of coffee, and then he gave expression to his thoughts.

"I can hardly believe it's finally true," he remarked.

"You must be talking about the church meeting you went to last night at Stener Paulson's," Johanna guessed.

"Yes, last night, May 18th, 1876, we took the final step. But such a time we had agreeing on a location. We finally voted to have it four miles south of the spot they were considering five years ago. A few have already been buried in the cemetery there, but so many of our members live farther south, we thought it only fair to have it more centrally located. Now we have to get pledges and see what size we can afford to build."

"Won't it be wonderful, having a church to worship in?" Johanna asked.

"Ja, it will be just a mile and a half west and a mile north of our place. The men will begin hauling lumber from Sioux City for it soon. I told them I'd help the carpenters over at the building site until you have the baby, and then I'll go down to Sioux City and haul a load of lumber also.

"I want to do my share. Hauling that much lumber will take many trips. Besides, there are other things we need in Sioux City, too."

"It should be only a few more weeks now, and then you won't have to worry about leaving me," Johanna said. "You men will really have to get busy if you are planning on getting it ready before fall."

"Well, the first step has been taken now, and that's the most important one. If you never start, you'll never finish," Ole pointed out.

He finished his coffee and jumped up. "Nei, I can't be sitting here when there is so much to do. Ja, it is going to be a busy summer!"

* * * * *

On June 14th, Johanna gave birth to a baby daughter. They decided to name her Helmina after Johanna's youngest sister. Everything went fine and Helmina was a healthy little girl.

After it was all over, midwife Ingeborg joined Ole at the table and Ragna poured them some coffee. Each successful birth brought her a feeling of satisfaction, as she felt very keenly the responsible role that she played in the settlement. She took a sip of coffee and then she got out her corncob pipe and filled it with tobacco and sat and smoked and relaxed.

"How soon do you think I can leave for my trip to Sioux City?" Ole asked midwife Ingeborg. "I have been putting it off for over a month now, and there are many things that we need. Also, I've promised to haul a load of lumber home for the new church."

"Oh, any time!" she assured him. "I'll send my daughter Anne over to stay with Johanna. She is good with newborns and at 23 years of age you can depend on her to look after your family. You men worry so. Don't you know that birth is a natural function? Half of the women that I deliver are out milking the cow the next day."

Ole packed for his trip to Sioux City. He loaded a couple of sacks of wheat which were to be ground into flour, and he filled a pail with feed for his horses, and threw some hay into the wagon box. Ragna got together a loaf of bread and some salt pork for him to eat on the way.

Early the morning of June 16th, he hitched up his horses, and made ready for his trip. He came in to say farewell to Johanna before he left. He stood looking at her lying in bed.

"You appear a little tired today. You'd better take it easy while I'm gone."

"Ja, I feel a little lazy today," she said. "I guess having a baby is too much excitement for me. I'll be all rested up by the time you get home again. Don't worry about us," Johanna assured him. "I have plenty of help here so we will be fine."

Ole bent over little Johnny's bed and softly gave him a kiss.

"Take good care of my family," he told Anne and Ragna. "I'll be back in about six days. If you need any help, or an emergency comes up, go across the field to Lisa and Nils. They'll help you."

He went out the door and climbed up on the wagon seat. With a "Giddap" to his team, he headed for the Eden river crossing from where he would go south on the stagecoach trail to Sioux City.

Everything went smoothly at home the first day. Ragna milked Guldenrosen and carried the water and took care of the pigs and chickens. Anne was a very good nurse and gently tended the new baby, together with Johnny and Johanna.

Towards evening Johanna weakly volunteered, "I should get up and make the supper."

"No," Anne told her. "You just feed your baby. We'll take care of things. You really don't look too peppy yet."

"Well, I am so tired. I can't understand it," she said.

The next morning Johanna was complaining about how hot it was. When Anne touched her, she said, "You've got a fever, Johanna! You just lie still in bed and I'll go down to the well and get you some cold water."

As the day wore on, Johanna's face became flushed and she alternated between fever and chills. Anne tried to keep cool, wet cloths on her forehead to relieve her.

By late afternoon Anne told Ragna to go across the field and tell Lisa and Nils that Johanna was sick and would Nils drive over and get her mother Ingeborg.

Ragna ran all the way, and was soon back home again to do what she could.

When Ingeborg came, she told Anne, "Ja, you are doing the right thing by putting cool cloths on her."

Ingeborg stayed and between Anne and Ingeborg they kept changing wet cloths all through the night. But in spite of this, the fever kept rising.

Ingeborg began to worry about food for the new baby. "The poor little child has to eat, even if her mother is sick."

By afternoon the next day Johanna was delirious. Ingeborg became more and more alarmed and sent Ragna over to Nils Larsen's again.

"Tell him he'd better send someone down to get Ole. I'm afraid for Johanna."

At home Ingeborg and Anne kept on with the cold packs. They washed her hot body with cool, wet cloths.

Everyone in the Overseth shanty had strained, worried expressions as they went about their duties. Only baby Helmina and little Johnny did not know that their mother had the dreaded childbirth fever.

Lisa came over to see if she could be of some help.

"Perhaps you could give the baby something to eat," Ingeborg suggested. "Your little Emma is almost six months now and won't miss it."

Nils got John Johnson to go on horseback to Sioux City and he left immediately.

He rode until it was too dark to see any longer, then he camped until the dawn started breaking and he was off again. That afternoon he pulled into Sioux City. He knew Ole would be loading lumber, so he went to the lumberyard and here he found him.

"Ole," John Johnson excitedly explained. "Johanna's sick. You must start home right away. You take my horse and I'll take your wagon load home for you. Hurry now! Ingeborg says to hurry!"

The trip home from Sioux City was the fastest one Ole ever made, but it seemed the longest. He took the pony express trail which followed the west side of the Sioux River, and then cut through the Big Springs community.

Fear possessed him. "Ja, perhaps it will go with Johanna like it did with her mother," Ole thought. "I shouldn't have left her so soon." He chided himself as if in some way he was to blame for what was happening.

When he had left home four days ago, he was a happy new father; now he was returning a worried man. Why, perhaps even now he was an **enkemand.** He almost dreaded to get there and find out. Tears rolled down his cheeks as he rode along. The dust raised by the horse's hooves settled on his face and left dirty streaks on his cheeks.

"Oh, Father-God, I beg you, help me," he pleaded. "You know how we need Johanna—the two little ones and me."

He finally galloped up to his house. Ingeborg saw him coming and met him at the door.

"Johanna has been very sick, Ole. We almost lost her, but I think she is starting to pull out of it now. The fever finally broke. She started sweating this morning and

I think she has licked this thing. She's a very strong woman. I guess it will take more than childbirth fever to finish her off."

Ole didn't wait to hear any more. He rushed inside and bent over his wife. "Oh, Johanna, my Johanna." She opened her eyes a few moments and weakly tried to smile.

"Just go to sleep now, Johanna," Ingeborg said. "That will be the best for you. Then you will get your strength back again."

Ole held her hand and with his big rough one he stroked her pale forehead and brushed back the hair around her face.

"Kjaere Johanna, Kjaere Johanna min."

When she was asleep, he went over to check on his new little baby; she lay there so tiny and helpless. Then he picked up little Johnny who hugged him tightly, seeming to sense that something bad had been happening.

"Thank you, Anne and Ragna, for being so faithful when I was gone. I guess you had your hands full, didn't you? And it was quite a scare for you. But you did what was best. Johanna's fever is down now and thank God, I pray that everything will be all right. I am indebted to both of you and you, Ingeborg, for your care of my family."

In a few days Johanna was sitting up and able to feed her baby again. John Johnson got back with Ole's team and wagon and Anne was able to return home. Now Ole was finally able to tell well-wishers, "Ja, Mother and baby are doing fine!"

But he knew well enough how close he came to losing his Johanna.

The church building project was in full gear. The loads of lumber were hauled whenever the members could take off from farm work for a trip to Sioux City. All the labor was volunteer, and done under the supervision of carpenters—Lars Sogn, John Skorheim and Solomon Mortenson. It was being built on a corner of Knud Ekle's homestead, with space laid out for a cemetery right south of it.

The church was built facing east and the final measurements had to be reduced from fifty feet long, thirty-two feet wide and sixteen feet high to forty feet by thirty feet by sixteen feet because of a shortage of pledges.

The work progressed and all the members contributed a day or half-day, whenever they could. Pastor Olsen wrote: "Although our church building will be both small and plain, we nevertheless have every reason to thank God that we will be permitted to erect a house that will accommodate our services, especially when we see how many hindrances are put in our way in the furtherance of God's Kingdom in our midst."

On July 9th, when services were held in the Ansten Odegaard home, little Helmina Overseth was baptized. Ansten and Elie Odegaard, together with Anne P. Hansen, who helped take care of their daughter those first few weeks of her life, and a neighbor, Lars Nilson Schulrud were the sponsors.

Another baby was baptized the same day—Clara, baby daughter of Iver Skeyens. Ingeborg Hansen was one of her sponsors. At almost every baptism this favorite lady, the midwife who delivered so many of the infants, was honored by being chosen godmother.

Later in July, after the wheat harvest was finished and the grain was safe in whatever building they had, another infestation of grasshoppers arrived. The settlers were glad they had planted their wheat early.

Thomas Tvedt moved his family out of the log house back into the sodhouse so that his wheat could be stored safely in there. Others used their old sodhouses, stables or loghouses to keep this precious commodity safe from the grasshoppers.

The church construction continued and on August 6, 1876, the first service was held in it, although there was much finishing left to be done. The members sat on planks which were set up in rows, and now there was room for everyone to sit.

That summer the women of the congregation often mentioned that they would like to have a **"kvindeforening."** "Well," Ole Overseth, Nils Larsen and John Skorheim told a group, "just start meeting together. That's all there is to it!"

These three men each contributed a fifty-cent piece for the women to purchase yarn and other materials to make items that could be sold and the money used for missions.

Else Margrethe Skorheim invited the church women to her house. Most of them walked, some carrying babies or knitting as they walked the two, three or more miles to her place. They had their hymnbooks along in their bags.

Sixteen ladies gathered that first forenoon. Else was elected president. She served sandwiches and small cakes at noon and then they all settled down to business on the slope outside the door.

"Perhaps we should read from the Bible," Else suggested.

"Yes, you must do that!" Ingeborg Hansen declared, her voice heavily accenting the last word, and then trailing upward.

Else turned to Matthew 28:19, and read, "Go ye into all the world and make disciples of all nations." She finished with a short prayer.

"Our Father, we would like to be a part of your world mission. We haven't much, but please use what we have to thy glory and bless our fellowship together today. In Jesus' name, Amen."

"Now," Else continued, "we must sing." They all opened their songbooks and sang many of their favorite hymns.

"Well, it is time to work!" Else instructed, and she got out the yarn and divided it among those who wished to make mittens and socks for missions. They began knitting.

Mari Dompedal remarked, "Singing the old Norwegian hymns was so good, I hated to stop and get to work."

"I have an idea," Johanna said. "You, Mari, have such a fine voice, why don't you sing while we knit? That shall be pleasant!"

Everyone chimed in in agreement.

Mari Dompedal loudly cleared her throat and gave several short coughs and then lamely said, "I am so hoarse today, I don't think I can sing very well."

"Oh, come on, Mari," they all encouraged. "Please sing for us."

She cleared her voice some more then opened her hymnbook and began singing,

"Hvor salig er den lille flok." Her clear, sweet voice with the beautiful words and music fell on the ears of the women who knitted as they listened.

Else made them some more coffee before they left for their homes. "It was good for us to be here today," they remarked to each other.

The group of women met when it was convenient and these were times that they all looked forward to. Mari Dompedal had a regular part in these meetings. She didn't like to knit as well as she liked to sing, and after a little coaxing as she went through the same routine of coughing and excusing herself, "because I am so hoarse today," she always complied with their wishes and her voice added to making these days both worshipful and beautiful.

*****

The grasshoppers had become a very serious, annual problem to all the farming area throughout the Midwest. The pioneers tried to cope with these pests, but found that beaters, fire or open plowed strips were of limited use against an enemy that could fly.

There were several cases in Iowa in which a flight of grasshoppers settled across a railroad track and stopped the trains. The crushed insects greased the wheels so that there was almost no traction.

On October 26, 1876, the governors of Iowa, Nebraska, Missouri and Dakota Territory, met and discussed methods of fighting this menace. Before adjourning, they adopted a resolution suggesting a public day of prayer.

1877 looked like it was going to be another bad grasshopper year, for the weather was warm that spring and perfect to speed the hatch of the grasshoppers.

John Pennington, the Governor of Dakota Territory, declared Friday, May 4, 1877, as a day of fasting, humiliation and prayer to Almighty God, "for assistance without which all human effort is made vain."

The day of prayer and fasting was observed by farmers and businessmen alike. And then something strange happened. A small, red parasitic bug appeared, destroying the embryo hoppers so quickly and completely that the annual grasshopper plague was prevented. And many credited it to the workings of God.

But, in some areas it was thought that these hordes of insects had moved off to the lakes of Minnesota and Wisconsin or to the Gulf of Mexico where they drowned.

There were people who declared the pan-fish of Wisconsin and Minnesota were not good eating for a year after the great infestation was over. They had gorged themselves on fresh grasshoppers and that was what they tasted of when caught and fried!

Chapter XVI

15 Aug. 1877

My dear brother Peder,
Greetings from Dakota Territory!

How is it going with you?

And how is the storekeeping job? You must know the business from top to bottom after these years of working behind the counter in Winneshiek County.

I have had something on my mind lately—and it concerns you. I think there may be a fine opportunity out here for you. The railroad is being built and will be coming into Eden next year. I'm sure many buildings and stores will be appearing there then. I feel this would be an opportunity to get in on the ground floor of a store business if you are interested.

With the coming of the railroad you are assured of supplies and there are many settlers in a very large area south and west of here who would appreciate a good general store. We are all tired of depending on those trips way down to LeMars and Sioux City for supplies.

If you are interested in this idea, perhaps you should come out here and look things over. The railroad expects to reach Eden some time next summer.

We had a letter from **Mor** Overseth last month. She mentioned that brother Johannes and his bride are thinking of coming to America—and brother Johan is making arrangements to buy the home farm. Her letter was full of news, and she also included a photo of herself and Pa.

It has been a very busy year here. This spring I got ahold of 3,000 seedling trees from down by the Missouri River and I have been having a job keeping them weeded. I am putting up a granary this summer so we have had several carpenters around here. We have hired them to build a house for us also. We are making plans now and I will begin hauling lumber when the harvest is over. The little one-room shanty we have is getting to be too small, and it is hard to keep warm in the winter. Really, it was built with the idea that it would only be temporary.

Johanna is not idle either, you can be sure of, with our two little ones and all the woman's work on a homestead. We have a young neighbor girl that helps her.

It would be so good to see you again, Pete!

Eden is only about eight miles from our homestead.

Think it over!

your brother, Ole

Later that fall Ole received an answer to his letter,

Kjaere Ole,

Thanks for the letter! It came just in time because I have been contemplating a move. Here I am only working for someone else and I can see no chance of a change in these arrangements.

The Eden opportunity sounds very good. I talked to my old friend from Toten—you remember Peder Dyste, don't you? He works in another store here in town and he is interested in this also. By the way, last year he made a trip back to Norway and got married to Elena Stikbakke.

Peder and I have been talking about working out some kind of a partnership and starting out on our own. I think I will plan to make a trip out to Dakota Territory in the spring. Then I can size up the situation. So, I'll probably be seeing you. In the meantime, I'll have to be saving my money if I am going to be able to go into this business enterprise.

greetings from
brother Peter Anton

Spring came with all the usual activities of planting and sowing. The first of May the two carpenters that Ole had hired returned and began building the new house. They slept out in the new granary, and Johanna gave them their meals. She now had another young girl helping her, for Ragna had married in the fall.

Brother Pete Overseth arrived in April, coming across Iowa by railroad. He had made his big decision and now was in Sioux City working out final arrangements for his store. He had sent for Peder Dyste and his wife and they wanted to get things going as fast as possible.

When Johanna awakened on this May morning, the first thing she was aware of was her bothersome tooth. It had been aching off and on for two weeks now, and it was getting more and more aggravating.

"Perhaps when I get busy, I won't notice it so much," she told Ole at the breakfast table. And there was plenty to do.

She got through the day but by the time she started on the evening meal, the pain was unbearable.

"That's enough of that!" she said as she grabbed her shawl.

"I shall put an end to this!" she angrily declared as she marched out the door. She called to Siri to keep an eye on the children and on the supper, and she headed in the direction of Nils Larsens.

"I can't stand it any longer," she told Lisa as she reached their place.

"Oh, Nils will take care of it for you," Lisa assured her.

"Sit down, and I'll go out and get him. He's still doing chores."

But Johanna couldn't sit down. She held onto the right side of her jaw and walked back and forth, back and forth, in the Larsen kitchen.

Anna, who was eight years old, and Lina, who now was six, stood watching, wide-eyed, their heads turning from side to side as Johanna paced the floor.

"Does it hurt?" Anna finally questioned, her little face full of sympathy.

"Ja, Ja," was all Johanna could answer.

Soon Nils and Lisa came, and Nils had his tooth hook with him. He had made it in his blacksmith shop and now had it pretty well perfected.

"You'll have to sit down, Johanna," he instructed. "Then show me which tooth it is."

She sat on the three-legged stool and opened her mouth, pointing to a molar on the right side.

"Well," Nils said, "if it is the wrong one, you can come back and we'll try another one!"

"Hurry up," Johanna urged, "and get it over with."

Nils worked his hook around the tooth and with several strong jerks and a twist he soon had the large tooth in his hand.

"Here it is," he said as he showed it to her.

"Throw it away. It's caused me enough trouble. I don't want to be seeing it any more." She started to get up.

"No, you sit here for awhile, Johanna," Lisa advised, "until the bleeding stops."

"Is the toothache gone now?" Nils asked.

"Ja, it hurts a little, but it is a different pain. All I can say is that it is a blessing that you have a tool small enough to get the teeth out."

"Nils is getting quite a reputation as a dentist," Lisa pointed out. "Yesterday a man from up by Canton came down to have a tooth pulled."

"Yes, Nils, you are doing a good work when you pull out those aching teeth. I do believe a person could lose his mind from a bad tooth," Johanna said.

She got up and put on her shawl.

"You shall have many thousand thanks!" she said, full of appreciation.

"Ja, I am glad if I helped you," Nils told her.

Johanna started back home, but now she walked at a relaxed steady pace, instead of the frantic half-run she had used when she arrived.

By the first of August the house was finished and Ole and Johanna moved into it. They needed the extra room because brother Johannes Overseth and his wife arrived from Norway and they were staying with them while looking for a farm in the area.

The new house was much larger than the old one, and it had a loft which was divided up into several rooms. Downstairs, a corner was partitioned off for a bedroom. And now she also had a cellar. Johanna would be using her old shanty for a summer kitchen and wash-house.

One noon, John Johnson stopped by with the mail. He had been to the post office and he had two letters from the Overseth **gaard** in Norway—one addressed to Ole and one addressed to his brother Johannes. Ole opened his letter; it was from his father.

10 June 1878

My son Ole,

I have sad news for you. Your dear mother Marte died June 6th of a stroke. The funeral will be next week. It is hard to believe she is gone because it all happened so suddenly. She was 65 years.

Ole called to Johanna who was busy in the kitchen. His voice choked up as he told her about it.

"I guess I thought there was plenty of time, and one day we would go back and visit her."

Brother Johannes spoke up, "I can't believe it! She seemed fine when we left the middle of May."

"Ja, so it goes!" Johanna sympathized.

"I suppose brother Pete at Eden got a letter, too," Ole stipulated.

"Ja, you can be sure of that!" Johannes agreed.

Now there was a heavy quietness in the room as each person sat deep in thought. Finally Johanna said, "You boys had a lovely mother. She was such a lady."

"Yes, and she tried hard to make gentlemen out of all of her sons," Ole added, and Johannes nodded his head.

"She seemed to have a longing for the beautiful, and was always creating fine things, and planting flowers," Inge Marie, Johannes' wife pointed out.

Ole brushed away a tear and Johannes sadly repeated Johanna's words, "Ja, so it goes!"

For supper that night Johanna got out one of the tablecloths that Marte had woven, and the napkins, and Ole brought in a few wild flowers for the table.

That night all of the conversation was of home as the two brothers reminisced, and memories were freely shared of Marte Ensrud Overseth, dear mother and mother-in-law.

* * * * *

Yes, so life goes! Some die and some are born and time keeps moving, moving, moving.

About a month later, on September 28th, Johanna gave birth to another son.

They gave him the favorite family surname of Petter Anthon.

On October 20, 1878, when he was baptized in the new church, Ole and Johanna had the opportunity to have relatives for sponsors—Ole's two brothers, Johannes and Pete Overseth. Inge Marie was too timid to participate.

"After I've been here awhile and know how they do things in America, then I will feel more brave," she commented.

So Ole and Johanna asked midwife Ingeborg Hansen and her seventeen-year-old daughter Rannaug to be the other two sponsors.

It turned out to be a raw cloudy fall day. A light drizzle had been falling during the night so it was cold and muddy traveling to church, but it was with joy and pride that Ole and Johanna brought their guests inside.

The church had now been furnished with benches that some of the men had constructed. Up in front was a stand built for Pastor Olsen to use as a pulpit. A stove had been purchased, and was in use during the fall and winter months. Last winter one of the men had carved out a fine baptismal font from a log.

When Pastor Olsen arrived, he looked out at his congregation. There wasn't as good a crowd as usual today—most likely because of the cold wet weather. Pastor Olsen had been very pleased with the attendance since they had their new church. Why, the communion records gave a good indication of the response—52 had communed last December and 43 in May, and the communicants were only a small percentage of those that gathered monthly.

He had chosen for his text the 18th Sunday after Trinity, a passage from Matthew 22:1-14.

"If the King sent you an invitation to his Son's wedding banquet, wouldn't you be excited?" he questioned.

"Of course!" he went on. "You would right away begin to make plans to go. But then perhaps you would look at your old suit, or your best dress which has become very worn and shabby after these years here on the prairie, and maybe you would have to say, 'I don't think I can go because I haven't anything to wear to the King's palace.'

"That would be a very sad ending to the story, wouldn't it?

"But that isn't what it says in Matthew. Here it says that no one's clothes are good enough—not the rich man's nor the banker's nor the fine lady from Chicago. We all must throw them out and take the fine garment the King has prepared for His guests—Or else He won't even let us in!

"You think this is just a story? No, it is not!

"It is the King of Kings that invites, and He is greater than the King of Norway or the King of England. When we come we must be willing to throw away our old life and put on the clean robe of righteousness, which we can receive through our Lord Jesus Christ. Amen."

That Sunday Pastor Olsen baptized two babies and administered communion to sixteen members.

* * * * *

It had been almost seven years since Ole Overseth made his application for homestead at Vermillion, way back on April 18, 1872. He had become a U. S. citizen on October 17, 1877, and received his naturalization papers from Judge Shannon when District Court met in Canton that fall. Now it was time for him to prove up on his claim and get the final papers and the deed.

On Saturday morning, March 15th, 1879, Ole drove his team and wagon to pick up his neighbors, Ansten Odegaard and John Johnson, and they set off in a northerly direction to Canton, Dakota Territory, about a fifteen- or twenty-mile ride.

They reached the office of M. Cuppett, Clerk of the District Court, as he was opening up after his noon lunch hour. The three men stood before him as he asked the questions and filled out the forms needed for homestead proof.

First he questioned Ansten Odegaard. Ansten was a rather small man, quite a few years older than Ole, with salt and pepper whiskers framing his face from beside his eyes and down around his chin, leaving a top which was very bald. A matching mustache filled in all the spaces below his nose, almost hiding his mouth. The hair that was growing around his ears and around the sides of his head also had a touch of gray.

As Ansten gave his testimony, the clerk quickly wrote down the answers.

"How long have you known Ole Overseth?"

Ansten looked at Ole and his merry blue eyes twinkled as he said, "I guess it has been about seven years now."

"How old is he?"

"Oh, he is barely 32 years."

"Is he head of a family, or a single person?"

"He has a wife and children."

"Is claimant a native-born citizen of U.S.?"

"No, but he has received a certificate of naturalization."

"When was claimant's house built?"

"He has two houses now, but the first one was built on or before April 18, 1872."

"What other improvements have been made?"

Ansten scratched the back of his head while he thought it over.

"Well," he began, "he has a stable and a granary. Then he dug two wells and set out 3,000 forest trees, and he has fenced 20 acres."

When he finished he nodded his head slightly as if agreeing with his own appraisal.

"What is the total value of said improvements?"

"That is hard to say," he said. "I would have to make a guess. I know they would be worth more than $500."

"How many acres have been broken and what crops does he raise?"

"Ole has a fine farm, and already he has broken 70 acres of sod and he has raised wheat, oats, barley and corn."

The clerk turned the paper over and asked Ansten to sign it.

"Is that all?" he questioned.

Ansten took the pen in his calloused, rough hand and signed his name, ending with a fancy flourish that curled back and forth beneath his signature, and the clerk certified its authenticity.

Two witnesses were needed for proving a homestead, so now Clerk Cuppett asked the same questions of John Johnson and had him sign a Testimony of Witness also.

Ole filled out his Homestead Proof, swearing that he had complied with all requirements necessary to obtain a patent on his homestead.

Ole and Ansten served as witnesses for John Johnson because he also needed the final papers filled out for his homestead proof.

The two men were given the papers and were instructed to deliver them to the Land Office in Sioux Falls, together with the balance of their payment.

Ole folded up the long sheets very carefully and stuck them inside his coat pocket for safekeeping. The three men reached home just as it was getting dark and Ole showed Johanna and Johannes and Inge Marie his precious papers.

"Next week John Johnson and I are going to have to make a trip to the Land Office at Sioux Falls with them," he announced.

Early Monday morning, March 17th, they started out, following the stagecoach trail that went by Lars Sogns and then west and north towards Sioux Falls. There were many ruts in the trail and it jolted the wagon as they rode along over the hard frozen ground. They stopped several times on the 40-mile ride to give the team a rest, and when they got hungry, they ate their half-frozen sandwiches.

Late that evening they pulled into Sioux Falls and went to a livery stable with their team and wagon and then they got a room in a hotel. The next morning as soon as the Land Office opened, they were there with all their papers. They each presented their $4.00 balance payment to the Receiver and they took the receipt he gave them, together with their other papers, to the Registrar where they received certificates. These, when presented to the Commissioner of the General Land Office, would entitle them to patents on the tracts of land they had homesteaded.

Now as they rode home, they were both relieved and proud to finally have it registered officially that they were landowners in America. Now they would have to start doing their share, by paying taxes.

Brother Johannes Overseth found a farm for sale that spring. Lars Nilson Schulerud, who lived right east of Paul and Ingeborg Hanson, was moving and after they had agreed on a price, Johannes made arrangements to buy it. It was located just a mile north and a half mile west of Ole and Johanna. But they wouldn't get to move on the farm until the last of May when he would give them a deed.

Now there were two Overseth families farming in the community, and brother Pete Overseth was not far away in Eden, where he was operating a growing general store.

By the end of March, the ground was bare of snow and the southeasterly winds had been drying the plowed land and the old prairie grasses.

"It won't be long now, Johannes, and we will be able to start the spring work," Ole mentioned at the breakfast table.

"Ja, I have a good team and wagon, but I will be needing a plow and other equipment before I can start farming on my own."

"You won't be needing much, if you believe what Lars told you about the land you are buying."

Ole chuckled and repeated Lars' statement to the women.

"He says the ground is so fertile that all you have to do is to scratch the soil, throw in some seed, kick a little dirt over it, and it will grow all right."

"That Lars!" Johanna exclaimed. "He's always kidding. No, Johannes, I think I'd buy myself a plow."

"The land is good enough, Johannes. It is fine land," Ole said. "It is fortunate that you can go ahead with the planting even if Lars is still living there. It would be too late to plant a crop after he moves out in June."

Ole and Johannes went outside to do the chores.

"There is a smell of smoke in the air today," Ole noted.

"Must be a prairie fire somewhere."

All forenoon Ole kept an eye on the horizon because the odor was becoming stronger. Just before noon he saw smoke to the south.

"I'm glad that I plowed a wide firebreak around the buildings and around our new grove last fall. The wind is so strong today, it is a bad day for a fire."

Soon they could see the flames as they came from the southeast and moved northwesterly. They were leaping along in a wide band. The fire raced along at over 30 miles an hour, eating the dry wild prairie grass, strawstacks and haystacks and whatever else lay in its way.

When Ole announced that it would pass west of them, both Johanna and Inge Marie relaxed and quit running from window to window, nervously watching the fire.

"If the edge of it moves a mile west of here the church will be right in its path, and also John Skorheim's home. I think Johannes and I had better go over and see if we can help." Ole threw some wet sacks in the wagon and the two men set out westward.

John Skorheim was already at the churchyard setting a backfire between the two widths of plowing that had been done in the fall.

"Aren't you worried about your place?" Ole asked. The Skorheim home lay one mile south of the church and about a quarter mile west.

"It's right south of here, and it looks to be in the fire's path," Ole explained.

"No, I plowed such a good firebreak I'm sure it can't jump that," John said and continued lighting the fires as Johannes and Ole beat them out. Soon the prairie fire was right up to the burned area and the men busied themselves pounding out the little flames that trailed along the edges. Often a little fire would start up here and there as a piece of burning grass blew across the plowing, and on to the ground around the church. Before long the wind had carried the fire on northwest and the men headed for home.

When they stopped by John Skorheim's place they were shocked to find that his sodhouse had been partly burned.

"I guess some sparks blew across and landed on the dry sod roof," Else said. She had wet her mop and pounded the flames out before they could do too much damage.

"It was awful! It is almost too much for me!" she moaned as she wiped her sooty, sweaty face with the bottom of her long apron.

"I was so afraid for our little ones. And with little Johan Richard lying inside sick with a fever too!" She dabbed at her eyes with her apron. "Why, it isn't even three weeks since our baby Else died."

John Skorheim put his arm around his wife and comforted her with a "There, there, Else! It is all right now."

While Ole and Johannes waited, Viktor Carlson came driving up with his mules and wagon. He had a sad tale to tell, for his sodhouse had been completely destroyed in the fire, and if he hadn't taken his mules and wagon with him out unto his plowed field, they, too, would be gone.

Ole and Johannes went back home, smelling of smoke, their clothing sooty and dirty.

"This has been a bad day," Ole said, his voice full of sympathy. "Here Skorheim was so concerned about the church, and he almost lost his own home. Yes, and his family. And poor Viktor! Thank God, no one was injured!"

Johannes commented, "The fierce way that fire moved westward, I really would be surprised if no one gets hurt today."

After evening chores the two men walked up to the top of the hill west of the house where they could get a better view of the country.

"We want to be sure that it doesn't move this way again," Ole said. "Sometimes sparks can start up a whole new fire."

When they looked northwest, they saw a tall column of smoke and flames in the vicinity of the church. The men wet their sacks and jumped in the wagon again but when they got to the church it was too late to do anything.

Solomon Mortenson, Stener Paulson and several other members of the church were already there, but all they could do was stand by and watch the building blaze with flames, its structure and beams falling as the fire weakened them, and soon the church was leveled—just a pile of burning boards.

"I guess a spark must have got into the straw that was banked up around the foundation," Ole conjectured.

The men stood around, quietly talking to one another, but they all had pained, sad expressions on their faces. The church they had sacrificed to put up, and had labored for, was now only burning embers. And the pride and joy they had had in this building had gone up in the smoke.

The men all dreaded to go home and tell their wives of the tragedy.

That night, as darkness settled on the land, little twinkling lights could be seen here and there along the ground, but now that was all that was left of the Dakota settler's most feared enemy—the relentless prairie fire.

Inge Marie kept shaking her head at the awfulness of the day. "Fire running across the land like the wind—**nei,** there was never anything like that in Norge!"

Chapter XVII

The little congregation **"ut paa landet"** was again without a church building. It had grown considerably and the need for a place of worship was greater than at any time before.

Immediately discussion as to the erection of another church began, but the spring season was a difficult time of the year to raise money, and besides, a dispute arose within the congregation as to whether or not the church should be erected on the old location or a new site.

The issue of where to build the new church was widely discussed in the community. Almost every conversation included the pros and cons of the question.

"Ja, we must be fair to all the members," Ole told Johanna. "There are many who live four, five and six miles southwest of the old site, and building farther east would make a long trip for them on Sundays. There already is a church there—the South Bethlehem **Kirke,** just a mile northeast of us. And then we should consider the many buried in the old cemetery there. No, I don't feel we should keep changing the church location every few years."

Finally action was taken at a meeting May 14th, 1879, in the home of Ansten Odegaard. Over seventy men gathered, many of whom were very adamant about their wishes.

It was agreed by all that the size of the new church should be larger than the old one—50x34x18—instead of the 40x30x16. Finally, when the decisive vote as to the location was taken, there were 44 voting for the old location and 29 voting against.

Because of the disagreement about the location, some people withdrew their support and the committee finally had to reduce the size of the building to 45x30x16. In spite of this discouragement, many took hold of the work with great zeal and sacrifice and pitched in to rebuild. The carpenters in charge again were Lars Sogn, John Skorheim and Solomon Mortenson, but others helped also. Again, members had to haul lumber. This time they secured it from Pattersonville,* about 35 miles away. Ole made several trips, as did Hans P. Hanson, John Skorheim,

*now Hull, Iowa

Thomas Ulrickson, Knud Ekle, Thomas Strand, Severt Mjoen, Stener Paulson, Andrew Lundstrom and Solomon Mortenson.

The cornerstone was laid in the fall of 1879, but the church wasn't completed until the summer of 1881. However, services were held in it. This church had a balcony. It again faced east, and there were four long windows on the south and four on the north, complete with shutters. A steeple was added in 1884, but not finished until 1885.

Pastor and Mrs. Olsen lived four and a half miles north of the church site, and the confirmants had to walk there for their confirmation training.

Dissatisfaction in the eastern part of the congregation because the church was constructed on the same location did not cease. Finally in 1880, some members left to organize a new congregation called Gran. A location was provided two miles east, but a church was never built there, and their services were always held in their homes. Both congregations, however, received service from the same pastor until 1895.

Ole and Johanna had friends in both church groups and often they would attend both services, for Pastor Olsen spent one Sunday a month with each congregation.

There was a nip in the September air, and the days were quickly reaching toward winter. The threshing of the 1879 crop had been finished at the Overseth homestead, and a golden stack of straw stood out behind the house.

Johanna and Siri had been busy filling the mattresses with clean fresh straw before Ole turned the strawpile over to the cows and horses for their lounging area. The family sat around the supper table, finishing their evening meal.

"Ja, that rabbit was a treat!" Ole commented. "I had been hungry for rabbit meat lately. It didn't take much hunting this morning to find one."

"It was nice and plump," Johanna said.

Ole took another helping, "Johanna, you do something special with the rabbit to make it taste so delicious," he complimented.

"Oh, I just stick it in the oven," she answered.

"Papa, I saw mama pour cream over it," Johnny volunteered. "Maybe that's what makes it taste so good."

Johanna watched her family clean up the food she had prepared.

"Did you get all the mattresses filled today? Ole questioned.

"We'll all need stools to get into bed tonight," Siri announced.

"Ja, the newly stuffed mattresses did make the beds pretty high, but it won't be long before they're flattened down again," Johanna explained.

"And we also filled two new mattresses. Any day now I expect to see sister Klara and Ole Grevlos and their family pull up to the door. Then we'll be needing some more beds."

Johanna turned to Ole as she asked, "Do you think Pete or the Dystes will give them a ride out here from the Eden railroad station?"

"I'm sure one of them will. It's hard for us to know just when to expect them."

"I can hardly wait to see Klara again. It's been eight years and now she's got three young ones just like we have."

"I've a feeling that there's going to be a lot of activity around here with six little ones."

"I'm not little anymore, Papa!" five and one-half year old Johnny spoke up. Ole looked into his eager childish face and smiled.

"Neither am I!" Helmina chimed in. She was a serious little girl of three now. His pretty little daughter had grown out of the toddler stage.

"And Petter Anthon isn't a baby anymore either now that he can walk," she added.

"Ja, you are all growing like weeds," Ole teased.

The Overseth home was soon a busy place because the next week Klara and Ole Grevlos and their three children—Christian, Julia and Helene arrived from Norway with their belongings and trunks.

"Make yourselves at home," Ole invited.

"You must stay with us at least until after Christmas," Johanna said.

While the women went about the housework and cared for the children, Ole tried to help his brother-in-law look for a place to live, and in turn Grevlos helped Ole with his work. The corn had to be picked, and soon October passed into November. They went down to the river to haul wood home for winter. Many of the farmers in the community had purchased a few acres of school land along the river near Fairview from which they would gather their wood supply.

When December came, Johanna and Klara began getting ready for Christmas. Working side by side in the kitchen was like old times, except that now there were always little ones underfoot, and often there was a toddler tugging at their skirts. They baked **fattigmand** again and **lefse.** A pig was butchered and they fixed blood sausage and head cheese.

Ole had invited all the relatives to the Overseth homestead for Christmas Eve. He told brother Pete, "On Christmas Eve you must bring along your trumpet so we can have some music." Pete had been playing in a band back in Winneshiek County.

Several days before Christmas, Pete sent out an evergreen tree from the store, and in the late afternoon of December 24th, brother Pete and Peder and Elena Dyste drove up in their sled. Johannes Overseth and his wife Inge Marie came over. Johanna and Klara had a big Christmas Eve supper prepared. One of Johanna's geese had been killed and spareribs had been fixed, and from her garden supply Johanna had boiled potatoes and carrots.

The Christmas tree had been decorated with what they could improvise—bits of ribbon and candles. After the supper was eaten, the candles were lit and everyone gathered around the tree. Johanna gave Ole the Bible and he read the Christmas story from the **evangel** Luke, chapter two. The children sat with folded hands, but excitement danced in their eyes, as they waited for the treats that were coming later.

Litte Petter Anthon, his thick brown hair curling around his face, toddled around. He spent the evening going from lap to lap, for when he turned his smile upon his aunts and uncles, they couldn't resist taking him in their arms.

Pete got out his trumpet and played familiar Christmas songs. The strong melodious tones reminded the grown-ups of the greatness of the evening. Their thoughts returned to past Christmases in Norway, while the little ones, enthralled with this shiny instrument, listened in awe.

Ole sat absorbing every note. When Pete had finished, he said, "Ja, the angels made music the first Christmas, but we have a trumpet to remind us to be joyful on this holy night."

They all stood around the tree, holding hands and singing favorite carols—the old ones from Norway. Verse after verse they sang from memory.

Uncle Pete had brought gifts from his store for the children. For the boys he had narrow black ties, and for the three little girls there were necklaces. Helmina slipped hers over her head and went to thank him. He lifted her up in his lap and pulled at her pigtails. He looked her over, and gave her his verdict, "My little Minnie is even prettier with jewelry." Minnie was the pet name that Uncle Pete had given to his niece, Helmina.

The storekeepers had brought a sack of candies and a box of apples from Overseth and Dyste General Store and the children kept begging until the last piece of candy was gone.

Johanna looked around at all of her loved ones, and remembered the times she had been lonely in this country. Now Ole and she had more of their families in America than they had back in Norway. She had received the news that her two brothers Peter Anthon and Martinus Narum had come over in 1878, and they were in St. Peter, Minnesota, with Christian.

Now here in Dakota Territory, she had Klara and her family, cousin Peder Dyste and his wife, Elena, and Ole's two brothers, Pete and Johannes and his wife Inge Marie.

Johanna had a feeling the hard, lonely days were behind her. Now their lives were becoming more civilized with stores as close by as Eden, and Ole had been progressing very well in his farming operations.

She found herself humming the melody of **In dulce Jubilo,** and the words they had just been singing with it were still repeating themselves in her head.

I sing a Christmas song
I am so glad, so glad

He my Savior is!
He my Savior is!
Yes, tonight Johanna's heart was overflowing with gladness.

Chapter XVIII

With the eighties a new era arrived. The years of 1878-1887 were called the "Great Dakota Boom." The railroads had opened up Dakota Territory to the rest of the world. Now homesteaders were coming on trains instead of by covered wagon. Now supplies and food and lumber were available and farmers had an outlet for their produce.

The economic conditions caused by the Panic of 1873 had improved. The weather during these years was favorable and the grasshopper plague had passed.

By the middle 1880's settlers' shacks and little towns spread north and west of the Big Sioux, Vermillion and James Rivers as the railroads stretched to the west and north.

The years of 1880-84, when Ordway was governor, were stormy years in South Dakota history. It was a time of organizing county governments. The selection of county seats was decided by popular vote and there were many fights when some towns made attempts to relocate county seats.

Beginning in 1881, ox teams gradually began to disappear and horses and mules took over with their horsepower. There were improvements in farm machinery and harvesting was revolutionized by self-binding reapers. Yes, a new era was arriving on the Dakota prairie.

Early in the summer of 1880, Johanna received a letter from her youngest sister, Helmine.

Vestre Toten, Norge
1 May 1880

My dear sister Johanna,

I have a great surprise for you! I will soon begin packing my trunk because brother Hans and I are leaving for America the middle of July.

The home here at Narum is brother David's home now, and since I am 25 I feel that I should leave to make a life of my own.

Papa is quite upset because Hans is going. He will only have two of his children left in Norge then—David here at Narum, and Helene Marie with her husband, Johannes Stikbakke and their family.

Papa could say goodbye to all the rest of us, but to have his youngest leave is pretty hard on him. You know as well as I that Hans has been Papa's comfort ever since Mama died. Remember how Papa even let him sleep with him because little Hans cried for Mama. Yes, Hans has always been Papa's favorite.

But I want to warn you, no more can you call Hans "Little Hans." He is the biggest and most muscular of all of our brothers—and strongest! That you shall soon see! He has changed a lot since you left nine years ago, and perhaps you will not even recognize him again.

I plan to take the railroad directly to Eden, but Hans will go to St. Peter where our other brothers are.

I suppose it will be the latter part of September before I arrive. I am so anxious to see my namesake, Helmina, and my two nephews. Perhaps you will let Auntie spoil them a little? It will be good to see Klara and her family again, also. Tell her my plans.

Till I meet you in person,

I am your sister,
Helmine

Even though Johanna was filled with happiness at the news, she sighed, "Poor Papa," as she thought of her father bidding goodbye to his youngest daughter and youngest son.

"But how fortunate I am!" Johanna told Ole as they sat at the dinner table. "Now I will have Helmine here to help me when I have the baby."

Two-year-old Petter Anthon was on Ole's lap and Johnny, now six and one-half, and Helmina, four, each had their own places at the table.

"Ja, I am happy to hear that, for it has been too busy for you since Siri left. I have noticed how tired you are most of the time."

"Can you believe it? Three of the Narum sisters will be together again. May God be praised!"

Johanna couldn't wait to tell Klara the news. Klara and Ole and family were now living on a farm southwest of the Overseths, but the families got together almost every week.

"Can we go down to Grevlos' tomorrow?" Johanna asked. "There is no church here tomorrow and we could have an early dinner and spend Sunday afternoon with them. Klara will be just as excited as I am to hear Helmine's news."

"Ja, Papa. Then we can play with Christian and Julia and Helene," Johnny begged.

"I guessed we can do that," Ole said as he gave Johnny and little Helmina a wink.

On September 20th, Helmine Narum's train pulled into Eden. The depot was a busy place because every train that came through nowadays was loaded with immigrants and homesteaders who were going to the end of the railroad line to take up homesteads.

Helmine was glad to get off the crowded train and she watched it depart with the heads of men, women and children leaning out of the windows, trying to get a look at this new land of Dakota.

Ole happened to be in town that afternoon and he loaded up Helmine's belongings and they drove out to the homestead to surprise Johanna.

Johanna had washed clothes and she was now following the practice of pioneer women and using the soapy lye washwater to scrub up the pine boards on her kitchen floor. This took all the grease spots out.

"Papa's home!" Johnny shouted, as he came running into the house.

"Don't step on the wet floor, Johnny!" Johanna warned as she wiped up the last spot by the back door, but he was gone again as soon as he explained, "I have to go out and see if Papa brought some candy home for us."

Johanna straightened herself up after being down on her knees. She glanced out the door and when she saw Helmine standing there with Ole, her mouth went agape.

"Oh, **kjaere meg!**" she exclaimed, and hurried out to greet her sister. They embraced, and their nine-year separation was ended. No longer were they big sister and little sister, for the age gap had even seemed to disappear. It was so good to be together again. The next few days they were busy sharing and bringing each other up to date on everyone and everything.

Helmine had brought along a piece of lovely plaid woolen material for a dress for her namesake, little Helmina. She was there to help Johanna when the threshers came and together they got ready for winter, digging up the potatoes and beets and carrots from the garden and making warm clothes for the children. She sewed a lovely dress for little Helmina from the red plaid. It had long sleeves and a wide ruffle at the bottom. She put a white collar on it and sewed white pantaloons to wear under it.

When Auntie Helmine wasn't busy, she was sitting in the rocking chair with three children around her. Petter Anthon would be cradled in her arms, little Helmina wedged in beside her and Johnny standing alongside, riding on the rocker runner.

Ole was getting ready for winter, too. He hauled home wood and had just begun to pick his corn when in the second week of October, the snow began to fall.

He came in after doing chores on the morning of October 15th, and said, "**Nei**, I have never seen weather like this in October before! The snow is getting heavier by the minute, and the wind is getting stronger and stronger. I guess there won't be any cornpicking today."

As the day advanced, the wind and snow increased in fury, and the area was soon enveloped in a fierce blizzard. It continued for twenty-four hours and left the fields of corn covered with drifts. It blocked the roads and even stopped some of the trains before they had a chance to get the coal hauled to their destinations before winter set in.

When Ole's horses could get through, he made a trip to Eden with his sled to get some supplies—coffee, salt, sugar, candles and kerosene.

"It's good you came when you did," brother Pete at the store told him. "Our supplies are getting pretty low. The trains haven't been through yet. I hope they come soon, before we get some more snow."

But this was the winter of the snows—the Hard Winter of 1880-1881. As soon as one snow settled down a little, a few more inches fell.

Because of this freak winter weather Pastor Olsen couldn't have services in any of his congregations for three weeks, but finally he was able to continue with his regular schedule again. On November 28th he had confirmation in the new church with 24 confirmands. Two weeks later, on December 5th, there was communion with 48 communing.

Piles of snow were still lying everywhere, but there was a hard crust on it so you could walk over it.

Ole's corn crop lay buried under the snow. All he could see were the tops of the stalks. His pigs needed the corn for feed, so almost every day that the weather permitted he had to go out in his cornfield with a sharp stick and dig down around the stalks until he could pull out a few ears.

"I think brother Johannes and I will have to try to make another trip down to the river next week for some more wood," Ole said as he sat down to supper.

"I hope the weather holds." He had spent the afternoon at the chopping block, splitting wood into stove-size lengths, and his wood supply was quickly diminishing. It was only the 8th day of December and most of the winter still lay ahead.

The family was gathering around the table.

"**Sette deg**, Johanna!" sister Helmine instructed, as she carried the bowls of steaming hot mush to the table for supper. There was cinnamon and sugar to sprinkle over it and creamy cold milk. Helmine sliced off pieces from the loaf of fresh bread and they commenced eating.

Ole turned to the children and asked, "Do you know what day it is today?"

Little daughter Helmina's eyes lit up and she guessed, "Is it Christmas already?"

"No," Johnny said to his sister, "Uncle Pete told me there were two weeks left when he was here Sunday."

"No," Ole explained, "it isn't Christmas yet. Today is **Mor** and **Far's** special day. It was eight years ago today that your mama and I got married."

He looked at Johanna and asked, "Can it really be that long already?"

"Is that something like a birthday? little Helmina asked.

Johanna smiled and agreed. "Yes, it is very much like a birthday."

After all the bowls were emptied, Ole took the Bible out for their evening devotions.

"Let's sing, 'So Take my hand, dear Father,' tonight," Johanna suggested. They went through several verses, the children joining in now and then. Then Ole turned the pages of the Bible to Psalm 128.

Johanna explained to her sister, "Pastor Johnson, who married us, asked us to read this chapter each year on our anniversary."

Ole cleared his throat and began. He read slowly and with meaning.

> "Blessed is everyone who fears the Lord,
>   who walks in his ways!
> You shall eat the fruit of the labor of your hands.
>   You shall be happy,
>   and it shall be well with you.
> Your wife will be like a fruitful vine
>   within your house.
> Your children will be like olive shoots
>   around your table.
> Lo, thus shall the man be blessed
>   who fears the Lord."

Ole looked at all the faces around the table. There was Johnny, his oldest, his thick dark hair hanging down over his eyes, his eager little face quickly turning into a smile as he caught his father's glance. And there was his serious little Helmina, her pigtails hanging down her back. And his precious two-year-old Petter Anthon, sitting with folded hands and with traces of milk and mush still around his mouth.

His eyes turned to his Johanna, her hair tightly pulled back from the center part, and her quiet beauty seeming to increase with each year. He could see how uncomfortable she was now, and he gave thanks for her sister Helmine who had come at such an opportune time now that Johanna needed help.

Ole bowed his head and thanked God for each of them, naming them one by one before the throne of God. Then he thanked his Heavenly Father for another year of His loving care.

One week later, on Tuesday, December 14th, Ole and Johanna's fourth child was born—a fine son whom they named Martin.

The excitement of the new baby and the excitement of Christmas all blended together as the days neared Christmas Eve.

"It will just have to be our own family this year," Johanna said, as Helmine and she tried to get ready for the holidays.

"Ja, you have plenty to do this soon, and with such a little baby to care for, too," Ole agreed.

"Klara and her family will be happy spending Christmas Eve by themselves. And the relatives in Eden can get together that night," but then Johanna got a thoughtful expression on her face as she asked, "But what about your brother Johannes and Inge Marie? Inge Marie has been so homesick and if they are alone on Christmas Eve that will only make it worse."

Ole shook his head. "I can't understand it. It is over two years now since they left Norway. I thought she would get over homesickness by now."

"Well, Inge Marie is a very sensitive person, and rather timid, and I know she has really been suffering. Sometimes she can't even eat. She told me that she has to try to keep busy so she won't think of Norway and of her folks there because, she said, she just can't bear to think about them. It hurts so much."

"I feel sorry for Johannes. He has tried everything to get her to be happy here. Maybe it is just that she can't adjust to pioneer life."

"Lisa Larsen has been so kind to her, too. She visits her often and last year they even had Johannes and Inge for sponsors for their little Nora."

Ole finally remarked, "I think what she needs is a little one of her own to keep her busy. Then she would get over it."

"It is hard to say. But they live so close by, I think we should ask them to join us for Christmas Eve. That will only be two more."

"Well, it's up to you," Ole concluded.

"Then it is all settled. We don't want anyone unhappy on Christmas Eve if we can do something about it," Johanna said.

Ole made a trip to Eden the week before Christmas and did his shopping. He purchased apples and candies and new shoes for Johnny, Helmina and Petter Anthon. Sister Helmine was busy making lefse and fattigmand.

"It wouldn't be Christmas without that!" she remarked.

When the magic evening arrived, Johnny came to his father with a puzzled expression on his face, "Are you sure it is Christmas Eve? There is no Christmas tree."

Ole tried to explain, "It can be Christmas without a Christmas tree. Last year Uncle Pete found one for us, but there weren't any in Eden last week when I was there. All the trains still haven't been coming through, and you know there aren't any of those trees growing around here."

Johnny didn't seem satisfied with his answer so Ole put his arm around his son and confided, "I tell you what we will do, Johnny. In the spring I'll try to buy some little evergreens and then we'll plant them outside and grow our own Christmas trees. And you can take care of them and water them and weed them. It may take a few years, but what do you think about that?"

"Well," Johnny said, as he slowly nodded his head, "but aren't there any presents either?"

"Oh, yes," Ole responded. "There is a box for each of you. You will see."

When Johannes and Inge Marie arrived they all sat down to the table, and feasted on spareribs and potatoes and beets and lefse and all the different cookies Auntie Helmine had baked.

When Ole finished reading the Christmas story, they all loudly raised their voices together in song.

"A babe is born in Bethlehem,
   in Bethlehem,
Therefore rejoice Jerusalem,
   Hallelujah, Hallelujah!"

The Christmas story seemed to take on more meaning this year because Johanna had a new baby boy of her own. She looked down at the little one in her arms and it was so hard to realize that her great Savior and Friend had come to this earth just as little and helpless as her baby Martin. Yes, the loving ways of God were sometimes beyond understanding.

Now Auntie Helmine told the children to sing the song she had been teaching them. Johnny and little Helmina lined up side by side and Petter Anthon quickly jumped down from his father's lap and stood beside them. He stuck out his chest and raised his head erect as he tried to join Johnny and Helmina in singing, "Thy little ones, dear Lord are We." Now and then Petter Anthon would repeat a word after his brother and sister.

Everyone sang the other Christmas favorites and then Ole came with the three boxes and gave one to each of his children. Johnny had his opened first, and exclaimed, "New shoes!" He looked them over carefully. They were made of cowhide and inside was a tin plate on which it said "oil me twice a week." He began taking his old worn shoes off so he could try these on.

Helmina also had found new shoes and was in the process of unbuttoning her old ones.

Little Petter Anthon became very excited when he found shoes in his box also, and he plopped himself down on the floor and began pulling at his old shoes so he could put his new ones on.

Ole smiled as he watched them and then he sat down on the floor by Petter Anthon and helped him. When Petter had his shoes on, he took several careful steps in them, and headed for his Mother. He tried to put his foot up on her lap so she could see his shoes, "Oh, so fine!" she declared, "but be careful for the baby, Petter."

After they all had had apples and candies, Johanna said to the children, "Do you think you could sing your song once more?"

They quickly lined up again, but it took a while before they were ready to sing because they kept glancing at each other's new shoes. Then her three little ones joined hands and began singing.

> "Thy little ones, dear Lord, are we
> And come they lowly bed to see.
> Enlighten every heart and mind
> That we the way to Thee may find."

Johanna watched and listened and then she thought, "Of all the Christmases in my life, this is the greatest."

* * * * *

Ole and Johanna decided to have Pastor Olsen baptize Martin when he had services with the Gran group at Iver Skeyans on January 2nd. "It will be warmer for the baby there than in the church," Johanna said.

"And besides," Ole added, "They only live about a mile from us, so it won't be so far to travel in all the snow."

They asked Ole and Anne Raasum and Nils and Lisa Larsen to be sponsors for baby Martin.

Johnny and little Helmina had developed running noses and Johnny had begun coughing, so Auntie Helmine insisted on staying home with them.

"It will only make them worse to go out," she said. So, on that first Sunday in 1881, Ole and Johanna and the new baby went to Skeyans for services.

The following week Johanna and Helmine were busy nursing the two sick children. They had fevers and coughs and Johanna cooked up an onion poultice and put on their chests to loosen up the congestion. Ole went into Eden and Dr. Avery at the drugstore sold him a bottle of Cherry Pectoral for the coughs.

About the time Johnny and little Helmina were up and around again Johanna noticed that baby Martin had a slight fever.

"Oh, **nei-da!**" she sighed. "It is worse to have such a little baby sick." But it didn't develop into anything serious.

In the midst of all this sickness, Ole picked up Petter Anthon and swung him up in the air. "Petter, my boy, You are a strong man! You don't sit still long enough for the germs to catch up with you!"

But later that week Petter Anthon became tired and listless. He wanted to sit in the lap and be rocked. He was very cross if he couldn't have his new shoes beside him wherever he went. Johanna noticed that he had a slight fever when he went to bed January 16th. It was worse the next day, and the next night when she got up to feed the baby she checked on him and his fever was climbing. The rest of the night he kept awakening and calling "Mama" and "Papa."

The following day Helmina and Johanna sponged him continuously with cool cloths, and they managed to keep the fever down, but by evening it shot up again.

"We'll take turns sitting up with him and sponging him. And we must try to get him to drink something," Johanna said.

They made a bed for him by the stove and Auntie Helmine was going to take the first shift.

About midnight Helmine came running in to awaken Johanna and Ole. "What shall I do? He has convulsions!" she rushed back to be with him again.

Johanna and Ole hurried from their bedroom. Johanna touched his hot, hot body and shook her head. "He is very sick!"

She began washing him again with the cool, wet cloth. Ole would not go back to bed either.

"Would it help if I held him?" he asked.

"No, he is so warm, I think he is better off lying on the cot."

He reached for his little son's chubby hand. It was so feverish. Petter Anthon began coughing and choking. There were worried expressions on all of their faces. None of their children had ever been this sick before.

"If we could only get the fever down!" Johanna kept saying.

She stroked her son's brow with her hand as she talked to him. "**Stakkars,** Petter Anthon. You are so sick."

All three hovered around him the next few hours, trying to think of things to do to counteract the fever and make him more comfortable. But once again he went into convulsions.

"**Nei,** I am going for the doctor," Ole announced and got on his boots and his big, warm coat. He lit the lantern and went out into the stable and began bridling his horse to ride to Eden. He hurried, and was ready to untie it when he heard his name.

"Ole."

He looked around in the faint lanternlight and saw his sister-in-law Helmine standing in the doorway of the stable. She came over to where he was.

"You won't need to go for the doctor," she said.

Ole was puzzled. "Why? Has the fever gone down?"

"Ole," Helmine had a hard time getting the words out. "I think he is dead." Her lips quivered and she bit them to try to keep her composure.

"No," Ole said. "That can't be!"

She quietly told him to go in and see.

It was getting to be dawn now. Ole ran into the house and there Johanna knelt beside the cot. Little Petter Anthon's body was no longer in the tense throes of convulsions. He lay there like he was asleep. Ole grabbed his hand and felt for his pulse. He moved his big thumb around on the little wrist, trying to discover a beat. Then he put his head down upon his son's little chest, but he could feel no movement—no breathing, no heartbeat. He thought, "It can't be," and again hunted for his pulse.

Johanna raised her head and looked at Ole. "It is true. He is dead." Ole took her into his arms and together they wept.

Then Ole picked up the little body and carried it upstairs and laid it on the spare bed. There he knelt beside it and tried to get his own life back into focus again and face the sad reality of this 19th day of January, 1881.

After an hour he came downstairs. Outside a light snow had begun to fall. He went to do the morning chores and began looking around for some wood to build a little coffin for his son. All day he kept on working outside in the stable with his saw and hammer. At times his eyes were so full of tears that he couldn't see what he was sawing.

That afternoon Auntie Helmine and Johanna washed Petter Anthon's little body and dressed him in his best suit.

When Ole came in, Johanna said, "You must go to the Pastor's and see about the funeral," but by then the snow had gotten heavier and the wind was coming up so they decided that he'd have to wait for the next day.

But the next day the area was in the midst of another blizzard and it continued for three days. When it had quieted, deep piles of snow lay everywhere, and Ole said, "I'm afraid it's too much snow to get up to Pastor Olsen's, and besides, people couldn't come to a funeral in all this snow," so he took his shovel and got on his horse.

"I am going to the cemetery to dig the grave," he said.

"I will stop at brother Johannes and see if he will help me."

The horse waded off through the deep snow with Ole on its back.

The next day Ole loaded the little coffin into the sleigh and Johanna and he went over to the cemetery alone to bury their son. They stood side-by-side at the grave, and then Ole looked up into the heavens and said, "Thank you for letting us have him. He gave us much joy."

Then he bowed his head and prayed, "Help us to remember that You gave him to us and You have the right to take him again. Even as David, I will say now, 'He cannot come to me, but I can go to him."

Then he put his arm around his wife, and she added, "Yes, that is so. That is so."

Chapter XIX

The first week in February, 1881, a fierce blizzard descended on the midwest, lasting many days and depositing a heavy accumulation of snow. All during the month the snows continued, leaving only a day or so of respite between them. Now the ground covering was so deep that no one could travel by horse or rail or oxen. Some used skiis. One man from near Canton, Anders Quien, went by skiis to Fairview, pushing a hand sled to get a supply of flour for his family and his neighbors from the Fairview mill.

By now everyone had shortages of everything—coffee, kerosene, flour and candles, and they had to improvise or manage with what they had.

Johanna's supply of coffee had almost run out and she watched it diminish until it just covered the bottom of the can.

"Oh, life will be still more bleak without coffee," Johanna predicted.

"Perhaps we could roast some barley or wheat and grind it and mix it with what we have to make it go farther," Ole proposed.

"Well, we can try," Johanna said.

She roasted some barley kernels in the oven until they were brown and then ran them through the coffee grinder and mixed them in with her coffee supply. Now she had twice as much left.

She cooked a batch of coffee from this mixture and poured up three cups, one for each of them to sample.

Sister Helmine made a face and commented, "This is not so good!"

"But it is better than none," Ole said.

"Ja, we must do the best with what we have," Johanna added.

Johanna and Auntie Helmine made candles by dipping wicks into tallow and cooling and redipping again and again until they had lights for the long, dark winter evenings, for their kerosene supply had run out.

In the first week of March, it warmed up considerably and the snow began to melt. This process wrought almost as much havoc as the blizzards, for the melting snow began running off and filling and flooding rivers and streams and left mud everywhere. In many places it did more damage than the blizzards. As the waters and ice floes started downstream they covered the lowlands and swept buildings, haystacks and animals with them. Many animal and human lives were lost.

The flooding was so bad the last week in March in the Sioux City-Yankton area that numbers of houses, animals, railroad beds and bridges and telegraph lines were destroyed, and steamboats wintered at Yankton were so badly damaged that they were a complete loss.

The town of Vermillion, then located on the flatlands below the bluffs, was inundated and later had to be rebuilt on higher ground.

Gradually the water disappeared and the ground finally dried so people could get around, but there was much repair work to be done and a lot of cleaning up. Dead animals and much debris lined the path the flood waters had taken. The railroads had to be repaired. The railroad bridge between Canton and Beloit had been washed out, so it was some time before people could travel directly from Eden to Canton by train. Instead, they had to detour by way of Rock Valley, Iowa, and then over to Canton.

Pastor Olsen had no services in any of his congregations from January 17th until April 3rd, when he once again met with the town congregation in Canton. On April 10, Palm Sunday, he was out in the country, but even then it was so muddy that not very many could attend.

The beautiful weather of May soon made roads passable again and a "Day of Prayer" was planned for the congregation on Friday, May 13th, in the new church **"ut paa landet."** Many babies that had been born during the long winter were baptized that day—Paul Gubberud's little girl Clara, and Blilie's daughter, and three baby boys.

Ole and Johanna and sister Helmine Narum were sponsors for Ole and Anne Raasum's son Oskar, who was one of the children baptized.

There was communion and then following the benediction they went out into the cemetery to have graveside services for little Petter Anthon Overseth and another member of the congregation who had died during the winter—Mrs. Ole Kitelson.

Pastor Olsen preached his sermon on his favorite "Day of Prayer" text. Every year in the spring he held such a day in one of his congregations and always he used verses from Isaiah 55. Today it was the seventh verse:

> "Let the wicked forsake his way
> and the unrighteous man his thoughts.
> Let him return to the Lord that he may have
> mercy on him and to our God for he will
> abundantly pardon."

After he read the verse, he looked out at his congregation and asked, "I suppose you are thinking, 'Ja, we have heard that before. Why is he preaching on that verse again?'

"Then I will ask you, 'Why do you return every spring to plow up your fields?' You have done it before, have you not? But again you dig up last year's growth and weeds and husks and mistakes and prepare the ground for a new, and you hope, more fruitful crop.

"This is how it is with God also. He must clean up our hearts before He can use them. Oh, my people, let the plow of God's Word dig into your hearts and make you ready to be fruitful. Yes, and willing to go His way."

Ja, Johanna thought, "His way." That is something that is so hard to understand. Her heart was still hurting. Especially today as graveside services would be held for little Petter Anthon.

Not that I am blaming God, she thought, although I know He could have healed my little boy, if He had deemed it best.

Then her thoughts turned to the blessedness of her son, for he was at home—yes, at home with Jesus. These past few months heaven had become very real to her because Petter Anthon was there waiting.

She heard Pastor Olsen conclude his message with:

"For my thoughts are not your thoughts, says the Lord. Neither are your ways my ways."*

How right that is, Johanna agreed. Then she went one step further and willingly consented, "I will trust that Your ways are the best."

* * * * *

On one of the first trips Ole made into Canton that summer, he ordered a gravestone for little Petter Anthon's grave. He chose a white stone that had a lamb carved near the top. Underneath he wanted to have inscribed the words:

"Here lies the remains of Petter Anthon Overseth, born Sept. 28, 1878, died Jan. 19, 1881. Blessed be his remains, and may he rest in peace"

When it was ready he brought it home and erected it in the Lands Church cemetery over little Petter Anthon's grave. That night he told Johanna, "You know, we don't even have a photo of little Petter Anthon to remember him by."

"I will never forget him," Johanna sadly vowed.

"Nor will I, but I think we should have had a photograph. It is too late for Petter Anthon, but not for the other children. I have decided that I will take Johnny and Helmina to Canton to the photographer. Perhaps Martin is too small yet."

Ole didn't waste any time accomplishing this resolution and several days later little Helmina was dressed in her new pretty red plaid dress and her new button shoes. Her ruffled white pantaloons hung slightly below the wide ruffle on her skirt.

Johnny had outgrown the trousers that belonged with his suit, but Ole said, "This new darker pants will look all right. No one will be able to tell the difference on a photograph."

*Isa. 55:8

Little Helmina slipped her prized necklace on and Ole carefully tied Johnny's narrow black tie. When they were ready, Ole and his two oldest children set off in the wagon for the shop of C. A. Delong, the photographer in Canton, South Dakota, where their images that day were imprinted for their parents and their relatives in Norway, and even for their posterity.

* * * * *

July 9th dawned with sunshine. Daylight revealed the puddles that were left after yesterday's thunderstorm. At least, it had cooled the hot July weather temporarily.

This summer storm had come when many of the settlers were putting up their hay. Much of Ole's hay still lay on the ground. A half-made haystack stood in the corner of the new field that Ole had just acquired. This field was eighty acres of land that lay a half mile west of their homestead on the north side of the road. John Johnson had sold it to Erik Rise in April, and then last month, June 25th, 1881, Erik sold it to Ole. It was mostly hayland and they had been putting up hay there yesterday when the electrical storm came up. Nils Larsen was helping him. They had let their two sons come along so they were quick to leave the field when the thunder and lightning got close.

When Ole finished his chores this morning he had gone over to check on his hay. Johanna and Helmine were busy with their Saturday work. Baby Martin was asleep. Johanna was baking bread and sister Helmine was ironing the family's clothes so everything would be ready for church tomorrow morning.

Ole came rushing into the house and announced, "Something terrible happened."

Johanna looked up from her kneading and was about to ask, "What?" when he explained.

"Thomas Tvedt stopped me over on the west eighty and told me his brother Ole Endersen Tvedt was struck down by lightning yesterday."

"Oh, no!" Johanna gasped. "Poor Ragnild! And she just had a new baby, too."

"Yes, it is true. He was putting up hay also. When it began to sprinkle he started home and had stopped to visit with his neighbor Rogness over the fence, and then it happened. A bolt of lightning struck, hitting Ole Endersen and the fence."

Ole sadly shook his head. "Why he was only 41 years old.

"The funeral will be this afternoon," he informed her. "With this hot, humid weather, they can't wait until next week. I think we should go."

"Yes, we should," Johanna agreed. "Ragnild will need all the support we can give her. Poor thing, left with five little ones to care for."

"Ja, that lightning is nothing to take chances with," Ole said.

Johanna again shook her head and muttered, "Oh, that is so sad! What a shock it must be to Ragnild, happening as suddenly as that."

"Thomas said the new baby will be baptized this afternoon, too. Ragnild decided to name him Ole Oleson after his father. Just think, the baby isn't even two weeks old, and he has already lost his father. Ja, it will be a hard road for Ragnild."

"Poor thing. Only 26 years old, and already an **enke**," Johanna sadly added.

"I'll take several loaves of bread along this afternoon. Yes, and I'll stir up some doughnuts. I'm sure she doesn't feel like baking, but they will have to eat, and her little ones will like to have some doughnuts. You can be sure people will be stopping by to see her!"

Johanna got back to her work and quickly shaped her bread into loaves and put them in pans.

"Ja, these are sad times," Ole commented. "Tomorrow graveside services will be held for Ole and Dordi Wilson's three children who died from diphtheria the last week of May. I guess the whole family is finally well again—those that are left. Just think, they lost all three boys within one week—a six-year-old, a four-year-old and one that was one and one-half. That diphtheria is some bad stuff!"

"Yes, there are a lot of heartaches today," Johanna agreed. "Sometimes I wonder how some people can stand such great sorrow. And with Dordi expecting another child, too, it seems like life and death are all mixed together nowadays. Sorrow overcomes the joys of birth, both in Ragnild's case and in Dordi's."

"Perhaps the new babies were needed to give them strength, hope and courage to go on," Ole suggested.

After a few moments of contemplation, Johanna asked, "What will Ragnild do now?"

"I don't know," Ole responded. "The five children will need a home, and it will be a long time till they are much help on the farm, the oldest being only seven. Perhaps she can find a hired man to do the work so she can keep the place. There are newcomers from Norge arriving all the time now. Maybe some of us neighbors can help so that she gets this year's crops in."

"I don't know what I would do if this had happened to me. It is too awful to think about," Johanna said.

"Yes, it is sad. But, Johanna, you forget that God promises that we are never given any more than we can bear."

Ole got up from his chair and headed for the door. "I told Thomas that I would let Nils and Lisa and Ansten and Eli know about it, so I'd better be going. Ja, Ragnild will need many of us for support this afternoon."

Johanna filled her big kettle with lard, and went out into the shanty to make doughnuts. Helmine was standing out there ironing clothes, because during the summer months the cookstove was set out in this building to keep the house from becoming so hot and uncomfortable.

Johanna went to work with the doughnuts, but she had such a heavy heart. Oh, the sorrows of life! And how much greater they were for Ragnild and Ole and Dordi. She sent a prayer up to heaven for them all.

> **"Kjaere Gud,**
> Dearest Jesus,
> Be their comforter today.
> Amen.

Chapter XX

The October sun was shining brightly in the blue sky, and Johanna decided that she would get out and enjoy it.

"There won't be many more of these days," she told Johnny and daughter Helmina. The memory of last year's long winter was still fresh in her mind.

Ole had left in the morning for a trip to Canton to pay his taxes and do some shopping. Auntie Helmine was staying at Grevlos' now, helping sister Klara with her new baby boy—Paul Andreas.

Johanna and her three children—Johnny, Helmina and baby Martin walked across the field to spend the afternoon visiting at Lisa Larsen's. The Larsen girls, Anna, Lina and Emma, entertained Helmina and let her play with their real dolls with china heads and china hands.

There was a special little doll about six inches long, made entirely of china, with an arm missing that Helmina took a liking to. The china face had such dainty painted features and such a pleasant expression. The girls let her play with it all afternoon.

Adolph and Johnny were outside investigating, and Johanna and Lisa, each with a little one on their lap, visited together and drank coffee.

Later in the afternoon when Johanna announced it was time to go home, Helmina pretended that she didn't hear. She was having so much fun and she didn't want to give up the precious little doll. Soon Johanna called again, and her daughter knew she must go. She quickly stuck the little doll with the pretty china face into her apron pocket.

On the way home Johnny and Helmina ran several yards ahead of their mother, who had baby Martin. He was now nine months old and quite a bundle to carry. Johanna shifted him from one hip to another, and from time to time, stopped and set him down so she could rest.

There was a faint trail between the two farms. This was the path the families traveled when they visited each other. The way by the road was almost twice as far. The grasses were now all brown and as Johanna looked ahead to the Overseth

farmstead, she could see how tall the trees Ole had planted had grown. Most of them now were bare of leaves and ready for winter.

As the two older children walked along, Johnny was telling Helmina about school.

"Adolph said the schoolmaster has a wooden leg," Johnny confided. This fall both of the Overseth children would begin school. Helmina was now five and one-half years old and Johnny seven. Last year there hadn't been many days of school because of the tremendous amount of snow.

"They call him '**Tre-fot** Sven'," Johnny went on. "Adolph thinks he can take his wooden leg off and spank naughty kids with it."

Helmina's eyes widened and she became very quiet.

"Has he really got a wooden leg?" Helmina asked.

Johnny matter-of-factly nodded his head and said, "Ja, that's what Adolph told me."

When they reached home, their father had already returned and he presented them with the things he had purchased—new slates and pencils for school for each of them, and new readers, too.

"Now, my scholars, you can go and learn your ABC's."

Johnny was very excited about his things, but Helmina didn't have much to say.

When it started to get dusk, she made a trip outside and took the little doll out of her pocket and hid it underneath the porch steps and went to bed.

The school year began two weeks later on November 14th. It was to be held in the Ansten Odegaard's home the first week.

"Get up now, Helmina," Johanna called. "Today you begin school."

When she didn't come down, Johanna went up to check on her.

"Are you sick, Helmina?" her mother asked, but by now her daughter was crawling out of bed.

Johnny quickly did his chores, got his book, slate and lunch and was ready to go, but Helmina wasn't in any hurry. Finally Johnny went ahead without her. The path north across the field was a little over a half mile.

"Hurry now!" her mother prodded. "**Skynde deg!**"

Helmina finally left the house with her book, slate and pencil under her arm, and carrying her sandwiches, but her feet were in no hurry.

When she reached the Odegaard home, school had already begun. Helmina peeked in the window to see if she could get a look at the teacher with the wooden leg. She sat down on the step and considered heading home, but she knew how disappointed her mother and father would be. She was afraid of this strange man called "Tre-fot Sven."

Finally, she got up her courage and opened the door. The school-master saw her enter and turned to her. She was ready to burst out crying when he spoke.

"You must be Helmina. Your brother said you'd be coming. Sit down by Emma and Lina Larsen, or over there besides Tina Odegaard."

Helmina took the seat by Tina. She watched the teacher carefully. She could hear the "clump-clump" as he walked back and forth across the pine floor on his peg leg. She listened as the older students recited from their books.

Helmina looked sideways at Lina and Emma, and then she glanced over at Anna Larsen. She wondered if they had discovered she had taken their doll. Oh, she was so unhappy and scared. Everything was wrong.

That afternoon when she got home, and her father and mother wanted her to tell them about her first day of school, she started crying and ran outside. Johanna went after her. She found her sitting on the porch step.

"What is wrong, Helmina? Were the big boys naughty to you today?" her mother asked.

Helmina crawled under the step and brought out the little doll with the pretty china head and the missing arm. She hung her head as she confessed, "I took the Larsen girls' doll home with me when we were over there."

Johanna realized the guilt that her daughter had been carrying.

"Oh, Helmina, that was stealing. You mustn't take things that don't belong to you."

Now her daughter was sobbing again, and Johanna comforted her.

"Well, let's get this straightened out, so you can be happy again."

"Give me a spanking, Mother," Helmina suggested, "and then I'll feel better."

"You know, Helmina, that God saw what you did. He says we should not steal, so let's first get right with Him."

Johanna took her daughter into the kitchen and she had Helmina kneel beside her by the rocking chair while Johanna asked her Heavenly Father to forgive the sin her daughter had committed, and to show them how to make it right.

Helmina thought that she would rather have had a spanking.

After talking it over, they decided that Helmina must take the doll back to the Larsens and ask for forgiveness.

"I think we still have time to go over there and get back again before it gets dark. I'll go with you," Johanna offered, "and Johnny can stay with Martin."

Helmina carried the little doll in one hand, and she held her mother's hand with the other as they hurried across the field.

"Helmina has something to say to your girls," Johanna explained to Lisa when they got there. Helmina went over to Anna and Lina and held out the doll to them.

"I'm sorry that I took it. But it was such a beautiful doll."

Anna and Lina looked at the little doll. "That old thing? You can have it! See, her arm is missing, and we have much nicer ones."

Helmina looked at them both to see if they meant it.

"Yes, you take it," they assured her.

Helmina began to smile and the load of guilt that she had been carrying for over two weeks fell off. And besides that, now the little china doll with the missing arm was her very own.

The second week of school was held in the Overseth home, and the teacher stayed there. By this time Helmina had decided that he perhaps wasn't strange and dangerous, and she soon was enjoying school. Even the "clump-clump-clump-" of his leg as he walked around the room didn't bother her. "This way you always know where he is," she told her mother.

Each week school rotated between different homes. Adequate room was getting to be a problem because this year nearly 30 pupils had enrolled. The school board, and the parent-pressure were pushing plans for building a school house. It was decided to locate it in the very center of the district. An acre had already been purchased from Knud Hanson Rise and his wife, Johanna, and if everything worked out, the pupils would be meeting in a schoolhouse by next fall.

* * * * *

The spring of 1882 arrived. The bright green leaves of the little cottonwood trees were opening. Johnny and sister Helmina had already spent many hours digging around the rows upon rows of trees that stretched north and west of the Overseth home. Keeping them weeded and tilled was their responsibility.

The pasture was green again and the creek that flowed through it was full. Today the milk cows, and even the horses lazily relaxed, for it was Sunday. The geese slowly waddled around on the banks of the creek.

The lilac bush that Ole had planted by the house had budded and a faint sweet fragrance could already be smelled.

Johanna had been up early killing and cleaning chickens and peeling potatoes. Today she was having a family get-together for sister Helmine before she went to St. Peter, Minnesota, to take up her new duties there.

The Eden folks were coming—cousin Peder Dyste and his wife Elena, and brother Pete Overseth. Sister Klara Grevlos and her husband and family, and Ole's brother Johannes Overseth and Inge Marie were invited, too. Several weeks ago, brother Hans Narum had arrived from St. Peter and this would be a chance for him to visit with everyone, too.

The reunion that Johanna had with her youngest brother two weeks ago was something that she would never forget. It brought back so many memories of their life in Norway when he had been a little boy. Now he was 23 years old, big, tall, husky and very muscular.

"And to think we used to call you "little Hans," Johanna said as she laughed about it. Now he was staying with Ole and Johanna and helping Ole with his work.

This 7th day of May, Pastor Olsen conducted church services in Lands Church and all the guests of the Overseths attended. Johanna knelt beside her cousin Peder Dyste at the altar rail as they communed, and her thoughts went back to the day in 1865, when they had both knelt together and confirmed their faith in Jesus Christ before the Kolbu **Kirke** congregation and Pastor Magelsen in Norway.

Johanna remembered what Peder had written in the front of the Bible his parents gave him that day. He was so serious about his commitment then. She could still recall the flyleaf with his handwriting on it:

"Peder Anthon Hansen Dysthe, born 2 Januar 1848, and confirmed by Prost Magelsen at Kolbu Kirke, year of 1865 in West Toten, Norway, Europe. This book is given by my parents in hope that I shall read it and live by it. So I pray to my merciful God that He will help me and give me desire to read it, and live according to its contents. May God by His Grace for Christ's sake. Amen

P. A. Dysthe."

"Ja," Johanna thought, "train up a child in the way he should go and when he is old he will not depart from it."

After church the women helped Johanna in the kitchen and the cousins ran and laughed and played together. Six-year-old Helmina and the Grevlos girls helped take care of baby Paul Andreas and brother Martin.

The voices of the men drifted in from the porch where they visited while they waited for dinner. You could hear Ole, in loud but friendly tones, address the storekeepers.

"And how is business in Eden?"

"You should see us!" Dyste replied. "The way we cash checks and buy produce and lend money at Overseth & Dyste General Store, you'd think we were bankers."

"That's right!" Pete Overseth agreed. "We can't complain about business. Eden is getting to be an up and coming town! It even has its own cornet band. We've been practicing every week for over a year and we are getting to sound pretty good. You must all plan to come to the July Fourth celebration there this year. We have uniforms now and will be marching then."

"Ja," Peder Dyste explained. "Pete is director and public relations man and everything!"

"Oh, that many instruments playing at once—that will be something to listen to," Ole commented.

"Ja, that shall be music!" Dyste remarked.

Then he turned to his cousin Hans and inquired, "How do you like Amerika by now?"

"Well, I've tried lumbering in Minnesota, but I believe farm work is more along my line," he answered. "I think I'm going to like it better here."

Brother Pete Overseth changed the subject. "I hear you folks out here are hauling lumber for a new schoolhouse."

"Ja," Ole replied. "It's about time we got at it. The district bought the land from old man Knud Rise way back in 1879. They paid $10 for it then. We were fortunate Skorheim and Hermanson and Erik Rise got it done when they were on the school board so that we can go ahead with the building now. The number of students has increased every year. They tell me there will be almost 40 students next fall. Of course, many of the older ones don't come very regularly. They are needed at home, you know."

"You mentioned Knud Rise," Peder Dyste interrupted. "That reminds me, how are the newlyweds—his son Hans K., and bride?"

"Oh fine," Ole answered. "When they got married last summer we thought with his wife Mary, a school teacher, living right here in the community that we wouldn't have to worry about hunting for a teacher every year."

"Ja," Johannes added. "They tried to hire her for this fall, but she told the school board they would have to find someone else because this summer she will have a little one of her own to care for."

"Yes, that is the way it should be," Ole declared. "But after we get a schoolhouse, it will be much easier to find a teacher. Of that I am sure."

By the last of August a nice one-room schoolhouse was standing on the Rise land. It was an oblong building with the entry on the east side. The three windows on the north and three windows on the south, made the schoolroom light. A fence had been put around the parcel of land. Now Ole Overseth, John Skorheim, Hans Rise and several other men were unloading wagons filled with handmade benches and desks. Mary Rise had come to oversee the arrangements.

"You must put the teacher's desk on the west end," she directed, "and the recitation benches should be up at that end also."

The men carried them in and set them in place.

"I think we'll have to make four rows of desks for the pupils—of course they must all be facing the teacher."

She sized up the space and then added, "Why don't we put the double desks in the two center rows and the single ones along the north and south walls?"

The men followed her instructions for they had asked her to advise them.

A stove would be set up in the back where the chimney was. On the east wall, on either side of the door, were places for the pupils to hang their wraps.

After the men had unloaded all of the school furnishings they looked around the new schoolhouse.

"Vel, it's all ready to go," Nils Larsen remarked as he stood with his hands on his hips and surveyed their work.

"Ja, we're glad that you changed your mind and decided to take the school," Ole said to Mary Rise.

"Our baby will be five months old by the middle of November when school starts," she explained, "and Hans' mother says she will care for baby Knud. We do live so close by that it's just a hop and a jump from the schoolhouse. I enjoy teaching and it will be a treat to do it in this brand new building."

She turned to her husband and said, "We'd better be getting back to our baby now."

After Hans and Mary left, John Skorheim confronted the rest of the men.

"Yesterday at church I was talking to some of the other parents of the district, and they think we should have parochial school for a couple of months now before regular school begins."

"I agree," Ole said.

"What about a teacher?" Nils Larsen asked.

"Well," John explained, "there is a newcomer in the community. He is a Bible reader from Norway. He only speaks Norwegian but that will be all right for Bible School. Of course, for regular school we must only use English."

"That sounds fine to me," Ole agreed.

"If it is all right with everyone," John Skorheim concluded, "I will get in touch with him and he can stay at our place the first week. I suppose he can take turns boarding at the different homes the way we have done before, only now they can hold classes in the new schoolhouse."

"Ja, go ahead," Nils suggested.

September 18th Bible School commenced and all the pupils that weren't needed at home gathered in the new schoolhouse. The school teacher began with the lessons from the Bible and the catechism. After only two days of school, the teacher showed up early one morning at Overseths with his books and his suitcase. Ole was out in the yards feeding his livestock. The teacher, with a very serious expression on his face, approached him.

"Mr. Overseth, I think we must close school."

"What do you say?" Ole exclaimed, thinking he must have misunderstood.

The schoolteacher went on, "The little Skorheim children are very sick. It looks like diphtheria to me. If it is, I have been exposed staying with them. I won't have it on my conscience giving that sickness to anyone if I can help it."

Ole looked at him in surprise. "Do you think so?" Then he shook his head and added, "Diphtheria is bad—yes, very bad."

"Tell me, what should we do?" the teacher questioned.

"If this is true, I agree with you that we must close school. I am sure the other parents will feel the same way. I can go over to the schoolhouse this morning and dismiss the pupils."

Ole's attention turned to this young man with the kind eyes and the worried expression on his face and he noticed the suitcase that he was holding in his hand. He asked him, "What will **you** do then?"

"Well, I don't really know. I suppose no one will want me around if I have been exposed. Maybe I can stay in someone's barn until I see if I come down with it."

"But it is late September already, and too chilly for that," Ole exclaimed.

"You sit here," Ole told him, "and I must go in and talk with my wife."

When Ole explained the predicament to Johanna, she became very solemn.

"Oh, **nei-da**!" she exclaimed. "That is a bad sickness!"

"Well," Ole asked, "what shall I tell this poor teacher? It is sad to think of turning him out in the cold after he has been hired to teach our children."

"Yes, it is too chilly to live in a corncrib or barn now," Johanna agreed. "It was to be our turn to keep him next, but, Ole, I don't want our children to get sick."

"Neither do I. This is a serious thing."

Ole put his hand to his brow and closed his eyes in deliberation. Suddenly he opened them and spoke to Johanna.

"I have an idea. Do you think it would be safe if he stayed upstairs in the bedroom at the end of the house? We could lock the door so the children couldn't get in, and I could put my ladder up to his window and he could get in and out that way."

Johanna looked at Ole in a puzzled way as she tried to follow his thinking.

He continued, "We could leave his meals at the bottom of the ladder. In that way there would be no contact with him and no danger to our children or to us."

Johanna asked, "What if he gets diphtheria? What then?"

Ole just shook his head. "We'd have to figure that out when and if the time comes."

"Why don't you tell the schoolmaster your plan and see if it is satisfactory with him?" Johanna suggested. "I hate to turn this poor man out in the raw fall weather when he came here to teach our children."

"Ja, and to teach them about God, too!" Ole emphasized.

Ole left and soon Johanna saw him returning with the schoolmaster and the ladder. Johanna went upstairs and opened the bedroom window for him. When she came out, she locked the door and carried the key down in her apron pocket. She started making plans. She would have to get out the old tin plate and cup, and they would have to leave these outside. Oh, they would have to be very careful! She fingered the key in her pocket. "Yes, they would have to be very careful!"

The following day a neighbor stopped out in the field where Ole was working and confirmed the schoolteacher's diagnosis. The doctor from Eden had been out to the Skorheim's and Johan Richard who was two and one-half years old and Andrew Theodor who was seven months were very sick.

A week later word was received that the little Skorheim boys had both died on September 26th.

"Oh, **nei-da**!" Johanna sighed, "and we were sponsors for little Andrew Theodor, too. Poor Else Margrethe! She has had more than her share of sorrow! Why, this is the second Johan Richard that she has lost. How can she take it?"

"And **stakkars** John! It isn't easy to lose a son," Ole sympathized. Now the possibility of the schoolteacher coming down with diphtheria was even more probable.

Ole hoped that this diphtheria talk had only been a scare, but now the heavy cloud of an epidemic hung over the community. Ole and Johanna gathered with their little family in prayer each evening. Upstairs the schoolteacher spent his time with his books and his Bible.

The memory of little lifeless Petter Anthon kept flashing into Ole and Johanna's minds, sending messages of fear concerning their remaining children's health. They both needed something to hold onto.

Ole found these comforting words in the 91st Psalm:

"He who dwells in the shelter of the Most High, who abides in the shadow of the Almighty, will say to the Lord, "My refuge and my fortress; my God, in whom I trust."

"Listen to this, Johanna!" he said as he read on . . .

"Because you have made the Lord your refuge, the Most High your habitation, no evil shall befall you, no scourge come near your tent. For he will give his angels charge of you to guard you in all your ways."

Ole and Johanna bowed their heads and dared to believe this for themselves and their children.

By the last part of October, the diphtheria epidemic seemed to be over. The Bible teacher had left the Overseth home and gone on to another job. English school was begun November 13th, and life had returned to normal.

On November 19th, people dared to come to church and mingle again. John and Else Margrethe Skorheim went that day to the Lord's Table to be strengthened by their Lord in their time of sorrow. Private services had been held for their two children on October 5th.

As they knelt at the altar rail they were a witness to their fellow members because they had come through hard times just like Job of old. After laying five of their children in the churchyard these past years, they seemed by this act to say, "Still will I trust Him!"

* * * * *

Ole examined the calendar on the kitchen wall. Only one week until Thanksgiving! He had risen while it was still dark, started the fire in the kitchen range, and now waited for the coffee to boil. He liked an early morning cup of coffee before going out to do the chores.

Soon Johanna appeared and began the breakfast preparations. The men were picking corn. Her brother, Hans, still in bed, was helping Ole. While the porridge was cooking, she sat and joined Ole in a cup of coffee.

"Well, it seems to be another fine fall day outside," Ole commented. "There is no moisture in the air so the picking should go well today. The husks on the ears of corn are very dry now. Perhaps today you should keep Johnny and Helmina from school so they can gather husks. You never know when the weather will change."

"I'm anxious to try them in our mattresses. Everyone says they are much better than straw," she replied.

Ole took another sip of his coffee. "The cornpicking is going quickly this year. The weather has cooperated, and that younger brother of yours doesn't get tired. We've been putting in some long days. Such strength as that man has! I think your folks should have named him Samson.

"Yesterday when we were unloading our corn, Hans grabbed the forepart of the wagon and raised it into the air. The corn came tumbling out the back, and we didn't have to do any shoveling. It didn't seem to take any effort on his part either."

Ole finished his coffee. "You know, I'm not the only one who has noticed Hans' strength. Every now and then some neighbor comments about some powerful feat he has done."

Soon they heard footsteps upstairs and brother Hans came down. He and Ole went out to feed the animals, milk the cows and harness up the horses. After breakfast, at the first rays of daylight, they would head for the cornfield.

Johanna awakened Johnny and Helmina.

"Get dressed!" she called. "There will be no school for you two today. You must go out in the cornfield and gather husks."

After the family had their hot porridge and bread and butter, Johanna bundled up six and one-half-year old Helmina, and Johnny, who was almost nine. She wound a long, wool scarf around each of them, covering their cheeks and necks because a chilly wind was blowing.

The children went out, each with a sack. All morning they kept at it, filling and emptying, and then warming themselves by the kitchen stove before going out again. By noon Johanna had enough for one bed. That afternoon little two-year-old Martin sat and played in the pile of husks outside the back door while she filled the mattress for the downstairs bedroom.

Everyone was curious to know how the cornhusks worked. That evening Ole, the children, and even Hans, sat on the bed and tested it. The general consensus was that husks were indeed superior to straw for filling mattresses.

* * * * *

December arrived. Ole and Johanna were busy preparing for Christmas. Finally school was dismissed for Christmas vacation, and then it was December 24th. Christmas Eve came on Sunday in the year of 1882, and the Christmas service at Lands was held that day. Ole attended alone because it was very cold.

When he got home, Johanna asked, "Did you see Lisa and Nils and their family there today?"

"No, Ansten Odegaard mentioned something about some of the Larsen children being sick."

"Poor Lisa!" Johanna sympathized. "My, what kind of a Christmas will they have with sick children?"

Johanna packed some of her Christmas baking into a box and that afternoon she sent Ole over to the Larsens with it. The doctor from Eden was just leaving as Ole drove up, and Ole heard the bad news—the Larsen children had diphtheria.

Now it was too close to home. Many times a day Johanna looked out to the northeast where she could see the Larsen buildings and her heart and thoughts were with her dear friends Nils and Lisa and their family. But what could she do to help? She didn't dare to go over there. She had her own children to protect.

Several days later Ole walked over and caught Nils outside doing chores. "Adolph is very sick," Nils said. "He is much worse today."

Ole brought the sad news back to Johanna. Eight-year-old Adolph. He looked at his Johnny, only a month younger than Adolph. The boys had grown up together, two peas in a pod, but Adolph had always been just a little taller. He could easily imagine what Nils was going through. And Lisa, too.

"Oh, this is dreadful!" Johanna moaned.

Several days later Ole again went to check on their sick neighbors, and he carried along several loaves of bread which Johanna had baked. When Nils saw him coming, he turned his face away and motioned for him to go. He didn't want to talk.

Ole could tell by these actions that something was terribly wrong. Finally Nils spoke, "Adolph died last night. My oldest son, my Adolph."

"Oh, I am so sorry, Nils," was Ole's response. What more could he say?

"Can I do something to help?" Ole offered. "Do you have lumber for a coffin?"

"I have enough," he answered gruffly.

After a few moments of silence, Nils added, "Perhaps you can help with digging the grave. It is so hard to dig when the ground is frozen, you know."

"Yes," Ole replied, "I know." And he remembered the cold January day that he had chiseled away at little Petter Anthon's grave.

He turned to Nils and offered, "I'll get my brother Johannes to help me. We will do it for you."

"We decided to bury him in the Gran cemetery just a half mile northeast of here," Nils informed him.

"We'll take care of it," Ole assured him.

One week later, on January 5th, when Ole again stopped at the Larsen's, he learned that Anna, too, had died.

"Oh, my poor friends," Ole thought. "How terrible it is for you."

When Ole got home, he informed Johanna and their thoughts were of twelve-year-old Anna. Pretty, happy Anna. She was almost like one of their own family. They had lived here going on ten years now, and during those years they had watched her grow up.

The children, Johnny and Helmina, also grieved for their friends.

"Oh, death, what a sting you have!" Ole thought.

Within the next month seven more children in the community succumbed to diphtheria.

But finally spring came and things got better. With the spring and sunshine came new hopes and new beginnings, and at Overseths on May 3rd, 1883, a new baby daughter was born.

On May 20th, Ole and Johanna christened her and gave her the beautiful name of Anna. Her godparents were Auntie Klara, Uncle Pete Overseth, Uncle Hans and neighbor Mikkel Gilbertson.

Now Ole and Johanna's family consisted of two boys and two girls.

Chapter XXI

Y ou must stand still now, Helmina," Johanna insisted, as Sigri, the seamstress, fitted her daughter for a new dress. It was a light-blue wool, made from
a piece of cloth that Johanna had picked out at Overseth and Dyste's General
Store.

Sigri Carlson had been staying at the Overseth's for one week now and she had
been very busy. Suits had been sewn for ten-year-old Johnny, and four-year-old
Martin, and dresses for Helmina, who was eight now, and one-year-old Anna.

"Next, I will have to get busy on a dress for you," Sigri told Johanna.

Johanna didn't answer immediately, but when she finally spoke, she suggested,
"Let's see if we can't remodel one of my old black taffetas, because," she confided,
"in a few more months I'm afraid that it won't fit me anymore anyway."

"Oh," Sigri replied, with a slight nod as she comprehended the full meaning of
Johanna's statement. She helped little Helmina take off her dress and then sat
down on the rocker in the corner of the room. Soon her nimble fingers were
hemming the blue dress.

By her side was the little collapsible table she could fold up and carry to her jobs.
On it stood her sewing machine that she would turn by hand.

Johanna seated herself on the other rocker and picked up her knitting. She was
working on mittens. It was now September 1884, and before long the snow would
be flying and every member of the family would need something to keep their
hands warm. As she got into the rhythm of the knit-purl, she struck up a conversation with Sigri.

"I am very pleased with Helmina's dress. It is beautiful the way you put the
smocking on the skirt and the wide ruffle below that."

"I like to sew for little girls," was Sigri's response. "I made this same style for a
little girl in Chicago this spring. They, too, liked it very much."

"You aren't getting to do much visiting with your sister when you put in such
long days with the needle and thread," Johanna commented.

"Perhaps you want to quit early this afternoon and spend the evening across the road with Lovisa and August."

"No. No. No. It is good for the newlyweds to be alone for awhile."

Johanna looked up from her knitting. "Our neighbor August Johnson really surprised us last December when he got married. It's been almost twelve years since we moved here and we have always called August and his brother "the Johnson batchelors." But your sister certainly changed that. Already she has made his batchelor house cozy, and she fits in so well at the South Bethlehem Church where he belongs."

"Ja, Lovisa seems to fit in well on August's farm, too. We Carlson women are well-built and strong! August is finding that out. Have you heard about the time the horses ran away?"

Sigri looked over her wire rimmed glasses to get Johanna's response. When Johanna shook her head, she continued. "The horses had been frightened and dashed ahead out of control. August tugged at the reins but to no avail. When Lovisa saw what was happening, she grabbed the reins from August, braced her feet, and with all her might pulled them tighter and tigher until the horses finally came to a stop. Hmmmm! I'm surprised you haven't heard it because August loves to tell everyone—especially Norwegians, because he points out that his wife is so capable because she is Swedish!"

"Yes, August always has liked to stress his heritage, but he has been well out-numbered in this community of Norwegians."

Then as an afterthought, Johanna added, "Although there are a number of Swedish families in the South Bethlehem Church."

Sigri talked as she continued with her sewing. "Now if you had one of those new machines that you speak into, then I could just ring up my sister and visit over the wire, and in a few minutes I could be right back at my sewing."

Johanna sat and shook her head, "I can't imagine anything like that."

Sigri interrupted, "Yes, it really works. I saw one in Chicago."

"What will they think of next?" was all that Johanna could say.

For awhile both women were occupied with their own tasks, and then Sigri spoke.

"I wonder what Lovisa has been busy with today. I hope August doesn't expect her to work like some of the women around here. At a place I stayed and did sewing last month there was an unmarried sister who lived in the home and I think she worked harder than the men. She did chores all day long. Over her shoulders she wore a wooden yoke."

Sigri again peered over her glasses to get Johanna's reaction. She looked Johanna straight in the eye as she repeated, "A wooden yoke, mind you—something like the oxen wear. She would wear this wooden yoke and hook a pail on each end and carry water to the cattle—and to the pigs—and into the house. And she carried the milk, too, and slopped the pigs. Come to think of it—she worked like a horse, all harnessed up like that!"

"She probably was accustomed to it from Norway", Johanna commented. "In

Norway the livestock are the women's responsibility. Except for the horses!"

Sigri, still thinking about the wooden yoke, shook her head and remarked, "Well, I wouldn't have believed it if I hadn't seen it with my own eyes!"

They both continued with their handwork in silence. Then Johanna asked, "When are you going back to Chicago?"

"I haven't made definite plans, but I'll stay around here until after Christmas. I have two other places to do sewing after I finish here. Inge Marie, your sister-in-law, has asked me to come over there for awhile. She wants some things made for their little baby girl, and she also wants a new dress for herself."

"Ja, their little Mina is already six months old! How time flies! Oh, Sigri, we are fortunate that you came out to visit your sister so we could all get our dressmaking done. Ole says when we have our new clothes ready he will take us into Canton and get a family picture taken."

"That's a very good idea. I'm sure the relatives back in Norway will be anxious to see pictures of your children and you."

"We'll have to get it done next month because school will be starting after that," Johanna explained.

Little grunts and noises were coming from the cradle in the corner and Johanna laid her knitting aside and got up to care for her sixteen-month-old daughter Anna, who was awakening.

Outside, Ole was up on a ladder painting. This summer an addition had been added onto the house on the south side. It was a big fine addition and on ground level it contained a sitting room and a bedroom, and upstairs above these rooms were three more bedrooms. A wide porch had been built all across the south side of the house, and was decorated with carved scrolls and supported by tall white columns.

Ole and Johanna's brothers, Hans and Christian Narum, were doing the finishing and painting. Christian had come to Dakota almost a year ago. He had been helping at Johannes Overseth's part of the time, and he was so much a part of that family that in March, when their baby Mina was baptized, he had been one of her sponsors.

Now the men were trying to finish the house because soon they would have to start cornpicking. And it would keep them busy for awhile because this year Ole had put many acres into corn.

* * * * *

Sunday morning could be the busiest time of the week, Johanna decided. This Sunday, June 6, 1886, there were to be services at Lands **Kirke.** Now that Pastor Olsen was having services twice a month in each church, this hurrying and rushing as she got her family fed and dressed, was getting to be almost a weekly occurence.

Husband Ole, 12-year-old Johnny, and her brothers Hans and Christian Narum came in from doing the chores and now were washing up.

Helmina, ten years old, was a lot of help to her mother now. Together they got five-and-a-half-year-old Martin and three-year-old Anna and baby Anthon

dressed.

Already the baby of the family was 16 months old. When this last son had been born on Feb. 6, 1885, Johanna had said, "Let's call him Petter Anthon after our little son who died. He can take his place in our hearts, and then perhaps it won't hurt so much anymore."

Usually he was called by his middle name—Anthon, and often it was just "Tony."

Ole helped his family get aboard the lumber wagon for the trip to church. Brother Christian guessed that he didn't feel like going to church. He settled himself in the rocker in the kitchen with his favorite pipe. Brother Hans harnessed up Lady, the brown mare, and took the two-wheeled cart.

Johanna sat with Ole on the wagon seat of the lumber wagon, and held baby Anthon. Ole had little Anna in his lap. He had placed a plank across the back of the wagon that the rest of the children could sit upon. They soon headed north on the path that led by the grove of young cottonwoods.

It was a pleasure to see how fast the trees were growing. Some of them were ten feet tall already. As they got to the crest of the hill, Ole looked back across his farm.

"See, Johanna, how beautiful everything looks now," he said.

To the south was the green wheat field and across the road, way down on the south eighty, the small corn plants made bright rows across the black field. The pasture along the creek was lush and green. The two other teams of horses and four milk cows, along with a large group of calves, were enjoying themselves this Sabbath morning. Several young colts were frisking about.

"Yes, everything is looking good," Johanna agreed.

Ole drove the team along the path that came out to the new road that had just been graded. In 1884, a surveyor had come to Lincoln County and marked out all the township roads and now farmers could work out their poll tax by digging out ditches and grading these roads.

No longer would you be following trails that criss-crossed the countryside, for all the new roads were straight, and ran north and south or east and west, and were marked out in one mile sections. In the newly excavated ditches along these roads, water often stood all summer, and contributed to the mosquito problem.

The road to church was dry now, but there were hard ruts here and there. Helmina, Johnny and Martin sat in back on the plank and bounced along as the wagon went down the bumpy road. Ole had the horses in a trot and on this nice June morning they all happily moved toward church.

Johanna had on her new hat. Ole helped her purchase it when they were in Canton last week. It was a straw hat with a wide brim. On the brim was veiling, with bunches of flowers tucked in here and there.

Ole stole a sideways glance at her as he commented, "I'm glad you bought that hat, Johanna. Ja, it's nice!" He nodded as he spoke.

Suddenly the tranquility of the day was shattered as Johnny hollered, "Stop, Papa! Stop!"

Ole tightened the reins and turned to see what was wrong. Running behind the wagon was five-year-old Martin. He was crying, "Don't leave me. Wait for me!"

The wagon had hit a rut that jarred Martin right off his seat and down onto the ground.

Ole jumped down and lifted little Martin into his arms.

"Are you all right, my boy?"

Martin wiped his eyes and tried to stop sobbing. "I thought you were going to leave me."

After Ole and Johanna were assured Martin hadn't been injured, they all continued on to church.

The 6th day of June, 1886, was a big day in Lands **Kirke.** The church was full. This was the day the newly organized choir sang, six little babies were christened, and communion was offered.

Afterwards, neighbors and friends lingered outside visiting and enjoying the lovely June weather.

All of the ladies had on their new summer hats. Some had wide and deep crowns that covered their coil of braids, while others wore very wide brims and shallow crowns that perched atop their buns of hair. A variety of veiling and flowers decorated them and they were quite a contrast to the men's black hats with the wide, pulled down brims. Johanna visited with Lisa and Klara and other neighbor ladies.

Ole approached Knute Nupen, the Rise schoolteacher, who was also the new choir director.

"Thank you for the fine music, Knute," he said. "It was a lucky day for us when you began teaching in our community. Now we can make use of all of your talents."

"You are welcome," was his reply. "We try to do our best. But it is the young people who are so willing to sing that they will walk to church every Sunday afternoon to practice that should have the thanks."

"Oh, we appreciate it. Music in church is wonderful. It makes me think of the choirs of angels that we read about in the Bible. Now maybe someday we can get an organ so we can sing the hymns with an accompaniment."

"Yes, that would be nice," Knute agreed.

On the way home, Ole held his horses tightly reined so they would have to keep at a walk. He hummed as they rode along. Some of the hymn melodies they had sung that morning were still with him.

They passed the driveway that went into brother Johannes Overseth's farm, and Johanna spoke,

"It seems so strange to realize that Inge Marie and Johannes and little Mina don't live here anymore."

"I suppose today they are on the train heading towards New York. Let's see now, it's next Friday that they sail back to Norway, isn't it?"

"Yes, it's hard to believe that they really are gone."

"Well, when Johannes finally got the land sold, it didn't take them long to pack and go."

"But Johannes is going to have a fine place in Norway, I'll have to say that!" Ole added. "Buruld **gaard** is one of the show places in Toten. Johannes was fortunate to get ahold of it."

"It is so sad that your father won't be there to meet them when they land. If he had only lived another year," Johanna commented.

"Yes, it was a sad day on October 4, 1885, when Pa was laid to rest beside mother in Aas churchyard . . . and only one son there to attend the services. Even my oldest brother was here in America."

Johanna slowly shook her head.

"Oh, your oldest brother! Will he ever be happy again? After losing his wife Marianne back in Norway, all his enthusiasm for living seems to be gone, but I guess brother Pete Overseth will look after him now that he has moved in with him."

A two-wheeled cart passed them and when the dust had settled, Ole remarked. "Johanna, that was Hans! That younger brother of yours doesn't let any grass grow under his feet. Did you see who was in the cart with him?"

Johanna ventured a guess. "I really only got a glance, but it looked like Elisa Odegaard."

"Ja, it was Elisa all right. He's giving her a ride home from church."

Ole scratched his head and commented, "You know, he's been spending a lot of time up at Ansten Odegaard's lately. I just assumed that it was the boys there that he was visiting."

"Well, I suppose it's time he finds himself a special girl," Johanna said. "Elisa is a nice young lady, and a hard worker, too!"

"Yes, that is true," Ole agreed.

"By the way, Johanna, this week I think Hans and I will try to make a trip to Sioux City. He would like to invest in a threshing rig. We need one in the community. We'll go down there and see if we can buy one."

Ole turned the horses into the driveway that came into his place from the north. After a few moments of silence, Ole added, "While I think of it, I want to tell you—don't let your brother Christian find an excuse to go to town while we are gone, I will be depending on him to do the chores, and when he gets to town, you know what happens! He has such a good time that he forgets about the chores!"

"Yes, it is a shame," Johanna admitted.

"Just keep him busy. If he doesn't have anything else to do, you can always have him chop wood."

* * * * *

On their trip to Sioux City, Hans made his big purchase of a threshing machine, and Ole came home with a new sewing machine.

"Now, Johanna, let Helmina learn to use it. She is almost eleven years old and I think she will enjoy being a seamstress."

He was right, for daughter Helmina immediately took to sewing and soon was making clothes for everyone in the family, which was a great help to Johanna.

Each time Ole was in Sioux City he went into the music store and looked at the organs. He was fascinated by them. "Some day we must purchase one for our church," he told Hans. The salesman always assured him that even he himself could learn to play an organ.

After the grain had been harvested and the bundles made into neat pointed stacks, Hans moved from one farmplace to another with his threshing machine. The grain bundles were run through, and he left the farmers with sacks of golden oats, barley and wheat and nice stacks of straw.

That winter Hans got a chance to buy 240 acres of land three miles west of the Lands Church, and when Spring 1887 arrived, Hans and Elisa Odegaard were married. Their wedding day was April 3rd, in the Lands Church, with Ole and Johanna as witnesses, after which the newlyweds moved into their new home.

Ole made a purchase of land that spring also. On March 30th, he bought a half section in Eden Township, several miles west of Eden. Brother Pete Overseth in Eden had told him the Jeraulds were trying to sell it.

"You know, with three sons already, we will be needing more farms," he told Johanna. They paid $3,500 for it.

Two more sons were born to Ole and Johanna. Jim's birth was February 25, 1888, one month after the terrible "school children's" blizzard. The day of the blizzard, January 12, 1888, the Overseth children hadn't attended school so they weren't caught out in the bad weather, but the Overseths had some excitement that day too, because that afternoon, at the height of the storm, a chimney fire started. Ole was out in the barn tending his animals and he could not be reached because of the intensity of the storm.

Finally the fire was put out, but the house became so cold that everyone had to bundle up to keep warm. And Ole and Johanna were always glad it wasn't the day that Jim decided to arrive.

In the community west of them, a young man lost his life that day. He lived near Hans and Elisa's farm. Edwin Kylling had driven a team and wagon a mile southwest of his parent's home to get a load of hay when the storm had struck. Edwin's parents, Lars and Mari Kylling, had hammered on pans and kettles throughout the night, hoping Edwin would hear them and find his way home. He was found frozen to death the next morning in a straw stack eighty rods from home.

On May 8, 1889, the last child was added to the Overseth family when Henry was born. Now Ole and Johanna had five living sons and two daughters. They ranged in ages from Johnny who was fifteen, Helmina, thirteen; Martin, eight; Anna, six; Tony, four; and Jim, fifteen months, to the new baby Henry. These days were busy ones for Johanna and also for daughter Helmina.

The majority of the families in the community were large families, having eight, ten, twelve and even sixteen children, but many had laid some of their little ones to rest in the churchyard. In those early years on the prairie from 75 to 80 percent of all deaths were children. Almost every home had known this heartache.

On November 2, 1889, Dakota Territory was admitted into the Union and the Overseth farm became part of the new state of South Dakota.

This was also the end of an era in the Lands congregation, because in 1889, Pastor Ellef Olsen resigned after 17 years of faithful service to the congregations of Lands, Canton, West Prairie, Eden, Gran, in South Dakota, and Beloit and Inwood, in Iowa. Rev. Tosseland, the new pastor in Canton, served the Lands congregation until a new pastor could be secured.

The statehood of South Dakota had barely been accomplished when in December 1890, the headlines across the state told of the massacre at Wounded Knee Creek camp in the western part of the state, where 200 Indian men, women and children had been killed.

"Short Bull says he will capture Pine Ridge if he loses every warrior," the January 2, 1891, issue of the Canton Sioux Valley News announced. Ole read the entire news article in order to get all of the details. It stated that twenty men had been sent to meet the wagon train coming with supplies for the camp and when they got ten miles out they found the wagons to be besieged by a band of 100 Indians. They rode for help and three hours later, courier troops came to the rescue and escorted the wagon train to camp.

The January 23rd issue of the paper reported the conclusion of this episode. "Troubles with Indians drawing to a close." General Miles had given an order for a big issue of beef for the Indians—enough to feed 5,500 people, figuring 22 to a beef. He had contacted the Indians to let them know the soldiers would not fire upon them when they came.

"Ja," thought Ole, "it has been twenty years since I first came to Dakota Territory, and a lasting alliance with the Indians still hasn't been worked out."

Chapter XXII

The young pastor glanced out at the solemn faces gathered at Lands Church on the cold 11th day of February, 1892. L. J. Hauge was a fine looking **prest** with a full, but neat beard which made him look older than his years.

It had been almost twelve months since he had been installed here. Because he had helped as an assistant to Pastor Ellef Olsen in 1887, it didn't take him long to work into his new responsibilities. But funerals still were hard for him.

In the front row was Dordi Wilson and her children, two girls and two boys, stair-steps in age, ten years and under. Behind Dordi sat another **Enke** Wilson—Britha and her family.

The past two weeks had been hard on Dordi. You could see how drained and weary she was. It began the day her husband Ole Wilson Bru went to Canton and bad weather had come up. She waited all night for him to return. His team finally brought him home, but he had been badly frozen and lay in the stable the rest of the night because it was blizzarding. This exposure to the cold had brought on pneumonia and now his life was finished.

Pastor Hauge opened his Bible to the Gospel of John and read just one verse for his funeral text—John 8:11. "The Master is here and calleth for Thee."

He paused a moment and then announced, "Jesus is in our midst today . . . and He cares."

"It is so sad," Johanna thought, and brushed a tear as she watched the bereaving family. Poor Dordi!

The Pastor led the funeral procession outside to the graveyard, the widow following the wooden coffin, her arms reaching around her little brood.

Behind Dordi and the children, walked Britha Wilson and her seven children. It wasn't five years ago that Ole's brother Bertil Wilson had been killed in a runaway accident on his way home from a business trip to Canton. That was July of 1886. Now there were two **Enke** Wilsons and many, many fatherless children. Yes, life can be so grievous for some, Johanna thought, as they went out and laid Ole Wilson Bru to rest beside his children's graves.

Oh, Jesus must be weeping again as he sees and feels Dordi's sorrows, Johanna felt. "**Stakkars,** Dordi!"

Both Johanna and Ole were heavy-hearted as they climbed into the sleigh for the ride home. They pulled the horsehide robe up over their laps. Franz gave a whinny as if complaining about the cold, and overly-anxious to get home to the barn. Two streams of white breath trailed from the nostrils of Ponyset and Franz as the horses headed east.

Both Ole and Johanna were silent for a time, and then Ole began reminiscing.

"Ja, Ole Wilson came about the same time that I came to Dakota. I guess I really got to know him the best when we attended the church services in the homes in the early days."

"Yes," Johanna recalled. "Ole and Dordi and their children were almost always at those services."

"And Ole Wilson was only 45! It is hard to believe; he seemed older."

"The same age as I am," Johanna pointed out. Then she shivered, as much from the sad emotional strain of the afternoon as from the cold.

The horses plowed through a stretch of deep snow, and then they turned south towards home.

"Jens Bjorlie, the Norwegian Bible School Teacher, and choir director, got ahold of me for a minute," Ole reported.

"You know what a fine musician he is—plays the violin and everything. Well, he's trying hard to get an organ for the church. He says a salesman wants to bring one out but the organ fund isn't big enough to pay for it yet. It will cost more than $300. I told him he should bring the matter up at the congregational meeting set for March 8th. They have to make some decisions then about building a new parsonage now that Pastor Hauge is getting married this summer."

Johanna pulled her shawl up around her cheeks. "Oh, it is so chilly! I'll have to fix something good and hot for supper so we can get warmed up. Helmina is churning butter this afternoon. Maybe we can have buttermilk soup. How does that sound? We haven't had that for a long time."

"Good hot buttermilk soup should be just the thing on a cold evening," Ole agreed.

After Johanna got home, she busied herself in the kitchen and soon the supper was ready. Tender kernels of rice floated about in the hot buttermilk broth. She called the family, and after Ole had asked the blessing, Helmina brought in the bowls of hot soup.

Now it happened that buttermilk soup was not one of the Overseth boys' favorite foods. Little four-year-old Jim looked at his, made a face and asked, "What is this?"

Seven-year-old Tony studied his and remarked, "It looks like swill."

This hit the funnybone of all of the younger Overseths and they all began giggling. Even Anna covered her mouth and daintily tittered. Three-year-old Henry decided to join in on the merriment and noisily added several guffaws.

Soon Father Ole's voice boomed out. "That will be enough of that! You will eat what your mother has prepared or you will go to your rooms."

The atmosphere quickly changed. Each boy lowered his head and began eating. With many bites of homemade bread mixed in with the buttermilk soup, they finally got it down, and the meal was finished in silence.

But before everyone left the table, Father Ole quoted a verse from a song that he liked to sing:

> Some have bread and cannot eat.
> Others can eat, but have not bread.
> We have bread and we can eat,
> Therefore we will praise our God.

* * * * *

There was much excitement at the Eden depot on Wednesday, February 24, 1892. For two days, eight Lincoln County farmers had been driving fat cattle into Eden and loading them on freight cars at the depot.

A special Lincoln County cattle train, consisting of 13 cars, was going to Chicago. O. Helvig, Ole Overseth and Erik Jacobson, from Norway township, each had two carloads. The other owners were from other parts of Lincoln County.

A banner had been attached to the side of the center car announcing, "Train of Fat Cattle from Lincoln County, South Dakota."

Just before it was time to board, Ole stood back and looked at the special train, with its banner. His mind went back to the day twenty years before when Johanna and he had arrived in Dakota Territory with one cow and six chickens. Today he was hauling out over forty fat steers. Ja, it was a far cry from that day!

This trip had taken much preparation. Besides getting the cattle into Eden, hay and feed had been hauled in and loaded because the livestock would have to be fed on the slow trip to Chicago. The eight owners went along to care for their property.

Food also had to be prepared for the men. The wives had been busy packing lunch baskets that would last until the men reached Chicago. Johanna had stuck in a chunk of **spekekjøt** and several loaves of homemade bread, and a slab of **ost.** She picked out some of the nicest apples from the barrel in the cellar. Last year the first two apple trees that Ole had planted back in the 80's had borne a fine crop. She washed and polished them and placed them into the basket. She hard-boiled some eggs and tucked in some doughnuts and cold waffles, and a good supply of sugar lumps. Coffee could be purchased on the train.

Johnny and Nordlie, the hired man, were at the depot to see the train off. Ole Nordlie had been working at the Overseth farm for three years. Many different newcomers had worked for Overseths when they first arrived in the United States.

Ole Nordlie had come from Hurdal, Norway, in 1888, at the age of 23. He had gone to the Lars Sogn home in Dakota Territory because Mari Sogn was a relative through marriage. His first job was with Stener Paulson the summer he arrived, and then Ole Overseth had hired him. Now he had become Ole's right-hand man.

Also on this Wednesday, in February, 1892, sixteen or seventeen miles northwest of Eden in the town of Canton, Nils Larsen was leading a procession of teams and they were heading out to his farm. The wagons were loaded with lumber for his new buildings which would be constructed during the summer.

An era of building had begun in Norway Township. In 1891, Hans Rise had erected a fine big barn, costing between $1,200 and $1,300. Also, last year Hans Narum and Lars Kylling, neighbors living several miles west of Lands Church, each built new homes on their farms.

* * * * *

The congregational meeting was held on March 8th, 1892, as planned, and the matter of the organ was again brought up. "A salesman wants to bring a pump organ out so we can try it and see how we like it," Jens Bjorlie announced.

A man in the back row stood up and said, "We older folks are used to singing without an accompaniment, so it doesn't matter so much to us. I think we really should leave this organ business up to the young people. I make a motion that we keep it one month and if the young people want it, they can get out and raise the balance needed."

Someone else spoke up. "If they bring an organ out here, we will need a platform to put it on."

Another person questioned, "Who will be organist?"

Finally all the details were ironed out. A platform would be built, Anna Johnson (Rodway) would be organist and be paid $25 a year, and if the young people wanted to keep the organ, they would raise the balance of the money.

The building committee was chosen to start work on the parsonage. It would be erected across the road north from the church and cemetery. Work should begin as soon as possible.

Next, plans for the layman's meeting were discussed, but a date could not be agreed upon.

"Constable" Nelson, clad in his big old fur floor-length coat, stood up and made a motion, "I move that we wait until summer when it is warmer."

Faint smiles came across many faces, and even a snicker could be heard in the back row, for "Constable" Nelson was known to wear his big coat to church until summer, and anytime before that was considered cold to him.

The young people were enthusiastic about the organ and pitched in to raise the money that was needed. Sixteen-year-old Helmina Overseth and her friend Matthea Raasum rode around the neighborhood in a two-wheeled cart soliciting money for it.

* * * * *

The September sun was shining on the countryside, making the fields of golden stubble and the pointed stacks of grain all shimmery. Johanna was busy in the kitchen. With growing boys and hired men, she seemed to be cooking and baking all the time.

Ja, vel, with such good appetites at least she knew they were not sick, Johanna decided. That was one thing to be thankful for.

Tomorrow brother Hans would be coming with his threshing machine and it would take a big crew to get that job done. And a lot of food!

She could hear Ole singing as he puttered around outside with his flowers and hoed around the new trees in his orchard. Every spare minute he had, he was tending his orchard and strawberries and gooseberries and other plants. There were row upon row of fruit trees now on the south and east sides of the house, about two dozen.

If Ole was not in the orchard, he was working with his flowers, and watering and weeding, or swinging his scythe around the yard, making everything neat and trim. He always had a little flower bed by the back door.

The melody of "Haul the Water, Haul the Wood" came drifting in through the kitchen window. "How happy and content he is when working with his plants," Johanna thought. She hadn't heard that old song for a long time and it brought back memories of old days.

Daughter Helmina was in the other room, working at the sewing machine. Johanna had bought a bolt of black and white figured wool and Helmina was sewing dresses for both herself and her mother from it. She hoped to have them ready for next week when they would be having the Layman's meetings.

Ole had invited Bragstad, the visiting Layman in charge, to stay at their house. Johanna had been looking forward to these meetings all summer. They would take their lunches along and spend the whole day at church, singing, sharing and studying God's Word. Ja, it was good to set aside several days to study and pray together. The soul needed food and refreshing too.

Henry and Jim were playing outside on the wide front porch and Anna was out there looking after them. Johnny and Nordlie were working down on the Jerauld farm. Martin and Tony had gone to pick up the mail.

The post office had been located in the Paul H. Hanson Grastadmoe's home for several years and had become known as the Moe Post Office after Paul Hanson's name—Graestad**moe.** Now his son Hans P. had taken over as postmaster.

"Ole," Johanna called from the kitchen door, "Coffee is ready!" Soon he was inside sitting at the table.

"I am trying to get ready for the threshers," Johanna explained, as she wiped her floury hands on her apron. Loaves of bread were rising in the pans and a big kettle of meat was boiling on the stove. She was going to serve boiled pork with her special sweet-sour gravy.

"Ja," she sighed, as she sat down across from him. "It isn't so bad to cook the food, but where is everyone going to sit? We'll have to eat in shifts again."

Ole swallowed the coffee he was sipping, and then slowly poured his saucer full again. "I was in the lumber yard when I was in Eden the other day . . . ," he began.

Johanna interrupted him. "You must call it 'Hudson' now. Remember?"

"Oh, well, I don't know why it was so important to change the town's name. Just because someone else called a little town up north Egan, I really don't think there would be that much of a mix-up."

"Well," he continued, getting back to his first thoughts, "I went into the lumberyard to get an estimate on adding a dining room onto the house. We would be wanting a second floor over it too, wouldn't we?"

"Yes, we need more bedrooms. Why Henry is still sleeping in the crib in our room, and he's two and a half years already. Yes, we really need more bedrooms."

"Well, I figured on tearing down this room that we use for a kitchen and adding a new dining room here. Another kitchen could be built on the north side of that again."

"And an entry," Johanna added. "That would be a blessing. We need a place to hang the coats and put the boots and dirty shoes."

"I will talk to a carpenter right away and see if we can get it done next spring." Ole put a sugar lump into his mouth and took another swallow of coffee.

"It was strange to go into the Dyste and Overseth Store the other day. I always expect to see Dyste there. I guess brother Pete will be changing the name of the store now that Peder and Elena Dyste have gone back to Norway."

"I suppose they are already in Christiania. It must be almost two months since they left. Elena told me that America never seemed like home to her. I can't understand that after living here for fourteen years."

Ole studied Johanna carefully as he asked, "What about you, Johanna? Don't you sometimes wish you could go back?"

She slowly answered, "Well, I would like to go back at some time and see Papa and brother David and his family and sister Helene Marie and her family, but I would be a stranger in Norway now. This is home."

Ole smiled as he agreed, "**Ja, det er sikkert, det!**"

The fall of 1892, was a great time in Lands Church. Jens Bjorlie, the newcomer who came from Norway in 1890, had started a Sunday School at Lands that year and in October, a big Sunday School Festival was held with badges for the participants to wear.

He also arranged a big Choral Festival. Jens Bjorlie was director of the choir, and soon was directing choirs in two of the neighboring churches also. Sometimes he accompanied the choirs with his violin. At Lands the fine new organ was in use.

Chapter XXIII

Ole slapped Ponyset's flanks with the ends of the leather reins to get her to hurry as she drew the buggy up the driveway to home. They splashed through several puddles, and the mud and water sprayed in all directions.

Ole was glad to see rain had fallen while he was gone. The crops had been marvelous the last few years. He was just returning from a trip to Sioux City. It was the last of September, 1893. He looked with pride at his cornfields, and at the new addition to the house, which had just been painted a sparkling white.

Ponyset pulled into the farmyard and Ole tied the reins to the hitching post by the shanty and hurried into the house. The family had finished supper and gathered around him when he entered.

"How did it go?" Johnny was quick to ask.

"The hogs sold better than I expected," Ole replied.

"What about it? Did you get any feeder cattle?" Johanna questioned.

"No, I didn't, but Erik picked up a few."

Ole Overseth and Erik Rise had shipped hogs to Sioux City by train, leaving from Hudson, and they had also been looking for feeder cattle at the stockyards. Ole had left his horse and buggy at the livery in Hudson.

"You'll never guess what Erik told me. He is talking about moving out west of the river by Presho," Ole reported.

"It seems like that Erik is always buying or selling or trading land," Johnny said.

"He is planning on raising horses," Ole explained.

"Horses?" Johanna exclaimed.

"Ja, I told him he should raise cattle and then we could buy our feeders from him."

But Ole wasn't through with his news.

"And now you must hear this!" he exclaimed, for he could keep it no longer.

"I have a big surprise."

Everyone turned to him with a look of anticipation.

"What do you think?" He paused a moment and then he announced.

"I bought an organ for us in Sioux City."

"Oh, Papa!" Anna gave a cry of delight.

"Wonderful!" Johanna agreed.

Then with childish forthrightness, Tony asked, "But who in this house knows how to play an organ?"

All the faces around him had questioning expressions.

"Oh, Tony-boy," Ole spoke to his eight-year-old son. "We shall all learn to play it. The salesman gave me a book with a chart of the notes and full instructions. Helmina will learn, and Anna, and your mother . . . . . and I am going to learn, too."

"You, Papa?" Anna questioned.

The whole family enjoyed music, and each evening when they had family devotions they always sang a hymn or two.

"Have you had supper?" Johanna inquired.

"**Nei,** I hurried home as soon as I got off the train in Hudson."

"Well, sit down and we'll find you something," his wife instructed.

Ole turned to the hired man, "Nordlie, would you go out and put Ponyset in the barn?"

Helmina poured up coffee for her father, and Johanna set the bread and butter and cheese on the table.

Ole turned to Martin, "Perhaps you can help take the packages out of the buggy."

Turning to his family, he said, "You should see what else I bought. I tell you it shall be beautiful around here! I stopped at the nursery and picked up some peonies and a rose bush and more strawberry plants, and some grape vines."

"You can leave them in the shanty tonight," he instructed Martin. "I'll have to get them planted tomorrow. I am going to make an arbor."

"What?" Tony asked.

"An arbor?" Anna questioned. "What is that?"

"You will see. We shall make a fine outside house, where we can sit in the evenings and get the breezes, with vines for walls. When the grapes are in season, we can just sit there and help ourselves."

Ole looked around at his family, and then asked, "Well, how have things been here at home while I was gone?"

"You should have seen what happened at Parochial School yesterday," Anna volunteered.

"Schoolmaster Bjorlie got after some of the big boys. He told them to spit out what they had in their mouths, and when he held out his hand, they spit tobacco into it. Oh, did Bjorlie get angry then! Those boys have been sitting in the corner ever since."

"I had better not be hearing anything like that about you children," Ole sternly advised.

Tony had some news to report. "Do you know what some of the big boys said? They saw Bjorlie and Osmund Steensland riding their bicycles near Sogn's last Sunday."

"Well, what is wrong with that?" Ole asked.

"They think they were going to see the Sogn girls."

"Well, there is nothing wrong with that either," Ole explained. "You children at school certainly keep good track of your teacher. Tell me this. How about it, are you learning your lessons?"

They looked at each other, and none of them seemed anxious to talk about that.

Finally Johanna changed the subject. "I stopped over to see Lovisa Johnson's new house yesterday. It is going to be a lovely place when they get it finished and painted. I am so happy for Lovisa and August."

Johnny spoke up. "And they are almost finished with the Trinity Church. Nordlie and I walked over there last night and looked around. We came back by Nils Larsen's and checked on the progress of the addition to his barn."

"When will the organ come?" Helmina asked.

"They said it would be here in about a week," Ole answered.

"Then we can have singing when we have the Ladies Aid auction here this fall," Johanna said, delighted at the thought.

She explained, "I offered our home this year. Since we have the big dining room and kitchen we will have plenty of room. It will be held in December."

"I'm glad you did," Ole concurred. "Why have a nice home if we don't share it? That's how we will get our enjoyment from it."

Fall passed quickly, and in December Johanna wrote a Christmas letter to her father in Norway.

Dec. 15, 1893

Kjaere Papa,

Glade Jul! I suppose it will be past Christmas when you get my letter. I will be thinking of you during the holidays as memories of Christmases in Norway are always strong then.

How are you feeling, Papa? We are all fine here in South Dakota.

I now have a big dining room, three more bedrooms upstairs and a large kitchen and entry. I am so happy with the addition that we built on to our house this summer. I even have a hand pump in the kitchen so I don't have to go outside to carry in water anymore. We now have room for a big table so everyone can sit and eat at one time. We always have one or two hired men besides our own large family and very often a newcomer or two that Ole has invited to stay until they find a job.

Johanna stopped writing. "How very true that was," Johanna thought. She recalled the recent incident they had just heard about. A newcomer directly from

Norway had come to the community and knocked on the door of a neighbor's house. The newcomer was a young man whom their neighbor did not recognize, and he quickly tried to get rid of him.

"I'll tell you what you can do," **Stor Johan** said to him. "You can go over to the Overseths. They take everybody in."

The stranger knew this was his older brother who had left their home in Norway many years before and he finally told him, "But I'm your little brother!" Of course, then he was invited in.

"Ja," Johanna reflected, "Ole has never forgotten what it felt like to be a newcomer. He has a soft spot in his heart for them, and everybody knows it."

She picked up her pen again and got back to her letter.

December has been a busy month. On December 5th we had a **kvindeforening** auction at our home. The sale was a big success. The Ladies Aid is raising money for missions. Daughter Helmina had sewed several aprons and I had knit stockings and mittens and we tied a wool quilt. My neighbor and friend Lisa Larsen brought her famous date cake, which all the men like and the bids really came fast then. Pastor Hauge opened up the evening with prayer and we sang some Norwegian hymns. Ole bought us a pump organ this fall and a neighbor girl, Minnie Sogn, played for the singing. Helmina and Martin and Ole are practicing on the organ and I think they all will master it soon. Martin already can play some melodies.

I have finished my Christmas baking, except for the lefse. Helmina and I made **fattigmand** and **berliner krans** last week, also **flatbrød.** With many little boys around, I had to hide it, or we wouldn't have any left for Christmas. I put it upstairs in my old immigrant trunk. I didn't think the boys knew anything about the cookies because we did the baking while they were in school and Henry was out with the men. But I do believe, Papa, that little boys have a special nose that can smell out sweets.

It was little Henry that gave away their snooping. He came into the kitchen with sugar from the **fattigmand** on his hands and around his mouth. I asked him what he had been eating, and your little four-year-old grandson said, "Oh, Mama, you should see what we found upstairs. A whole trunk full of cookies!" You can be sure that I hurried upstairs to see that they had not broken the cookies. Boys will be boys, and boys never seem to get enough cookies.

Helmina will be going to school in Canton after Christmas at the Augustana College there. She has been sewing clothes which she will be needing. Ole is making plans to build a big barn next year. After Christmas he will begin hauling stones for the foundation and lumber for the building. There will be room for 12 horses and pens for colts and calves and stalls for many milk cows. I understand brother David has been building a fine big house there at Narum.

We will be together with Klara and her family some time during the

Christmas holidays. Brother Christian has been staying at Hans' this winter but he stops over to see us often. Brother Peter Anthon and family have moved to Minneapolis from St. Peter, as have brother Martinus and sister Helmine. Helmine is running a boarding house for lumberjacks, and Martinus has a hiring agency and finds jobs for those in the lumbering business. Helmine gets down to visit us about once a year.

Uncle Peter Hilstad was down from Christiania, Minnesota, to visit us for several weeks this fall. He is in good health. He still travels and conducts Laymen's Meetings.

Do you ever see Peder and Elena Dysthe? I really miss them. I always used to stop in for coffee when we went to shop in Eden.

Greet David and family and sister Helene Marie and her family. Merry Christmas! and God be with you, Papa!

Love, your daughter,
Johanna

The barn was the big project at the Overseths in the year of 1894. But all the other activities of farming and living also continued. On Saturday, March 17, 1894, a special train of 11 carloads of fat cattle left Hudson for Chicago. Ole Overseth had three carloads. Erik Jacobson, P. T. Gubbrud, and others from the community filled the other cars.

Peter Gubbrud, Erik Jacobson, Ole Nordlie, Johnny Overseth and G. Skartvedt went along to care for the cattle. Most of the steers sold for $4 a hundredweight. Cattle prices were low then, but they sold better than expected.

Ole Overseth and Thomas Hove were road overseers for the township of Norway, in Lincoln County, and responsible for building the roads in their area. A lot of time was spent on this, for farmers worked out their poll tax in this manner. It was reported in the Canton Sioux Valley News of June 15, 1894, that these two men had been doing a fine job on the highways in their township.

Ole Overseth and Hans Rise had been hauling lumber and stones all winter. In May, Paul Loe and John Hanson came to lay the foundation for Ole's barn. Hans Rise, the Overseth's neighbor to the west, was building a magnificient house. The Satrum Brothers and Company were carpenters for the Rise house and toward the last of June they finished it and began on the construction of the Overseth barn. The barn set back of the Overseth house to the north, an enormous structure, sixty feet by sixty-four feet.

In the fall of 1894, all of the Overseth children returned to Rise School except the two oldest who had graduated, and the youngest, Henry. Gunda Jacobson had been rehired to teach for the second year. Five-year-old Henry spent most of his time around the house now that his brothers Jim and Tony were at school.

One day a buggy drove up the Overseth lane and two ladies stepped down. It was two of Johanna's maiden lady acquaintances that she had not seen for some time.

"Velkommen! Velkommen! Come on in," she invited.

Little Henry stood beside his mother as she welcomed them. There was a flood of chattering as the ladies exchanged greetings.

When the larger, heavier woman noticed Henry, she exclaimed, "Johanna, this is your baby?" She beamed at him and added, "Such a sweet child!" Then bending down, she planted a wet kiss on his cheek. Henry put his hand over the damp spot and rubbed it dry, then hid behind his mother's skirt.

"Henry is a bit bashful," Johanna explained.

Johanna ushered the ladies into the parlor and Helmina brought them coffee and cookies.

Henry sat on the bottom step of the staircase and did some thinking. Finally he quietly crept up the stairs and disappeared.

The ladies had a long visit. When they said their farewells at the door, Johanna's friend asked, "Where is your baby boy?"

Johanna, too, realized she hadn't heard anything from him for some time and called, "Henry! Yoo-hoo, Henry!" After no response, the ladies said their goodbyes and left.

Johanna and Helmina began searching for Henry. They called inside, going from room to room, and then went outside. When Johanna was on the south side of the house, she heard a faint, "Here, Mama." Looking up, she saw Henry perched on top of the south porch roof. She hurried inside and ran up the staircase. There, in the south bedroom, the window was open.

"Henry, what are you doing out there?" Johanna scolded. Henry was crying and shivering.

"D-d-did that lady go?" he asked.

"Yes, but why are you out there?"

"I hid on the porch roof so that lady couldn't find me and kiss me again," he explained. "I've seen the big boys climb out here, but I couldn't reach to climb back in again."

"You mean you have been sitting out there all afternoon, with the raw fall wind blowing on you?"

Johanna helped him inside and took him into the kitchen. She set him in front of the open oven door. Soon he quit shivering. This thorough chilling brought on a bad cold, and Johanna kept him in bed. She got out her brandy bottle, which she kept hidden from the children, using it only for medicinal purposes, and gave him a dose. She became worried about her youngest as his fever rose.

"Oh, Ole," she confessed to her husband. "He is worse today." She shook her head. "I should have noticed that he was gone that afternoon and found him before he got so cold."

"Now, don't blame yourself! And I don't blame Henry either. I don't know why some of these old ladies have to kiss every little boy that they see."

"You know, Ole, I was just thinking, we have never had a photograph taken of Henry. We just must get that done as soon as he gets well."

Henry was pale and weak for some time, and they seemed to think it was "the English sickness." As Johanna and Helmina cared daily for him, he gradually improved. His fever disappeared, and his appetite returned.

When he was strong again Johanna and Ole brought him to the photographer in Canton. Henry, dressed in his best suit, with a big wide bow at the neck, was a handsome young lad. The photographer couldn't get him to smile, but nevertheless, it turned out to be a fine photo of Johanna and Ole's youngest—Henry, age, five and a half, going on six.

Two institutions had been begun in the Canton community. A school, Augustana College, which had originated in Illinois in 1860, and later moved to Beloit, Iowa in 1881, was finally established in Canton in the late 80's.

During the 1890's, the Canton area Augustana College Association gave it enthusiastic support and a large number of young people from the Norway Township community attended. Often the young men only went during the winter months when they were not needed on the farm.

Helmina Overseth took in one term during the winter and spring of 1894. Professor Tuve was the president of this institution, and worked very hard to get it going in Canton. He often travelled in the rural communities soliciting for it, and finding new students.

In 1891, the old Lutheran Theological School building at Beloit, Iowa, was converted into an Orphan's Home. Two sisters of the Lutheran Church were put in charge. An infant and a little boy were the only orphans in the beginning, but it gradually was filled and the Beloit Home became a favorite charity for organizations and individuals to support. Basket socials were held with proceeds going to the home, and teas were given to raise needed funds.

The people of Norway Township were very much interested in it. The Trinity Church began having mission festivals in the Paul Gubberud grove in the summer of 1897, and all the people of the area attended.

Music, speaking and fellowship were the order of the day, and often the orphans from the home were taken there to have a day's outing.

As the home continued to grow, there were children of all ages. The older ones had to help with the work on the farm that was connected with it, and soon the accommodations became crowded with orphans of many age groups.

When Ole and Johanna heard of this problem, it troubled them, and since they had built for themselves, they felt the desire to provide a cottage for the home. They donated funds to be used for a building for the older boys. It was thereafter known as the Overseth Cottage.

Ole and Helmina Overseth Nordlie, wedding date, April 30, 1896.

Chapter XXIV

Nineteen-year-old Helmina had been fussing around in the Overseth kitchen all day. Now she placed two large homemade buns filled with ground roast, and two big pieces of white layer cake into the square box that set on the kitchen table. She tucked in some Christmas cookies and several pieces of lefse, then put the cover on. Helmina took a wide red plaid ribbon and tied it around the box, finishing it up in a puffy big bow on the top.

"How does it look?" she asked, as she rearranged some of the loops.

"Fine!" her mother assured her.

Sister Anna was watching Helmina put the finishing touches on the box. She was now twelve years old and growing into a slim pretty young lady. Her hair was a lighter brown than her older sister's and it hung long and wavy down her back, almost to her waist.

"Are you sure Nordlie will know which box is yours?" sister Anna questioned.

"Well, when he takes me to the Rise Schoolhouse tonight, I'll make sure he notices this bright plaid ribbon on top."

Martin, now fifteen years old, came downstairs on the run, all dressed in his Normanna Brass Band uniform. It was dark blue and trimmed with gold braid and gold buttons, and there was a jaunty cap with a visor to match.

This past summer of 1895, the group had been outfitted with uniforms and the Normanna Brass Band was the pride of Norway Township. The city of Canton had its Gate City Band, but Norway Township was not to be outdone. This band was composed of twenty musicians from Norway Township community and directed and taught by O. K. Indseth.

Martin Overseth was one of the young men who had taken cornet lessons, and now he was finally a member. Brother Tony had just begun instruction on the trombone from Indseth and had hopes of one day joining the group. Tonight the brass band was to entertain at the Basket Sociable at Rise schoolhouse.

Martin put on his cap, grabbed his cornet and left.

"I wish I could go," Anna said.

Her mother spoke, "You and I and the little boys will stay home and eat layer cake. I'm afraid it will be so crowded we'd have to stand all evening. You'd soon get tired of that!"

"Is Papa going?" Anna wanted to know.

"I guess so," her mother replied. "If the band plays he has to be there to listen—especially since Martin became a member."

When Helmina and Nordlie, the Overseth's hired man, arrived at the Rise schoolhouse, the Normanna Brass Band was tuning up. Helmina brought her box lunch over to the table in the front of the room and Nordlie found a seat for her.

"I'll stand," he said. Already most of the seats were taken and the men let the women have the chairs. People kept coming, and soon it was even hard to find a spot to stand.

O. K. Indseth took his place before the musicians, held up his baton, and the music began. The silver cornets played fanfares and the mellow tones of the trombones came in with the melody. The band filled the schoolhouse with music, and even those standing outside the door could enjoy it.

Included in the band's repertoire were stirring marches composed by John Philip Sousa. The audience was delighted, and after each number they noisily applauded.

The Rise schoolhouse was packed. This basket sociable was given for the purpose of raising money for the Fremad Library. It was just before Christmas of 1895, and the older boys and girls who attended college in Canton were already home for Christmas vacation.

The room was filled with young ladies who had brought baskets of lunch for two, and young men and boys who had come to bid on them. Ole Steensland, of Highland Township, had brought Emma Larsen, and Gunder Schiager was there with Matthea Raasum.

Martin Odegaard was the auctioneer and he worked up the bids on each basket until he got the very last penny the men were willing to offer.

When Helmina's basket came up for auction and Nordlie began bidding, some of the boys in the back of the room began shouting, "Make him pay, Martin! Make him pay!" Nordlie outlasted the other bidders and later Helmina and Nordlie ate the lunch together.

There was excitement, teasing, joviality and music! A total of $22.25 was raised that night for their project.

During the Christmas season of 1895, the weather was mild and October-like, with no snow upon the ground. On the evening of December 26th, Ole and Johanna and their entire family dressed up and took off in the buggy for the **Trefoldighed Kirke** Christmas festivities. This church was formerly known as the South Bethlehem Church, but it had separated from the Canton group in 1895, and later the Gran congregation had also joined with them. Its English name was **Trinity Church,** and it was located in the same section as the Overseth farm and only a mile and three-fourths by way of the road. A new edifice had been built in 1893.

Lands Church hadn't begun to have Christmas tree programs and so this special event at Trinity drew a crowd from far and wide. The church was packed—and overpacked—and many persons had to be turned away. Pastors Berge and Thormodsgaard spoke, the Sunday School children performed and Bjorlie's Normanna Choir presented several numbers.

This musical group, under the direction of Jens Bjorlie, played an important role in the community life of Norway Township. They met regularly in the homes of the members, and musical harmony and fellowship was the purpose of this organization, which consisted of members from the entire community.

At one of the meetings at the August Johnson home, a resolution was drawn up (in fun) that none of the members could marry before the year 1900, and break up this group. They sang at churches, schools and other social events.

Yes, during the 1890's, there was music in Norway Township. Besides the Normanna Brass Band and Bjorlie's Normanna Choir, many homes were getting organs, and a number of people possessed violins and many were very proficient in playing them.

In the early nineties, a general store was built north of the new Lands parsonage by two business partners, Button and Olson. This country store filled a great need in the community as housewives had to go to Canton or Hudson for supplies, and often they had to walk to town and carry the groceries back because the men needed the horses in the fields.

Later the post office that Paul and Hans Hanson Grastadmoe had operated in their home was moved to the new store. After several years, Olson sold his interest in the store to Knud Ekle and his son Oluf.

In 1895, a creamery owned by local stockholders was built near the store. Cream was bought and churned into butter and either sold locally or shipped out. The buttermilk was divided among the stockholders.

In the early part of 1896, an icehouse was constructed for the creamery and the stockholders hauled ice from the river at Beloit to fill it.

The corner north of the Lands Church was becoming a busy rural marketplace.

During the months of January and February of 1896, the weather was splendid. There was no snow on the ground and the rattle of the wagons could be heard for miles around as people came to this little community center of Moe. When farmers brought their milk and cream to the creamery, they made the Moe Store their favorite trading and visiting spot, and the proprietors Button and Ekle were kept busy.

*****

Ole Overseth stuck his head in the kitchen door and called, "Yoo hoo! Mama, I'm going over to Moe to get the mail. Do you need anything from the store?"

"Perhaps you can pick up a pound of coffee and maybe you can get me a small sack of black pepper," she answered. "I'm all out of that."

As Ole turned his horses north at the church corner, he saw the stars and stripes waving from the front of the store and post office. "Ja, those storekeepers don't miss anything," he said. Today was February 22nd, 1896, and the flags were waving in honor of the father of the country, George Washington.

Moe Store was a large building, facing the east, with a long wooden porch all along the front. An iron railing ran the whole length of the porch. Here Ole tied his horse. Above the store were living quarters for the owners.

Inside the store were shelves and tables filled with food, clothing and hardware. Towards the back was the pot belly stove where the customers gathered to get warmed after a long chilly wagon trip.

Ole went over to the stove, where a good fire was burning, pulled off his mittens and held his hands up to the warmth of the stove. Several men were sitting around the stove. One had his feet propped up on the nail keg.

"You look comfortable," Ole told him. "Been here all day?"

"Just about," he answered. "I suppose I'll have to move soon and head home to do the chores."

Ole winked at him and teased, "The molasses must be running slow today, hah?"

The black strap molasses was kept in barrels. During the winter months the molasses became so thick it could hardly be poured. When the menfolks arrived home late after having overstayed at Moe Store their standard excuse was, "It took so long to fill the molasses jug."

Much of the merchandise was contained in wooden boxes and barrels. There was salt pork, and always there was a good quantity of salt fish on hand. A display of cigars, tobacco and chewing tobacco was on the counter. Also a machine that clipped the ends from the cigars.

One day an inquisitive man, who was browsing around, put his finger into it and was rather shocked to discover how effective it was when the end of his finger was trimmed.

Cuspidors were situated in convenient places for customers who made a practice of chewing tobacco. Here at the store the latest news and gossip was quickly passed along, and politics was discussed and argued during the long winter evenings and dreary winter days. Music could be heard almost every night at Moe Store, for Oluf Ekle was excellent on the violin.

This year of 1896, was election year and the St. Louis convention in July was already bringing much discussion. W. J. Bryan was running on the People's Party and the issue and topic of conversation everywhere was "free silver and Bryan."

"What can we do for you today, Ole?" proprietor Oluf Ekle inquired. He had a white flour sack tied around his waist, and Button, the other owner, was wearing his white grocer apron. The storekeepers could be quickly distinguished from the rest of the people in the store.

"Well," Ole said, as he walked up to the counter, "I guess our coffee supply is a little low."

"Today our Best Golden Rio is 30 cents a pound, and No. 1 Rio coffee is 25 cents," Oluf informed him.

"Scoop up two pounds of the Golden," was Ole's response. "Johanna is needing some black pepper too. Wrap me up half a sack full."

"Now that is the kind of business we like," Oluf said. "We are very happy everytime someone orders black pepper because back in the warehouse we've got 600 pounds of it. It had been over-ordered, and at the rate we sell it, I think we will still have a good supply twenty years from now."

"Go ahead and fill up the sack, if it will make you happy," Ole told him. "We like to have good-natured storekeepers around here."

"Now," Ole said, "I'll pick up my mail, and then go home and read my Norwegian newspaper. That's the reason I came over today."

* * * * *

There were only five days left of February, 1896, and still the ground was black and bare. So far this winter Ole had not had snow to shovel, the thing that made winter chores so difficult. Shoveling out snow so the cattle could get over to drink and eat, with bitter winds that made him hurry so he could get back inside again, that was the kind of winter weather that he hadn't missed a bit.

But today fog hung like a heavy veiling over the land, leaving a frosty covering on winter grasses and trees and fences. Even Ole's cattle had white whiskers around their faces.

During this mild winter weather, Ole took his time as he did his morning chores. He stood and watched his cattle eat. He could tell if one was sick or weak. "Ja," he thought, "in another month I'll have to get ready to haul some of them out."

He thoroughly checked all the other animals and puttered around fixing something here and there, and when he had his morning chores finished he came into the kitchen for his forenoon lunch.

"You'll have to wait a bit while I warm up the coffee," Johanna said.

She filled the firebox of the kitchen range with several handfuls of cobs from the cob basket and set the coffee pot on the front part of the stove.

Ole took off his coat and boots and went into the parlor. Johanna could hear him at the organ. He was playing a hymn and singing along. Next he labored through his, "**Noen har brød**" song.

When the steam began rising from the coffeepot Johanna called, "**Vaer saa god!**" and filled the two cups on the table. She still had some Christmas bread and placed several buttered slices on a plate.

Johnny and Nordlie and Helmina had gone to Hudson to do some shopping. Helmina needed some materials for sewing, and the men needed nails and other supplies. "You never can tell how long this fine weather will last," Ole told them, "so you had better get the things that we will be needing." The other children were in school.

It wasn't very often that Ole and Johanna were alone and could sit and discuss things freely over their coffee cups without an audience.

Johanna quickly shared what was on her heart.

"I wonder how Papa is today."

At Christmas time they had received a letter from brother David in Norway, saying that her father, Paul Andreas Narum, was ailing. He had had a stroke which had left him partially paralyzed so he could no longer get around.

"I wish we weren't so far away," Johanna remarked. "If we were closer I could go and see Papa now and then."

Ole didn't speak for awhile, and then out of the blue, he asked, "Why can't we go?"

Johanna stared at him to see if he was joking.

He explained, "We have always said that someday we would go back for a visit, and I think now is the time while your father is still living."

Then he added, "Helmina and Nordlie are talking about getting married anyway, and they could look after things. I would feel free to go and leave them in charge."

"Yes, but . . ." Johanna protested, "how could we make such a long trip? What about the little boys?"

"Oh, we could take Jim and Henry along. They would enjoy that! Why, they could go for half price!"

Ole took another drink of his coffee, then dunked his sugar lump and quickly stuck it into his mouth. He seemed very pleased as he grinned at his wife.

"You know, Johanna, this is a very good idea. The more I think about it, the more right it seems."

As Johanna cleared the table, he remarked, "But if we are going to get to Norway this summer, we'll have to begin making plans right away."

When Helmina and Nordlie got back, Ole brought up the subject.

"Instead of you two going to a place of your own," Ole began, and then paused to elaborate, "I know you are looking around for something to buy. Well," he went on, "you could live here this year and take care of things so Mother and I and the little boys could take a trip to Norway. It would be good for your mother to get to see her father again before it is too late."

So plans were made. April 30th was decided on as the wedding date for Helmina Overseth and Ole Nordlie, and Ole and Johanna and the boys would leave for Norway after the corn was planted, about the first part of June.

The month of March, 1896, came in with a touch of winter. March 2nd the snow was flying and sleighbells could be heard for the first time during the winter of 1895-1896.

Nils and Lisa Larsen were glad the weather had held off until after February 26th because at twelve noon of that day their daughter Emma, had been married to Ole Steensland of Highland Township. The wedding was in the Trinity Church and the whole Overseth family had been invited. Lisa and Nils had just had a new kitchen added to their house the fall before so they had the wedding reception in their home afterwards, and they had plenty of room for entertaining.

In March, Maggie Sorlie, the dressmaker from Highland Township, spent several weeks at the Overseths and sewed Helmina's wedding dress. It was a soft plum color and made of a rep silk. The bodice was designed with a cross-drape, which ended with a large self-cloth bow at the waist. Similar bows were attached to the skirt in six different places. It had billowy elbow length puff sleeves, and white lace filled in the "V" neckline and a wide ruffle of this lace lay over the shoulders like a bertha. The floor length veil had a headpiece of orange blossoms.

Maggie also sewed several dresses for Johanna to take along on her trip and new suits for Jim and Henry that had wide ruffled shirt collars and big plaid bows at the necks.

Invitations went out for Hemina and Nordlie's wedding, which was set for 12 o'clock on Thursday, April 30, at Lands Church. Minnie Sogn and Johnny Overseth were to be their attendants. A big dinner was planned to be served afterward.

"We must have roast beef," Ole had insisted, for feeding cattle was his main livestock operation. A fine animal had been butchered in preparation for this wedding celebration.

Angel food cakes had been baked in large pans and cut into squares and individually frosted. Norwegian cookies were baked—**fattigmand, berliner krans, krumkakke** and **goro kakke** and **totenkringler.** Sister Klara had come and helped with the preparations.

Close friends and neighbors and relatives gathered at the appointed time and place. Pastor Hauge officiated at the marriage ceremony. The groom had written a wedding poem which was sung. The bride was attired in her plum-colored wedding dress with white veil and white elbow length gloves, and a corsage of white flowers. The groom wore a black formal cutaway suit with tails, and white gloves and a spray of flowers on his lapel.

After the wedding, the guests attended the reception which followed at the Overseth home. When people congratulated Ole Overseth on his new son-in-law, his response was, "Ja, I gained a son-in-law, but I guess I will be losing a good hired man."

And Johanna was praising God because her oldest daughter had married a Christian man, and they were establishing a Christian home.

Chapter XXV

N ei, we are not moving back to Norge!" Ole's voice was jolly as he teased Johanna who kept coming with more items to pack in the trunk. She had presents for her father, and for her sister and for her brother's wife, and for the Dyste's and for the wives of Ole's two brothers.

"But we will be gone for three months," she argued, "and besides, there is a lot in there besides clothes for the three of us."

Ole finally closed the trunk and loaded it into the lumber wagon and hauled it to the Hudson depot. Johanna packed the things they would be needing on the voyage into their suitcases. Yesterday they had all attended church at Lands where Ole and she had partaken of the Lord's Supper. After services, all of their neighbors and friends had gathered around and wished them a fine trip.

Only seven-year-old Henry would be taking the Norway trip with them. Jim, who was eight then, had decided he didn't want to go.

"Why, when haying and harvest come, they'll be needing me," he pointed out. "And besides, if Tony doesn't go, I don't want to either."

So he was staying behind, but Johanna was a little apprehensive about it. "Jim is still just a little boy, so you'll have to keep your eye on him, Helmina," she instructed.

The morning of June 9th, 1896, the whole family was at the Hudson depot to see them off. Pete and Hans Overseth were there, too.

"Greet brothers Johan and Johannes and their families from me," Pete requested, "and be sure to look up Pete Dyste and Elena."

They travelled by train to New York and then went by ship to England. As they pulled out of New York harbor, Ole, Johanna and Henry stood on deck, looking at the vast expanse of ocean, and Henry was overcome by the sight. Coming from the land where water was a precious commodity, he exclaimed in little-boy wonderment, "I bet there is enough water there to water all the cattle in the whole world!"

In England they transferred to another ship that took them across the North

Sea. They docked in the capital city of Christiana, almost three weeks later.

All of their relatives lived in the area to the north of Christiana, and on the west side of Lake Mjosa. They visited there for several months.

Far Narum was mostly confined to his room at the family **gaard** of Narum. Tears rolled down his cheeks when he saw Johanna and Ole.

"I didn't think I'd ever get to see you again," he told Johanna.

Above his bed was a swing-like contraption that **Far** Narum could grasp and move himself about in his bed. He held out his good hand to his American grandson Henry.

"How is it going with you, **Bestefar?**" Henry's happy little voice inquired.

A smile came over **Far** Narum's face and he said, "Ja, I shall thank God for this—that I got to see one of your children, Johanna."

They visited Ole's brother Johan on the Overseth **gaard** and his brother Johannes at Buruld **gaard,** and Johanna's sister Helene Marie Stikbakke and her family, besides **Far** Narum and brother David and his family, and other aunts, uncles and cousins.

It was harvest time while they were in Norway and Ole was surprised to see that Norway had the same farm equipment they were using in America—even modern McCormick Deering reapers.

"I guess things haven't been standing still while I have been gone," Ole commented.

But it was true that some things in Norway still were the best. "Oh, the taste of clabbered milk in Norway!" Ole couldn't seem to get his fill of it. It was prepared by spreading the bottom of individual glass bowls with one teaspoon sour cream; the bowls were set on a tray in the warm part of the kitchen and carefully filled with milk. By the next day the milk had set, and it was placed in the cooler to chill, and then served with sugar and rusks which were crumbled and sprinkled on top. Johanna went through the same process at home, "But," Ole pointed out, "it just doesn't turn out as fresh and delicious in America's hot climate."

And the cherry trees of Norway with their uncomparable tasty fruit! Brother Johan gave Ole a little cherry tree to take back home with him.

And the strawberries! So plump and juicy and sweet. They still were his favorite fruit, and he considered it fortunate that they were in Norway during the strawberry season.

Before they returned to Christiana, all of Ole and Johanna's brothers and sisters and their spouses and children gathered at the photographer's to have a picture taken of the relationship in Norge.

When they got to Christiania, they spent some time with Peder Anthon Dyste and his wife Elena before they boarded the ship for home.

During the homeward voyage across the Atlantic, Ole and Johanna often stood and watched the mob of immigrants down on steerage deck. During the day, young women sat in their crowded quarters and combed their long hair, and Johanna shuddered as she noticed some of the mothers picking lice from their children's hair.

With evening, the steerage deck really came to life. There were some fiddlers aboard and the dancing would keep on late into the night. Seeing the life of the steerage passengers brought back memories of the rough trips they each had taken on similar decks almost thirty years earlier. This time they travelled in comfort as second-class passengers.

Jens Bjorlie also took a trip back to Norway in the summer of 1896. He sold his violin to Oluf Asper of Norway Township before he left because he was not planning to return.

Ole and Johanna were glad to get home to America again and back to South Dakota to see how their family and farm were getting along.

During the year of 1896, hog cholera spread throughout Lincoln County, and across Norway Township, where it wiped out almost all of the pigs. Many farmers didn't even have a hog left to butcher for Christmas. Knud Ekle was one farmer that suffered a great loss because of this disease in his swine herd. Besides, he had gone into debt when he and his son went into the Moe Store venture. Now his son had taken on a new partner in the business, Solomon Mortenson.

As soon as Ole Nordlie heard rumors that Knud Ekle was considering the sale of his farm, which was located alongside the Lands Church, he contacted him and they agreed on a selling price. Nordlie paid $1,700 cash and took on mortgages of $3,000.

"If you will pay the back taxes," Knud told Nordlie, "I guarantee that you will never have hog cholera on this place."

The Knud Ekles purchased another farm near Fairview and when the Overseths returned from Norway the first of September, Nordlie began getting his new farm fixed up, and Helmina and Nordlie moved into their own home. However, they didn't get their deed until after Christmas. On February 23rd, the Knud Ekles signed the deed, and about the same time their son Oluf and his partner Solomon Mortenson, sold the Moe Store to Claus Hegness and Knute Jacobson.

In the fall of 1896, Pete Overseth ran for state legislature and won the spot as Senator from Lincoln County in the November election.

Helmina and Ole Nordlie were nicely settled by November 1896, and offered to have the prayer meeting at their home on November 28th. About a dozen people attended. The chairs had been arranged around the parlor and Pastor Hauge began the meeting with scripture reading and they sang some hymns. Several people had already raised their hearts and words to God when Nils Ekle, the neighbor to the southeast of Nordlies, arrived.

He had come on foot across the fields. He quietly found a place to sit and reverently became a part of the group. When it was his chance to pray, he got off his chair and down upon his knees beside his chair, his head bowed and his folded hands resting upon the seat.

Nils had been sitting across from Ole, and when he began his prayer, Ole glanced across the room at a sight he would never forget. This man in his plain plaid flannel shirt and loose fitting dark wool trousers which were held up by the wide suspenders, was kneeling, in complete unconcern of the people around him.

In those precious moments it was only himself and God. The words poured out from his heart to his Lord, with thanksgiving, humility and praise. This was his prayer posture and when he was on his knees praying, everyone could hear that he was on familiar ground.

The year of 1896 had been a bad year for hog farmers but these people promised to still trust their Heavenly Father to take care of them and provide for their needs and for the needs of their little ones.

The Overseths often attended the Trinity Church on the Sundays when there were no services at Lands. The **klokker** at Trinity was usually a Swede and the boys, Henry, Jim and Tony, always waited for him to announce the hymns in his Swedish accent.

One Sunday Johanna noticed Tony poke Jim, and Jim poke Henry as the **klokker** loudly and with a heavy Swedish brogue said, "We shall sing **hyt-ti hu!**" The syllable "**hyt**" was gurgled and slurred upwards and heavily accented while the last syllable ended as a very windy "hoo".

Johanna gave the boys a very stern look, and they stared straight ahead, trying to hold back their amusement, almost bursting in the process.

But a faint smile crossed Ole's mouth, for he could understand why the boys enjoyed the Swedish "77's". The sounds were strange to their ears after hearing the Norwegian **"syv og søtti"** all of their lives.

"Ja," he thought, "we all have our roots in the North countries, but we do have our little differences."

Often when they attended Trinity Church services they were invited to John Hegneses for dinner, or else they would entertain the Hegneses at their home. Ole Overseth was very hospitable and there weren't many Sundays that he didn't invite company home for dinner no matter which church they attended.

The women would go down into the cellar and come up with preserved meat and sauce and potatoes and carrots, and the older girls helped them prepare it while the men visited and the children played. After dinner the boys got the men to join them in a ball game. The ball was made of tightly wound yarn, and covered with denim, while a narrow plank was used for a bat.

Ole Overseth was gracious even to Arabian peddlers who made regular visits to the Overseth home. They knew they could find a room to sleep there, and he would feed their horse too. One room was kept just for strangers like them.

In 1895, Ole bought Johanna her own little mare named "Daisy". On days of Ladies Aid, or when she wanted to go to Hudson shopping or visit her sister Klara or her friends Mari Rogness or Ann Raasum, she would ask her sons to harness up her horse and hitch it to the buggy and then tie it to the post so it would be ready for her.

Ole and Johanna's family was enlarged on December 16, 1897, when a son was born to daughter Helmina and Ole Nordlie. This first grandson was named Obed Joel Nordlie.

On October 12th, 1898, a daughter-in-law was added to the family when Johnny Overseth was married to Erik Jacobson's daughter Rena. They moved onto the Eden farm.

Standing; Henry Overseth, Jim and Anna Overseth; seated Helmina Overseth Nordlie and son, Obed Joel.—circa 1899

Chapter XXVI

The last of February 1899, Johanna received a letter from her sister Helmine Narum who lived in Minneapolis.

Dear Johanna,

I have a surprise for you! Ole Opsahl, a widower from Minneapolis, has asked me to marry him. He originally comes from East Toten. I have consented, and I would like to have my relatives at my wedding, so Opsahl and I are coming down there and would like to be married at your place. March 30th is the date we have chosen. I hope this is all right with you folks.

I am anxious for you to meet him. He is a very fine man. I know you will like him.

We will be arriving several days before the wedding date.

With love from your sister,

Helmine

"Oh, nei-min!" Johanna exclaimed. This news really did take Johanna by surprise, but she was delighted that they would be able to have a part in Helmine's wedding.

Opsahl and sister Helmine arrived at the depot in Hudson, and after all the arrangements had been made, a quiet service was held in the Overseth home on March 30th, with Pastor Hauge officiating. Both bride and groom were 44 years of age. A nephew and a niece, Martin Overseth and Marie Grevlos, served as their attendants. Sisters Klara and Johanna had baked cakes and cookies and the immediate family had a wedding feast afterwards.

"Now," Ole said, "it is brother Pete Overseth's turn!"

Pete had reached the age of 38 and still was unmarried, but Pete was much too involved with politics and business to have time to get serious about a young lady.

Pete Overseth had sold his general store in Hudson and after serving as senator from Lincoln County in the state legislature at Pierre during the terms of 1897,

1899 and 1901, he went into the banking business. In 1901, a new bank, the Farmers State Bank of Canton, was organized and on October 1, 1901, it opened for business with Pete Overseth as its first president. His brother Ole Overseth was one of the stockholders, and on the board of directors.

Ole, too, was a businessman. He bought himself a fine roll-top desk where he kept all of his papers and records. Besides his farming activities, he was involved in many transactions concerning his cattle feeding operation.

In 1897, he had gone into partnership with Ole Byhre. They purchased a ranch out west of the river at Presho, South Dakota. Ole sent out stock cows and Byhre cared for them and when the calves were big enough to fatten, they were shipped back to the Overseth feedyard. Every fall in about September or October, Ole went out to Presho and came back with about 60 or 70 head.

By the year 1902, Henry, Jim and Tony were able to be a great help on the farm. Johnny and his family were living down on the Eden farm and Martin and Anna were attending school in Canton.

Tony was 16, Jim 14 and Henry 13. Besides the field work, they all had their assigned chores. Ole always liked to feed his cattle and hogs himself. The boys milked the cows and tended to the horses, currying them and watering them, and also looked after the calves. There were usually one or two hired men to help with all the work on the farm. There were barns and hog houses to clean and animals to be fed and watered. Johanna looked after her chickens and geese herself.

In 1895, Ole had put in waterworks, with a windmill and a tubular well and pump, together with water tanks.

Even on Sunday mornings Ole would call up the staircase, "Henry, Jim, Tony! Time to get up and do your chores!"

The woodpecker in the cottonwood tree by their bedroom window was already busy pecking away at the tree trunk, but their dad had been up before the birds and by that time he had been outside and fed his cattle and hogs.

At the breakfast table Johanna always read a portion from the Bible to start off the day, and after breakfast the boys went out to do their tasks while Ole, on Sundays, cleaned up and dressed for church. He sat at the organ in his suit, white shirt and tie, his fingers upon the keys, as his feet pumped the pedals and he played hymns while the rest of the family got ready for church. Ole sang his favorite Norwegian hymns and usually included his special song, "**Noen har brød**":

> "Some have bread and cannot eat.
> Others can eat, but have not bread.
> We have bread and we can eat,
> Therefore we will praise our God."

During the summer of 1902 in June—a tornado struck in the community and destroyed the Romsdal Church to the west and the Trinity Church to the east, and it also took the steeple from the new Lands Church, which had been built in 1901. This new Lands Church was an eight-sided structure and provided much more room than the old one.

Pastor L. J. Hauge had resigned in the summer of 1899, to attend medical school in Sioux City, Iowa, and Rev. Strass was serving as interim pastor.

The seasons came and went, but the Sunday time at the organ was a routine that both Ole and Johanna looked forward to. Johanna, while busy in the kitchen, could hear the melodies.

Today, December 7th, 1902, Ole was playing **"Oh, hvor salig det skal bleve naar Gud's barn skal komme hjem,"**—the hymn that was sung most often at their evening devotions.

Johanna stopped her work and went into the parlor and stood and listened. She watched her husband as his big hard-working hands touched the keys and made music. At his last birthday, on September 30, 1902, he had reached the age of 56. She noticed the gray that was appearing in his hair and noticably in his full whiskers, and even in his bushy eyebrows. He had a few deep furrows across his wide forehead, and his hair was not as thick as it once had been.

Why, tomorrow, December 8, 1902, it would be thirty years since their wedding day! Daughter Helmina had hinted that her family and Johnny's would be stopping in later in the day to help them celebrate.

Brother Christian Narum was staying with them now and served as their wood man. He had a full time job chopping wood for the cook stove and the heating stoves. At times he became tired of it and grumbled about it, especially after he had been into town and had inbibed a bit, but it was always to the children that he would confide, "All they make me do is chop wood! Chop wood! I think I will go back to Norway." Then he would put his finger to his lips and say, "But don't tell your mother though."

At this time of the year all of the men worked on the wood supply and felled some of the trees in the thick grove to the northwest of the farmyard. In order to be assured of a wood supply, Ole had to plan ahead, for the trees needed to dry before they could be chopped for firewood.

On Sunday afternoon, December 7th, 1902, Helmina came over with a big cake. Anna and Martin were home from Augustana College for the weekend and the whole family helped Ole and Johanna celebrate their 30th anniversary a day early.

They all gathered in the parlor. Soon Ole was at the organ and the boys got out their instruments—Tony his trombone, and Martin, his cornet—and there was music!

Uncle Christian was enjoying the family concert too. During a break in the musical numbers, he spoke up, "Ja, that was a cold day, thirty years ago! But the weather didn't seem to get the newlyweds down. You should have heard your dad singing on the way to the wedding dinner at the hotel." He could report on their wedding, for he had been there as one of their witnesses.

"What did he sing, Chris?" Henry prompted.

"Well, why don't you see if your father still knows all the verses of that song?" Christian suggested.

"Ja, Pa," Jim begged. "Why don't you sing it for us. We weren't there, you know!"

Ole was in a jovial mood and he began pumping the organ as he played and sang **"Kjøre vatten aa Kjøre ved"**. He went through all of the verses, ending with . . .

> "She's the one I want,
> She is so good, she is so kind
> I can never get tired of her,"

and he finished with a flourishing "So now is it fun to live!"

Christian was sitting in the rocking chair smoking his pipe, and when Ole ended, he began clapping. All the family joined in.

"Ja, that was the smartest thing I ever did!" Ole announced, as he beamed at Johanna from behind his whiskers.

"And now we even have three grandchildren to show for it," Johanna pointed out.

Daughter Helmina and husband Nordlie had a son and daughter. Baby Thelma Louise Marie was born March 3, 1901. Obed was now almost four. Johnny and Rena had a son, Enok Oliver, who was born October 26, 1899.

Ole took the two youngest grandchildren upon his knees and he put his arm around Obed who was standing beside him.

"Ja, now I am **Bestefar**," he said in proud tones. "Is not that so, Obed?" he asked his oldest grandchild, who vigorously nodded his head.

After the lunch and the fun, Johanna asked Ole if they could have devotions before everyone went home. She got the Bible and gave it to Ole. It was time again to read Psalm 128, the portion that Rev. Johnson had used at their wedding.

Ole gave the little grandchildren back to their mothers, and everyone settled down to listen.

"In Jesus' name," Ole began

"Blessed is every one who fears the Lord,
 who walks in his ways.
You shall eat the fruit of the labor of your hands;
 you shall be happy, and it shall be well with you.
Your wife shall be like a fruitful vine within your house;
 your children will be like olive shoots around your table.
Lo, thus shall the man be blessed who fears the Lord."

Here Ole stopped.

"Ja, God has been faithful and good to these two newcomers who got married thirty years ago."

He first looked at Johanna, and then his eyes slowly took in everyone in the room. They became watery and his voice choked up as he finished the psalm:

"The Lord bless you from Zion!
May you see the prosperity of Jerusalem all the days of your life!
May you see your children's children!"

"See, here they are!" he said as he motioned to Obed, Thelma and Oliver.

The last verse was like a benediction upon his family as he meaningfully concluded,

"Peace be upon Israel! Amen."

＊ ＊ ＊ ＊ ＊

At Christmas time Johanna received a letter from her brother David in Norway, informing her of her father's death.

Dear sister Johanna,   30 Nov. 1902
    Father passed away Saturday, November 22nd. Yesterday all the relatives and neighbors gathered for funeral services. He now lies in the Kolbu cemetery beside Mother.

> your brother,
>
> David

    Johanna sat in the quiet house by herself. The letter fell to her lap and her mind tried to draw back memories of her father. Again, she could remember his happiness at seeing them when they visited Norway in 1896—and his delight at Henry.
    "Yes, I am so glad we went back," Johanna thought. "Yes, so very glad."
    Her heart was full as the thoughts of Papa came flooding in. Now his earthly remains were resting beside Mother's. In Johanna's mind's eye, she could see her mother's gravestone and the words upon it—**"Vi skal mote i himmelen!"** Papa had chosen that himself.
    "Yes, Paul Andreas Davidson Narum was a good man, and I thank God that I had him for my father."

Chapter XXVII

The big kettle of apple butter bubbled on the back section of Johanna's black cast-iron cookstove. Mouth-watering aromas filled the Overseth home today. It was late September, 1903, and harvest time. The apples had been picked and the perfect ones had been carefully packed into barrels in the cellar and Johanna was using the others for jam and juice.

The grapes on the arbor also were ripe and today she was in the process of extracting juice from some of them. A large cloth bag, filled with cooked grapes, hung from the end of the cookstove and underneath it was a crock that was gradually filling with deep purple-colored juice. Drop by drop the liquid drained from the bag and splashed into the container below. This juice would be used for tasty puddings during the winter ahead.

Daughter Helmina bent over the stove, a long wooden spoon in her hand, continually stirring the thick apple substance. She was helping her mother today, as her two children played on the floor of the Overseth kitchen.

Johanna came running down the stairway.

"I see them coming! They're just turning the cattle into the driveway now," she announced. She had been watching for the men on the cattle drive. The fruit orchard around the house obstructed the view to the south so Johanna had gone upstairs to get a better look.

"I'd better get busy with the lunch for the men. They'll be hungry, that is for certain!" she said as she began slicing bread and carving off slices of cold roast.

Last night, Ole Overseth had returned from a trip out to the ranch at Presho. Erik Jacobson had gone with him. They had helped Ole Byhre with the fall round-up and then had loaded about 65 steers on the train. Both the men and the steers had arrived at the Hudson depot last night. Today the cattle were being driven the eight miles home to the Overseth feedyard. Jim and Henry had been kept out of school to help, and Nordlie was assisting, along with Johnny, Erik Jacobson, his son, and several other neighbors.

Johanna pulled the big blue speckled enamel coffeepot to the front of the stove and filled the firebox with cobs. Then she turned to her grandchildren, Obed and Thelma.

"Go and look in the downstairs bedroom window. Soon you'll see all the cattle go by," she said. The children ran through the dining room to the bedroom to watch.

It wasn't long until the sound of mooing and bawling could be heard as the confused animals tried to find ways to escape the men on horseback. Finally the herd thundered past the house on the way north to the barnyard, raising clouds of dust, and were corralled and turned into the Overseth feedlot.

The men were dusty and stiff after sitting astride their horses for so many hours. They got down and stretched their legs, then filed into the house for food and coffee.

"Sit yourselves down!" Ole instructed. All the chairs around the dining room table were quickly occupied. Johanna carried in bread and butter and cold roast and set a big bowl of fresh apple butter on the table. Doughnuts had been stacked on a large plate. "Help yourselves!" Johanna invited as she began pouring up hot coffee.

"Well, what do you think of this bunch of cattle?" Ole addressed his son-in-law Nordlie.

"They are the finest you've gotten so far," he replied.

"Ja, Ole Byhre is doing a good job out there at the ranch. He can't be beat!"

After taking a swallow of coffee, Erik Jacobson spoke. "Well, Ole, now you can relax; you made it in time!"

He turned to the rest of the men to explain.

"We've been rushing ever since we left on the trip to Presho. Ole was afraid he wouldn't be back in time for the Augustana College dedication in Canton on Sunday. Of course, I didn't want to miss it either."

"Ja, it will be a big day, you can be sure of that!" Ole said. "We all must go. With Tony at school there this year, I'm sure Mother will want to take it in, too."

He looked at Henry and Jim. "You boys have to go along. Why, soon you'll be attending that fine school."

"Yes, we'll all have to go Sunday," Johanna agreed, "and we must bring Martin's clean shirts and socks along when we go into Canton."

On the first of September, Martin had begun working as a bookkeeper at the Farmers State Bank of Canton. He had accepted the position at his Uncle Pete's bank when Joseph Anderson had left.

The Sunday before, he had stopped by home with a group of young people who were taking the editor of the Dakota Farmer's Leader of Canton on a tour of the countryside. They had inspected the new Trinity Church which was being rebuilt after the tornado of 1902 had demolished the previous building. Also on the outing were his sister Anna Overseth; Anna Wilson; Knute Jacobson, the Moe Store proprietor; Ed Linde, who clerked there; and a Mr. Ericson of Inwood. As a result, the editor had written up a detailed description of the Trinity building project in the September 25th issue of his paper.

Johanna went on, "Everything is all washed and ironed, and Martin will be needing those clothes now that he must dress up every day."

Uncle Christian Narum took out his pipe and lit it, then leaned back, balancing his chair on its back legs. "Ja, you all go and take it in. I'll stay home and look after things here on the farm."

The noisy sound of the bawling calves came from the direction of the cattleyard to the north.

"That would be fine, Chris," Ole said. "It sounds like these cattle will be restless for awhile, and it would be bad if they broke out when no one was home."

On Sunday, October 4th, at 2 p.m., the dedication of the new Augustana College Main building at Canton was held. When Ole, Johanna and family got there about an hour before it was to begin, the large tent that had been erected west of the new building was already filling up. The tent had been secured from Mr. Forrest because a larger attendance was anticipated than could be accommodated in the new building's chapel. Planks had been set up for seating.

People kept coming. Soon they were standing around the sides and finally the south wall of the tent was raised so people outside could be included. Some sat in their carriages and listened. Over 2,400 people attended.

President Tuve announced the program. First the Harrisburg band played and then Rev. Kildahl from St. Olaf College was introduced. He spoke in the Norwegian language. For 45 minutes he held the audience spellbound. Men and women of all ages, shed tears as the speaker moved them with his words.

Another dignitary gave an address in English, and the Grieg Men's Choir sang. When an offering was taken from the crowd, $1,500 was gathered to help pay for this beautiful new addition on the campus of Augustana College at Canton, South Dakota.

It was a big day for Ole Overseth and Erik Jacobson and many other farmers from Norway Township, who had at a meeting of the Augustana College Association held several years before, stood up and individually pledged various amounts towards this new building. Now they looked at this imposing structure of red colored stone and felt the satisfaction and pride that comes from having had a financial part in the erection of such a fine edifice.

The last few weeks of October 1903, provided beautiful weather. The sun shone and day by day the countryside took on its fall colors. The cottonwoods were especially brilliant as their leaves dangled from their branches like gold coins, gently turning in the breezes.

Finally, the leaves fell from the trees. Then the big cottonwoods and the smaller fruit trees all stood bare. The weather gradually got cooler and more crisp. Frost turned the cornfields whitish and then light brown as they dried. The ears of corn hung loose in the husks, ready for picking. This year of 1903, there was a splendid corn crop.

Ole hired two young men to help with the cornpicking. It was time to get the crops from the field into the crib. Day after day, early in the morning, all of the men went out with their teams and wagons to pick corn by hand, tossing the yellow ears against the bangboards, and coming back with loads about noon. After dinner they went out into the fields to fill their wagons again. Yes, cornpicking was proceeding very well.

On Saturday, November 7th, Ole had to make a trip into Hudson on business. Johanna went along to do some shopping. When they returned in the middle of the afternoon, they were met by the sound of mooing, bawling cattle. Ole immediately went to the feedyard to check on the reason for the disturbance, and discovered that the water tank was empty. There was no water coming out of the pipe even though the windmill was turning.

Ole had to get water for the thirsty cattle, so he began hauling water from the old well. He filled wooden barrels and hauled them back to the tanks. When the other men came in from the fields, they helped but it was hard to get the tanks full because the thirsty cattle, over one hundred head of feeders, calves and milk cows, all had to satisfy their need for water.

Ole explained the siutation to Johanna. "Something is wrong down in the well, but we'll try to manage until Monday. Then I'll have to go down in the well and see if I can't get it fixed."

Monday, November 9th, was a gray cloudy day, with a raw wind blowing. Ole set to work repairing the well. It wasn't long before he was wet to the skin. The pumping apparatus down in the well had to be cleaned out and some pipes had to be disconnected. When he finally had it working again, he came into the house, wet and shivering with cold.

"Take off those wet clothes right away, and get into something dry!" Johanna instructed. "Then come and get warmed up with some hot coffee."

There was a good fire in the kitchen range, so she opened the oven door and had her husband sit by it and benefit from its heat. But a severe chill came upon him and he began shaking. His teeth were chattering so that he could hardly speak. Johanna put some more wood on the fire and soon the heat was radiating throughout the kitchen, and even the tea kettle and the coffeepot setting on the back of the stove began to boil.

Johanna got a big quilt and wrapped it around her husband, but he could not stop shaking. Finally she told him she thought he should get into bed.

"I'll go up and get the sheepskin robe and cover you. That ought to warm you up!"

After he was settled in bed in the downstairs bedroom with the woolly heavy robe covering him, Johanna dug out her bottle of brandy and gave him a big dose.

"Now you'll soon be sweating," she said. "Then you'll be feeling better."

Tuesday was not a good day. A light rain was falling and it was gloomy and gray. The men could not pick corn and they sat about the house a good part of the time. Ole was running a temperature and didn't feel well. Johanna had a difficult time keeping him inside.

"I should go out and check on my cattle," he said.

But Johanna was very insistent, "You sit down and keep warm. That's the best thing you can do. With all of these men around here, I'm sure the outside work will be done."

By Thursday, Ole had a tight pain in his chest and was very miserable. His fever had gone up, and he finally agreed to have one of the hired men go to Canton for the doctor. When Dr. Holmgren came, he listened to Ole's chest and took his temperature, and pronounced the case serious. "It may be your heart," he told him, "or you may be coming down with pneumonia." The doctor took some medicine out of his black bag and gave a dose to Ole.

After the doctor left, Ole told Johanna, "When I swallowed that medicine I could feel that strong liquid going down through my chest and I had such a funny feeling—it was like I was being galvanized."

Johanna was worried as Ole's health rapidly worsened. His breathing became labored and difficult. She sent for another doctor, Dr. Hetlesater. He did what he could, but there was no sign of improvement in the patient.

Rev. Numedahl, the new pastor who had come to shepherd the Lands congregation in March of 1903, stopped over to see Ole. Ole had always been so strong and always in such good health that Johanna couldn't believe that he wouldn't snap out of it.

Ole lay in their bedroom downstairs, and Rev. Numedahl comforted him with some words from the Psalms.

"The Lord is my strength and my song; He has become my salvation."*

*Psalms 118:14

"Ja," Ole weakly spoke between his labored breathing. "I cannot sing now, yet there is a song inside."

Again, he struggled for air, and continued. "It says that the Lord is with me."

"Yes," Pastor Numedahl agreed. "That's what He has promised."

Brother Pete Overseth consulted Dr. Holmgren in Canton and then talked it over with Johanna and the rest of the family. There was a specialist in Sioux City, a Dr. Warren, who perhaps could help Ole.

When they agreed to call him in, Pete arranged for a special train from Sioux City to bring him to Hudson. It travelled at almost a mile-a-minute and he arrived Tuesday evening, November 17th, at 7:30, and stayed until Wednesday noon. Now Ole was delirious part of the time. Dr. Warren consulted with the other doctors on the case and reported to the family, "There is nothing more that can be done. He has a severe case of pneumonia and it is very critical."

Ole continued to fight for his life, but finally lapsed into a coma. A kerosene lamp burned all through the night in his room, and Johanna sat in her rocking chair and kept watch. During the early hours, just before dawn, she knelt beside his bed. The tears began to fall.

She whispered, "I am here, Ole. Open your eyes and look at me." But there was no response. His big hand lay limply upon the quilt. She placed it in her hands. It was calloused from hard work—a lifetime of hard work—caring for her and their family. Underneath his nails there still was a trace of grease which he got while working on the well.

Johanna gently stroked his hand. This hand that loved to make music. This hand that had grabbed hers a hundred times as Ole had said, "C'mon, I want to show you something."

Perhaps the apple trees were in bloom, or the sow had had a big litter of pigs. Just several weeks ago he had grabbed her hand and invited, "C'mon and see how beautiful and golden the corn is this year."

She remembered that day almost 31 years ago that they had arrived on this spot, and he had grabbed her hand and helped her down to the ground, exclaiming, "This is our land! Step on it, Johanna!" and then he had swung her around and around in excitement.

Johanna buried her head in the quilt and quietly sobbed. The doctor's words, "There is nothing more that we can do," had filled her with fear.

Yes, already Ole was leaving her. She brushed her hand across his forehead, but there was no reaction. He didn't even know she was there.

All she could hear was his labored breathing, and the big clock loudly ticking in the parlor.

Johanna studied his face, as her mind kept asking, "What if this really is the end? How will I get along?"

She tried to look back and it seemed that all of her yesterdays had included him. Through good and bad, she had always depended on him and had his hand to hold, his shoulder to lean upon.

"Our lives are so involved in each other's. We know each other so well. How can this 'one flesh' that is both of us be separated?"

She closed her eyes and tried not to think about it. "Part of him will always be with me—his thoughts, his ideas, his words will still be in my tomorrows."

Johanna raised her head to heaven and cried, "Oh, Father-God, **Kjaere Gud,** dearest Jesus, give me strength to go on."

Saturday evening, November 21st, 1903, at 9 o'clock, Ole Overseth's heart beat its last beat. At his bedside in the downstairs bedroom on his homestead all of his family were gathered. Martin had his arm around his mother. Beside them were daughter Helmina and her husband. Johnny was there, and Anna, Tony, Jim and Henry, as were Ole's brothers, Pete and Hans Overseth, and brother-in-law Christian Narum.

For several days they had known it was coming, yet while there was life it was only natural to hold out some hope. But now it was over.

They stood silently looking at their dear husband, father and brother, each person deep in his own thoughts, each thinking through his own farewell, for the adventuresome pioneer, Ole Johanneson Overseth, aged 57, had gone on to explore a new country—the one his Friend and Savior had written him about in John 14, verses two and three:

"In my Father's house are many mansions. If it were not so, I would have told you. Lo, I go to prepare a place for you. And if I go to prepare a place for you I will come again and take you unto Myself, that where I am there you may be also."

The End.

Epilogue

Tuesday, November 24th, 1903, Ole Johannes Overseth, age 57, was laid to rest in the Lands cemetery. Prior to the funeral, devotions were held in the Overseth home for close friends and relatives. A procession of buggies followed the carriage bearing the coffin to the church where final services were held.

Pastor Numedahl spoke in Norwegian and Dr. L. J. Hauge, former pastor who now was a medical doctor, gave a sermon in English. Floral tributes covered the coffin and a choir of little boys and girls sang several numbers. A comforting letter of sympathy was presented to Johanna from the Lands congregation. Rev. Numedahl worded it thus: "He has left the Church Militant for the Church Triumphant and we will miss him in our assembly."

Afterwards a large gray stone was erected over his grave, inscribed with these words "Rest in peace—Blessed be your memory." Near the bottom was engraved, "Blessed are the dead that die in the Lord."

The widow Johanna rented the farm to Nordlie and daughter Helmina for four years while she lived down on the Hudson farm with Tony, Henry and Jim. Johnny later moved back on this Hudson farm when Johanna bought a house in Canton, and Jim got married and farmed the old Overseth homestead.

Martin and Tony bought a hardware store in Fairview, South Dakota, and besides running this, they kept up on their music and with the help of Indseth organized a musical group which played at different events.

On Johanna's 60th birthday, a big party was held for her on the old homestead where Nordlies were living, and all the relatives gathered. A platform rocker was purchased for her, and Martin and Tony had a musical group there to entertain. They brought the piano out on the porch, and with Miss Skartvedt on the piano, Martin on cornet, Tony on trombone, cousin Hans Bekke (Stikbakke) on the clarinet and his brother Anthon Stikbakke on the flute, together with several other young people, they made enjoyable music.

While living in Canton, Johanna visited often with her sister Klara Grevlos who also lived there, and with daughter Anna, who when she was married, made her home there.

In April of 1912, Johanna suffered a stroke, and after lingering a week, she passed away on April 9, 1912, at age 64, at daughter Helmina's home on the Nordlie farm. Funeral services were held in the Lands church and she was laid to rest beside her husband.

Daughter Anna was married to Hans M. Dale at the old homestead on June 30, 1908, while sister Helmina and Nordlie were living there. He was Lincoln County Superintendent of Schools, and later professor at Augustana College in Canton. Anna died while still a young woman in July of 1920, at age 37, leaving four daughters, Eunice, Jeanette, Hazel and Evelyn.

Jim Overseth also died while a young man. He contacted typhoid and was operated on for appendicitis. He died from peritonitis on August 16, 1914, at the age of 26. Jim had married Alma Hegness, of the John Hegness family, and left behind three daughters, Gladys, Helen and Agnes Julie.

Johanna sold the homestead to Jim. After his death, his wife rented it out for a number of years, and later sold it to one of the renters, Ingvald Ekle, a son of Nils Ekle, so it is no longer in the Overseth family.

Martin, Tony and Henry later moved to Minneapolis. Martin and Tony were in the insurance business, and played in the Minneapolis Symphony from time to time. Henry also was in insurance in Minneapolis for awhile and then moved to Sioux Falls, South Dakota, where he bought a grocery store. He was married to Millie Chraft and they had five daughters and one son: Eileen, Mae (who died at 13), Lillian, Nyla, Jim (who died at 17) and Marilyn. Henry passed away December 6, 1974, at the age of 85.

Martin married Stella Sime in Minneapolis, and they had two daughters, Muriel and Adys. Martin died in 1965, at the age of almost 85 years.

Tony married Laura Pederson in Minneapolis, and they also had two daughters, Arlene and Lois. Tony died in 1931, at the age of 46.

John and Rena had two more children. Besides Enok Oliver, there were James Maurice and Anna. John died in 1945 at the age of 71.

Daughter Helmina and her husband Nordlie lived on their home place by the Lands Church until Nordlie passed away in September of 1935. Then Helmina moved to Canton for a few years, then to Moe, and later to Sioux Falls, where she died at the age of 86, on July 12, 1962. Besides Obed and Thelma, they left behind an adopted daughter Catherine.

For many years, the little rural center of Moe continued to be a thriving, bustling place. At times, different businesses sprang up in addition to the country store, but toward the end of the 1930's the store was closed and now only a home remains.

The Lands congregation is still very active. The eight-sided church building has now been replaced by a large brick structure, and the pasture that the pastor used in early days for his cow has now been made into a park for the youth of the parish.

As you walk through the Lands cemetery today you may recognize many of the names that have been included in this book. And when seated in the sanctuary on Sunday mornings you can look about and see a great number of the descendants (now the third and fourth generations) of these pioneers who struggled to make a community from the prairie way back in the 1870's.

Glossary

berliner krans—rich wreath-shaped cookie
Bestefar—Grandfather
bukse—trousers
enke—widow
enkemand—widower
evangel—gospel
Far—Father
Farvel—farewell
fattig—needy
fattigmand—thin cakes fried in hot fat
fjells—mountains
flatbrød—thin, crisp bread
gaard—farmstead
Glade Jul—Merry Christmas
God dag!—Good day!
God Morn!—Good morning!
goro kakke—flat cookies made in special iron
Her Komme Dine Arme Small—Thy Little Ones Dear Lord Are We
Herr—Mr.
Hva skal vi gjøre?—What shall we do?
Hvor Salig er Den Lille Flok—How Blessed is the Little Flock
hytti-hu—77 in Swedish
Ja, det er sikkert, det!—Yes, that's for sure!
Ja, vel—Yes, well
jente—girl
Jul—Christmas
Kirke—church
kjaere—dear
Kjaere Gud—Dear God
Kjaere Johanna, min—Dear Johanna of mine
Kjaere meg!—Dear me!
Kjøre vatten, kjøre ved—haul the water, haul the wood
klokker—deacon who announces songs
kroner—dollars
krumkakke—scroll-shaped cookies
Kvindeforening—Ladies Aid
lapskaus—stew or hodge-podge mixture
lefse—soft thin potato pancake-like food

Mange tusen takk!—Many thousand thanks!
middags—dinner
Mor—Mother
nei—no!
nei-da!—Oh, no!
nei-min!—Oh my, no!
Nordamerika—North America
ore—penny
ost—cheese
post—mail
prest—preacher
seters—mountain pastures
Sette deg!—Sit down!
snakke—speak
skynde deg!—Hurry up!
spekekjøt—dried beef or mutton
stabbur—outdoor pantry
stakkars!—poor!
Stor Johan—Big John
syv og søtti—77 in Norwegian
Trefoldighed Kirke—Trinity Church
Takk for sist!—Thanks for past favors!
Tante—Aunt
Takkedag—Thanksgiving Day
toten kringler—sweet yeast wreath-shaped rolls
Tre-fot—wooden leg
tykemelksuppe—soup made of clabbered milk
Uff-da!—Norwegian expression with many meanings
ut paa landet—out in the country
Velkommen!—Welcome!
Vaer saa god!—Help yourselves!
Velt Alle Dine Veie Paa Ham—Leave all your ways with Him
Vi Skal Møte i Himmelen—We shall meet in Heaven

"Noen har brød men kan ikke spise
Andre kan spise, men har ikke brød
Vi har brød og vi kan spise
Derfor vil vi Herren prise!"

"Some have bread and can't eat
Some can eat but have no food
We have bread and we can eat
Therefore we will praise the Lord!"

"Oh, Hvor Salig Det Skal Bleve
Naar Gud's Barn Skal Komme Hjem"

"Oh, how blessed it shall be
when God's Children Come Home"

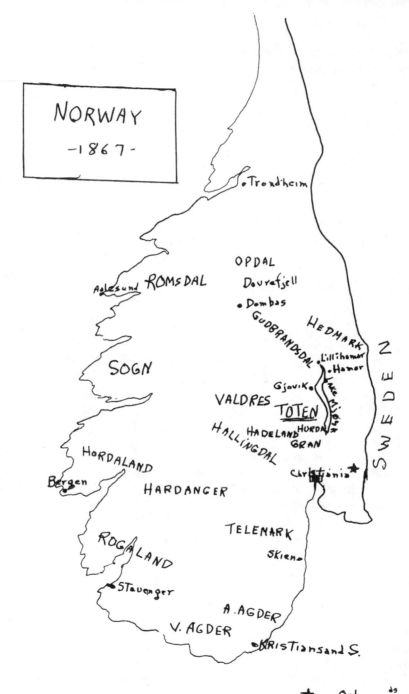

NORWAY

-1867-

• Trondheim

OPDAL

Dovrefjell

ROMSDAL

Aalesund

• Dombas

HEDMARK

GUDBRANDSDAL

Lillihamer

• Hamar

SOGN

Gjovik •

VALDRES

TOTEN

HALLINGDAL

HADELAND

HURDAL

GRAN

HORDALAND

Bergen

HARDANGER

Christiania

SWEDEN

TELEMARK

ROGALAND

Skien •

Stavanger

A. AGDER

V. AGDER

• Kristiansand S.

★ now Oslo

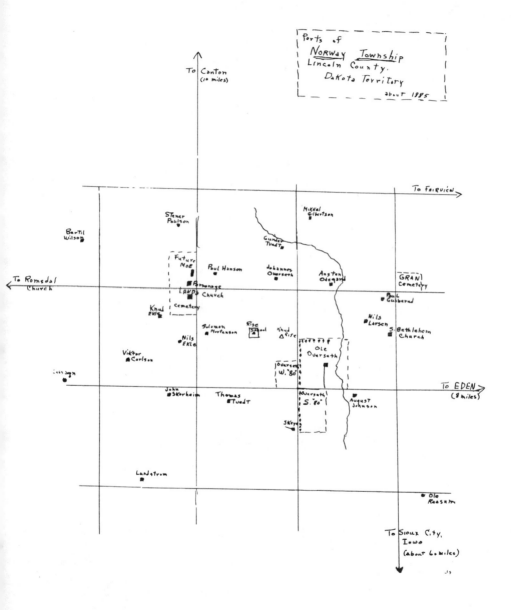